JOURNEYMAN

An Inspector Marshall Mystery

Emma Melville

ISBN-13: 978-1-8380344-0-5

A splash of logic, a touch of magic... a recipe for a good life as well as a good book. This story is for all those who look for both.

CONTENTS

CHAPTER 1 1
CHAPTER 2 34
CHAPTER 3 57
CHAPTER 4 82
CHAPTER 5 112
CHAPTER 6 135
CHAPTER 7 157
CHAPTER 8 191
CHAPTER 9 215
CHAPTER 10 231
CHAPTER 11 248
CHAPTER 12 260
CHAPTER 13 273
ABOUT THE AUTHOR 280

ACKNOWLEDGMENTS

Thanks to Paul for a superb cover and to all family – whether related by blood, Morris or folk music – who have supported me in my writing. And always, and forever, to Jon.

CHAPTER 1

January 3rd

The vacuous blonde on the early evening news had claimed that the gale would let up by morning. Inspector John Marshall squelched across the ploughed ridges towards the will-o-the-wisps of distant torches and cursed weather girls and mobile telephones. He could have been safely tucked up in bed listening to Marion's snoring and the wind in the wires when instead he was suffering the violence of a January midnight because an idiot had gone out for a stroll with a phone. It was at times like this that he wondered, though only briefly and with no real seriousness, why he'd left London for the rural delights of Fenwick.

The mud sucked at Marshall's wellingtons, clinging to each foot as if reluctant to let him go further from the road. Having no wish to lose his footwear in the country dark, Marshall resisted the urge to fight against the soggy ground and worked on freeing each foot carefully while the rain gradually soaked through his cagoule and trickled down his back.

"John!" Sergeant Mark Sherbourne waved his torch unhelpfully to and fro, signalling where to head whilst simultaneously blinding his superior. "Over here."

Marshall staggered on against the unrelenting wind. "Someone better be dead," he muttered as his foot slid dangerously sideways and he narrowly avoided sitting down for the umpteenth time.

"Haven't you got a torch?" Mark waved his own at the ground along the hedge. "Ditch is here."

"Back there." He'd dropped it the first time he'd nearly fallen and hadn't fancied grovelling in the mud to find it. It had, of course, switched itself off on landing.

"What's in the ditch, Mark?"

"Body." The minimal light showed a figure lying peacefully amongst the nettles. The face was turned towards them, the eyes closed, and the hands folded across the chest. The chin showed the beginnings of a beard.

"We need more light."

"They're working on it, John. The generator's stuck in the mud."

Behind his sergeant he could just make out three officers manhandling a lighting rig which was swaying dangerously with each fresh gust of wind. Two others were attempting to heave a small generator into place beside the ditch. He went back to his perusal of the body.

"Man?" He peered closer but it stayed resolutely male. "That's not right, is it?"

"No," Mark agreed.

Marshall looked around, doing his best to make out features of the landscape in the dark and the pouring rain. The ditch ran along the edge of a ploughed field, filled with bramble and weed so that only the presence of the body identified the dip in the ground. Any fool straying this way in the dark might well fall in before they realised.

Marshall checked down again; this body hadn't fallen. Even if it had he couldn't imagine anyone dying from slipping a foot and a half into a patch of nettles, but they certainly didn't then lay themselves out like a medieval effigy.

"We're going to need everyone's shoes." Mark was watching the ongoing struggle to erect the splay of lights. "Unfortunately, we've probably done for any tracks."

"Hickson enjoys a challenge." Marshall wondered what was keeping Fenwick's forensic specialist. Craig Hickson was usually first on any scene, his compact frame scurrying here and there, poking into cluttered corners and complaining about the time Liza Trent took in examining and removing the body.

Marshall looked back towards the road. Doctor Trent should also be here by now though he had trouble envisioning the neat, pretty doctor ploughing across the muddy field.

He tried to see his watch but Mark was examining the ditch again and the orange glow from Fenwick town centre two miles to the east wasn't enough to pick out the hands.

"Where is everyone?"

"You live closer than anyone else," Mark said reasonably, "and the number of reports of trees down we've had so far means they could be a while."

"So I spend longer standing in the blasted rain. I should have stayed in bed."

"Sorry." Mark didn't take Marshall's words too seriously. Even after their relatively short time together, they both knew that Marshall would never have stayed at home while a murder needed supervision. They went back to their pointless study of the ditch.

"So, not a woman then," Marshall said.

"No."

"Not even blonde." The short hair showed brown in the torchlight.

"Any other bodies?"

"Haven't found anything so far but it took uniform half an hour to find this one. I told them to hold off searching until we had lights up."

"Makes sense." It was about the only thing that did. Mark had been quite clear on the phone; they'd had a 999 from out by West Cross about a woman lying dead in a ditch. A blonde woman, hair almost white. The caller had used the term albino though how they'd managed to see such detail or why they'd been on the hill above West Cross in the middle of the worst storm in twenty years Marshall couldn't fathom. The fact that the body was male and dark haired and there was no sign of the caller suggested that someone was messing with them. Marshall wasn't fond of hoaxers at the best of times and the middle of a very wet and windy January night was a long way from being the best of anything. On top of which he was going to have to waste valuable time and resources on searching for what he suspected was a non-existent dead albino.

"John, nice night." Doctor Liza Trent clung to Hickson's arm with one hand, the other clutching her big, black bag. "Where is she?"

"He." He grabbed Mark's arm and directed the torch.

"Someone need anatomy lessons?" She put her bag down. "Light, John?"

Marshall opened his mouth to explain that they were working on it and then shut it again as the body and its encompassing ditch were suddenly floodlit. The night was filled with the chug of the generator.

"Light," he said unnecessarily as if he'd managed to conjure it just for her.

"Neat." She didn't look up from her search of the bag's contents. She pulled on latex gloves and grabbed her own small torch to add extra illumination, highlighting the recumbent figure. The man looked barely asleep, his eyes momentarily shut, his whole body relaxed.

"He is dead?" Marshall couldn't help asking.

"Oh yes." Liza Trent wiped the rain from her forehead, pushing her short curls back. "Not long dead, I'd say, but definitely dead."

"Cause?"

"You're joking, right?"

"I'm wet and I want to go back to bed. Tell me something to make that possible."

Hickson laughed. "She's a pathologist, John, not a miracle worker." The forensic expert had also donned gloves and was now holding up his white overalls. "Seems a little pointless," he said as he struggled into the wet material, "but rules are rules."

"Liza?" Marshall crouched down, the mud from his wellingtons spreading liberally up his trousers as he sat back on his heels.

"No readily apparent cause of death." She handed Marshall her torch so she could use both hands to lift the body once Hickson had blinded them both with his camera flashes.

"Nothing underneath obvious either. You'll have to wait until I get this one back, I'm afraid." She held the body still so Hickson could photograph behind it as well.

Marshall handed the torch back and left them to it, following Mark to where he'd collected several uniformed officers together beside the severely rocking light column.

"See what you can find," Marshall told them. "Work from here out and take care. It's more important that you get back to the station in one piece and I can't see there'll be hordes of people up here tampering with evidence on a night like this." Above them on the hillside he could already see one tree leaning at an alarming angle and the new illumination showed several branches had already come down into the field they were standing in.

"Looking for anything in particular, sir?" The woman constable looked cold and miserable; her short, dark hair plastered to her head.

"Anything unusual, anything that shouldn't be out on a night like this and, possibly, a second body; female, blonde."

"Us?" Mark asked as the officers set about their search.

Marshall checked his watch. It was two thirty. "I want to hear that 999 call and I want to be dry. I'm going via home to get a change of clothes and I'll see you at the station." He'd put in his fair share of years walking the beat and searching in the rain; rank had to have some privileges. It also gave him the chance to reassure Marion and warn her not to expect too much from the coming weekend. Murder enquiries were a non-starter as far as social life was concerned and he couldn't see this one solving itself by Saturday.

*

The ear-splitting crash just above his head brought Connor jerking to full consciousness, his eyes suddenly wide open. Something, possibly his subconscious registering what was happening above, stopped his initial surge to a sitting position. Without thought, he threw himself sideways off the bed as the giant branch slammed down through the caravan roof and impaled the mattress. Splinters of fibreglass rained down and a huge section of roof fell across the bed, slipped sideways and pinned him to the floor.

Connor's heart raced in his chest but by some miracle nothing seemed to be broken. He was going to be bruised but all right if he could manage to move the roof section or get out from under it. Ominous creaking suggested more of the structure was about to give way. If anything landed on the material above him, he was going to be crushed.

"Connor!" It was Luke. The travellers' leader was somewhere outside. "Connor! Can you hear me?"

A voice slightly nearer said, "The whole bloody branch must have landed on his head, Luke. His bed's this side."

"I'm here!" Connor yelled as loud as he could, inhaling dust and setting off a coughing fit as he did so. Material slid sideways, making the space he was in smaller as his body shook the caravan.

"We'll get you out!" Luke sounded relieved. "Are you hurt?"

"Only bruised, I think." Connor quelled the coughing fit. "But I'm trapped half under the bed."

"I'm coming in."

"You can't do that." The other voice was Terry, Connor decided. "You pull that door, the whole fucking thing'll fall back."

"You saying I should leave him in there?"

"No, course not."

"Back window's out," a third voice suggested. "Could go in that way if you're careful."

"Hear that, Con? I'm coming in the back," Luke yelled.

"I hear." Connor twisted his head round as best he could and gradually began moving his hands. Each small movement shifted the debris piled above him, but he managed to turn and push his hands above his head. The back window was that way if he could just clear a space. Carefully he pushed lumps of broken caravan out of the way, earning himself several splinters in the process until he could feel fresh air above his head.

Renewed creaking and a change in the motion of the caravan heralded Luke's arrival through the back and then a hand was grasping Connor's where he waved it about.

"Got you, mate. Now we could try this slow, but I think the 'van's going over so I'm going to heave and pull and I'm sorry if I hurt. Ok?"

"Ok." Connor gripped Luke's wrist tight.

"Ready, two, three, UP!"

The air suddenly cleared above Connor, the sheet of polycarbonate vanishing upwards, and Luke yanked hard on his wrist pulling him to upright.

Connor barely had his feet under him when he realised the redistribution of balance had sent the caravan into its death throes. The whole structure was heeling violently to the left.

Luke dragged him towards the back. "Jump!" The two men hurled themselves at the back of the caravan, flying through the space the window used to occupy and rolling out across the muddy grass of the field they were camped in.

Connor came to rest on his back, all the breath knocked out of him. The gasping beside him suggested Luke was in a similar position.

"Well," the travellers' leader said, recovering his breath first, "I think you better kip the rest of the night with me, mate. That'll teach you to park under trees."

Connor joined him in the relieved laughter of one rescued to begin life again.

*

"What shall I do?" her mother's plaintive voice grated on Zoe's nerves. She continued to stare out at the raging storm, unwilling to turn. The raindrops smashed against the glass above the sink, hurled by the screaming wind. It was a more comforting sight than her mother's pale face with its twin bruises.

"Zoe, you must stay."

"What, and hit you again?" She swung round, the rucksack on her right shoulder sending a mug crashing off the draining board to the tiles below. "I can't stay." The livid red on her mother's left cheek bone was beginning to shade towards purple; a rich counterpoint to the fading yellow along her jaw. The surge of guilt made Zoe angrier – with herself, with her mother. She wasn't sure which and neither was fair. She ought to be cross with the father whose daughter she was. She'd proved that tonight with that one blow.

Tears stood out in her mother's washed-out blue eyes. "Don't leave me, Zoe. Look at the weather. It won't happen again."

"How can you promise that? It won't happen because I'll be gone." She hooked her other arm through the rucksack strap. "Give me a bit of a start and then phone the police by all means. Tell them I've gone to find dad. Tell them anything you like."

Zoe turned away from the need in her mother's eyes and strode to the kitchen door, crushing pieces of mug underfoot as she went. She took a long last look around the farmhouse kitchen with its flagged floor and pine dressers; the old armchair pulled up beside the Aga. "I'm sorry I hit you, mum." She couldn't look at her again. "I ..." But there was nothing more to say, nothing that would make it right.

Yanking the door open she dashed through it and slammed it behind her before the weather could invade the cosiness of the kitchen.

The wind howled with animal-like fury and she staggered as a sharp gust pushed her sideways. Rain streamed across her vision, soaking her almost immediately.

Outside, away from the protection of the double glazing, the awful groans and creaks of the oak could be heard. The ancient tree in the meadow beyond the back garden had stood for hundreds of years and outlasted a thousand storms but was finally losing the battle. It leant at a crazy angle away from the house, its roots tearing themselves free of the soil in an agony of rending wood.

9

Branches clawed at the winter sky, grasping after handholds that weren't there as the mighty tree swayed towards the earth.

Zoe could see the ragged ends of the rope swing fluttering in a wild dance with each fresh gust.

She realised that when it finally fell it would crush the fence down the side of the field and block the road which ran past the front of the house.

For a second she paused. They ought to warn someone about the tree. Then she sighed and put the thought away to join all the other regrets her mother engendered.

Further down the hill there were lights in the traveller's encampment and even further below there looked to be lights in the bottom field. Zoe wondered about that briefly, but it was probably just some of the travellers – the wind had likely spread their possessions all over the farm. She didn't envy them chasing down the goods. If it was her, she'd give it up as a bad job and stay in bed. The thought brought a sharp laugh, halfway to a sob; she could hardly mock anyone else's foolishness tonight.

Turning away, she slipped down the side path, pushing against the wind with her head down. The ferocity took her breath away and she could barely see where she was going through the stinging rain.

She wrenched the gate open and tumbled out into the road, almost knocking down the young lady who stood poised to enter.

Zoe staggered to a halt, barely able to stay upright against the gusting wind.

The stranger did not look much over her own age. She was well wrapped against the storm in a wild assortment of clothes, the wind catching at her long skirt, coat and scarf which were all drenched through.

She also happened to be blocking Zoe's way out which wouldn't have been a problem were it not for the dog.

The girl's left hand rested lightly on the back of a giant wolfhound. It stood calmly beside her, unperturbed by the weather. It didn't look dangerous, but Zoe wasn't going to risk pushing past it.

The girl said something, the words blown away into the night.

Zoe shrugged, shaking her head slightly.

"I said that I was looking for shelter." The girl leant in to place her mouth beside Zoe's ear. "Do you live here?" Her breath tickled warmly after the cold of the wind.

The girl moved forwards in anticipation of an answer, pulling up the flap of the brightly coloured knitted cap she wore.

"Go in," Zoe said into the exposed ear. "Mum won't mind." It would take her mother's mind off her leaving. She stepped sideways to push the side gate open once more.

The girl didn't move.

"Where are you going?"

"Out," Zoe said, "away."

"Isn't your mum nice?"

"I'm not nice," Zoe snapped. What a pointless conversation to be having in such foul weather. She let the gate go, pushed past the strange girl as gently as she could and found herself facing the dog.

"We'll come with you," the girl said. "I know a place out of the rain."

"You said ..."

But Zoe found herself being dragged bodily down the road, the wind pushing her along from behind so that her feet scarcely touched the ground.

The rain hammered into her back and the huge dog pushed at her legs as they stumbled along. The girl's grip was surprisingly strong.

Zoe struggled to free herself half-heartedly. What would she do if she got clear? Go home? That would be an impressive start to her new life; running home to mum in under half an hour. Besides, when had her mother ever been any use?

Gritting her teeth, she went where she was taken and resolved to bide her time. Thanks to her father, she knew how to use her fists if the need or opportunity arose.

They didn't go far, not even off the limits of the farm or as far as the travellers. The strange girl pushed open a field gate after about quarter of a mile, the dog leaping the fence with ease. Just across the meadow was a sheep fold, deserted now that the animals were all nearer home for the winter.

It wasn't much – no windows or doors in the holes and the roof leaked in one corner – but it kept off the worst of the wind and rain.

Zoe was shepherded into a dry corner.

"This usually holds sheep," the girl said.

"Our sheep," Zoe pointed out, but the girl wasn't thrown.

"Sit down; we'll be ok here until it stops. I hope you've got food in that bag of yours."

"A little." Not a lot. The plan had been to hike the miles into Fenwick centre and find a place to stay. Zoe hadn't intended to spend the night in a field this close to home while sharing her food with two others. On the other hand, she was already soaked and would likely drown if she walked much further so perhaps it was best just to stay.

"I've got plenty of clothes," she offered grudgingly, "if you'd like something dry."

"Thanks, that'd be nice."

They could almost be sisters – one fiery, the other dark – Zoe thought later, watching the other girl sleep.

Her companion looked younger, fragile almost, in the borrowed jeans. Unruly auburn curls framed the sleeping girl's features, the hair falling halfway down her back.

Zoe ran a hand through her own dark tresses. They were still damp from the mad dash in the rain.

The two of them were snuggled up either side of the wolfhound who was, unaccountably, called Merlin. The dog was a gentle giant and Zoe had rapidly lost her fear of him.

She was more worried about his mistress. Under the delicate exterior there was a wildness to the girl, something slightly feral in the bright green eyes. Perhaps it was just the effect of the torchlight and the madness of the storm, but Zoe was happier with her asleep.

Nothing she had said had explained to Zoe why she was wondering about the countryside alone in a gale.

On the other hand, she couldn't really complain; she hadn't been very communicative herself. The explanations she could give were too heavy with anger and self-pity for her to want to repeat them.

They made her thoughts too weighty for sleep too. That and the strangeness of her bed. She gave Merlin a pat. It was the first time she'd ever had a pillow that snuffled in its sleep.

"Lacewing," she said softly. "What sort of a name is that?" It was the name the girl had given with a smile that half suggested she was joking. Following it with 'better than Zoe, at any rate'.

Zoe happened to agree but then she thought most names would be an improvement on Zoe. Perhaps she ought to change her name.

New start, new person.

She spent a slightly amusing half hour trying to think of a girl's name she liked before deciding that seventeen years of growing into

Zoe had ruined anything else for her.

She checked her watch for the hundredth time.

Half past three.

What would her mum be doing now?

Would she have called the police?

There'd been no sirens go past up the road so perhaps her mum hadn't bothered.

A shuddering crash, felt rather than heard, brought her upright. Merlin raised his head as well, a growl rumbling in his chest.

"It's all right," she said, realising, "it's just the tree going down."

The tree she'd climbed as soon as she could walk. The one she'd pretended had doors in to other, safer places. She'd kicked it, yelled at it, told it her secrets and now it was gone, taking her old life with it.

Overcome by the strangeness of the night and losses she couldn't put words to, she laid her head against Merlin and sobbed.

And, with the tears, sleep finally came.

*

Mark had tracked down two cups of strong coffee and two plates of bacon sandwiches by the time Marshall made it back to the CID office. Marshall spread his damp cagoule across the back of a chair in the partitioned cubbyhole he occupied off the main office and took a seat opposite Mark.

"No brown sauce," Mark said with a mouthful, pushing a plate towards him. "Sorry, canteen's out."

Marshall shrugged. At four in the morning after a trek in the cold and a nightmare drive amidst whirling twigs and leaves, any warm sustenance was welcome. "That tree's down above West Cross. I've had to come all round through the Manor Estate."

"Did you tell them downstairs?"

"Yep, they said it was number seventeen on the list of trees to be cleared so I might have a chance of getting home by Tuesday."

They ate in companionable silence for a while until Marshall could feel the damp receding. "Go on then, let's hear it."

Mark pressed a button on the small recorder in front of him.

"Hello, is that the police?" The voice was male and breathless. "There's a woman in the field ... well, the ditch ... I think she's dead."

"Where is this?" A female voice interjected, calm and business like.

"West Cross, up the hill, in a ditch. She's just lying there. An albino, all white hair when she isn't old."

"Can you be more precise about your location?"

"Hill Farm. I'll stand on the road." The man sounded increasingly agitated. "Please hurry. Perhaps she ... should I have called an ambulance?"

"We'll send one, sir. Could you give me some details about yourself—"

"But I've got to get to the road."

"As you walk you—"

"No signal, that's why I had to come up here. I'll give my details when you—" The signal broke up through the final sentence leaving Marshall to guess at 'arrive' as the missing word. The tape went dead and Mark stabbed the player to a halt.

"So?" Marshall put down his empty plate and leant back, cradling his coffee. He felt better but still residually damp.

"So, what was he doing in the middle of a field on a night like tonight if he wasn't the killer?" Mark said.

"Couldn't have put it better myself."

"So, my first guess is that we've got a killer who likes yanking our chains."

"Sounds plausible."

"My next guess is that my gut says he's going to do it again."

"I hope your gut is wrong." But Marshall agreed with his sergeant. He'd dealt with this sort of person before — killers who loved the publicity and had to be the centre of the policeman's world. The best way to manage that was to keep up a supply of bodies.

"May even have done it before?" Mark suggested. "Perhaps we haven't noticed and hence the call."

"OK, we ought to check M.O. I wonder why an albino?" Marshall drained his coffee.

"A trademark? We'll know it's him and he's killed again if we get more reports of albinos. It is an original calling card."

"Right, so now—"

"Now, Liza tells us off for hypothesising when we don't even have a cause of death and Hickson complains we've stomped all over the—"

"Top of the hill," Marshall slapped the desk, interrupting his sergeant's flow. "Get someone to try it. If there really is no signal from the road then he had to go up the hill and we haven't mucked up the traces up there."

"John," Mark began in the manner of someone wary of throwing cold water on an enthusiastic fire, "he could have phoned from anywhere. Killers aren't renowned for telling the truth."

"Well, get the phone records too, then. Check where the call was made from if that's possible." Marshall did his best to keep up with the stampede of modern technology but sometimes found himself wooed by televised possibilities that were still a policeman's dream.

"I'll check and I'll tell uniform to try phone signals and to stay off the hilltop until its light. Anything else?"

"See if Hickson's found any ID and I suppose we'd better look for a white-haired woman too, just in case." Marshall stood up. "I'll go see if Liza's got him back yet."

"You'll annoy her."

Marshall knew that but he couldn't help the desire to get started, to feel like he was progressing a case. He needed a name, an identity, a cause of death – something to grasp hold off to start unravelling the murder to a conclusion. Unfortunately though, Mark was right. "All right, I'll bother Hickson then, he doesn't snap. You talk to uniform."

*

Luke surveyed the mess. It wasn't as bad as he'd feared blundering about in the storm screaming into the night.

They'd only lost the one caravan – the smallest – bowled over and crushed by the branch torn down in the howling wind. Various other unsecured items had blown away. Already the children were out in groups scavenging what they could.

Much was ruined but very little was irreplaceable.

"We'll organise some 'shopping'," he said, hearing the door open behind him.

"Bit of a quagmire," Connor said, joining him at the foot of the caravan's steps.

Luke nodded. Connor impressed him. The man could have been complaining about the loss of a home – his caravan lying twisted and broken and, unlike most, it had been bought and paid for. But Connor wasn't a whinger.

Too many were; wanting Luke to provide everything on a plate for them rather than shift for themselves. He wasn't sure which was worse; those who expected him to supply or those who overdid it with their own supplying.

Take yesterday, for example. The letter had arrived from the council telling them they had to move on. Half of them had stood there just watching him as if he could perform some miracle; the other half had started building barricades.

Luke pushed the thoughts aside. After last night's weather there were more important things to consider. Like the man standing silently beside him who he'd dragged from the wreckage of his bed at three o'clock this morning.

"How are you?"

"Bit sore."

That had to be an understatement. The branch had crushed the side of the caravan, showering half the ceiling down on Connor's head.

"It's beyond help." They both looked at the sorry sight that had been Connor's home where it lay pinned into the mud.

"At least it wasn't that." Connor pointed away up the slope. The huge oak which normally stood silhouetted against the skyline now flattened the hedge and lay out across the lane.

"Too bloody right," Luke said. "I wouldn't have pulled you alive from under that."

"Thanks, I owe you."

"Wasn't looking for it, Con. Now, we need to find you a new home."

"What about the council?"

"Sod them. I'll talk to the bastards when I'm ready. Your home's more important." He slapped Connor's shoulder. "Our home's going nowhere. This is our field and will be so at least until we've got you somewhere to lay your head. Come on."

"Where?"

Luke grinned. "I bet we'll find a few going home after a Christmas away. We'll stake out the services for a couple of hours."

Connor nodded silently. Any doubts he kept to himself.

Luke almost regretted the decision. If he left it a couple of days, then they would share a 'van and he might get to know the other man better. Connor had been with them less than a year and, beyond his loss, Luke realised he knew next to nothing about the young man. Connor must be early thirties; competent, quiet and adept at keeping people at a distance. Nobody messed with him. He might make a good second in command if Luke could learn a little more about him.

Luke sighed. He missed Charlie but his recently incarcerated right-hand-man had become a liability of late, even before he was taken off for a spell at Her Majesty's Pleasure.

"Shall I drive?" Connor offered, sidetracking Luke's inner cursing at Charlie's incompetence.

"No, we'll take the truck for towing and set up a change."

They left, turning away down the hill to avoid the tree-blocked road.

*

Hickson wasn't around so Marshall wasted a fruitless hour trying to locate someone who could explain mobile phones and GPS systems to him at five o'clock in the morning. In the end he gave up and went in search of another bacon sandwich. Mark joined him in the canteen clutching two plastic bags.

"Present from Hickson." He placed them on the table. One contained a dark, water-stained wallet, the other a mobile phone.

"From the victim?"

"Yep. Bloke by the name of Philip Knight. He had a photo driving licence and everything. Definitely looks like him."

"Wonders will never cease."

"And the mobile phone seems to be his too and you'll never guess who his last call was to."

"Make my day, tell me he phoned his killer giving name and

address and discussing motive."

"Funny, I didn't notice any flying pigs tonight, John. No, his last call was here. This was the phone that made the call about the woman in the ditch."

"We're meant to think he made the call?"

Mark grinned. "Great, isn't it? He phones us, tells us there's a dead woman and then miraculously disappears her in order to lie down in a ditch and die himself. Bit coincidental not to mention far-fetched. Hickson says he'll fingerprint the phone to see if he can tell who really made the call, but he doesn't hold out much hope. Whoever did this is good."

"Possibly," Marshall said slowly.

"What are you thinking?"

Marshall frowned. "Well, that body looked unscathed which suggests it simply walked out there so our killer must have had a way of getting Mr Knight out in the middle of the night."

"In the middle of a bloody awful night," Mark corrected. "Yes, I see what you mean. Think it was someone he knew?"

"It's a place to start. I assume you have his address? I think we'll go there first." He checked his watch. It was barely six o'clock. "If we go now, we'll catch people before they go to work."

Philip Knight still lived with his mother in a detached house on Manor Estate. She answered the door to them in her dressing gown, her hair wrapped in a towel. Marshall judged her to be late fifties.

Confronted by the police on her doorstep, she seemed unperturbed, her lips tightening slightly revealed the only sign of emotion.

"What's he done this time?" she said, looking them up and down. "Something stupid no doubt."

"We're here about your son," Marshall began.

"I know that. Makes a change from men in uniforms and I assume it's serious this time because they normally just bring him home."

"Does your son get in a lot of trouble, Mrs Knight?"

She softened slightly. "He's just young and impetuous," she said, "all this animal welfare and stuff. He doesn't mean anyone any harm, but he feels he has a right to stick up for the creatures. So, what's he done now?"

"Nothing that we know of," Marshall said, though he filed the information away; perhaps there was a way to get Philip Knight into a field in the middle of the night. "I'm very sorry but we found what we believe is your son's body in a ditch out beyond West Cross this morning."

She didn't seem to understand. "In a ditch? Why? What was he doing there?"

"We don't know, Mrs Knight, though we hope to find out. I'm afraid your son is dead."

"Dead? But what about the shop?" she asked incomprehensibly and then crumpled silently to the floor. Mark picked her up and helped her through to a well-furnished living room where he sat her on the sofa while Marshall made a hot drink.

Once she was calmer, Marshall began the customary set of questions, trying – as usual – to forget how many times he'd asked them before.

"When did you last see your son, Mrs Knight?"

"Sheila. I saw him last night for tea and then he went out to the pub. He said he'd met some people who were interested in animal rights and he and Curtis were going to sign them up."

"Curtis?" Marshall prompted.

"Curtis Yates. A friend ... well, an acquaintance. I don't think many people liked him really, he was a bit of a wimp, Phil used to say, but he was good at the paperwork."

"Do you know what pub?"

"The Highwayman, I think, but I'm not sure. I didn't pay much attention to Phil when he was on about his animal things."

"What did Philip do when he wasn't caring about animal rights?" Mark asked. "You said something about a shop?"

"He worked for his uncle – my brother – in Calver's Hardware. Joe, that's my brother, had just arranged for him to take over the shop as manager once he'd finished training. He was going to go and do accounts and things at college. How can he be dead?"

"We're going to find out," Marshall assured her. "We have no evidence yet that there was foul play; it may just have been a tragic accident. Would you like your brother to come and be with you?"

"He'll be in the shop already."

"Your sister-in-law?"

"I'll phone and get her, Inspector," she said. "I'm sure you have better things to be doing."

*

The motorway services just north of Fenwick were surprisingly full. Hundreds of cars filled to the brim with suitcases and new gifts disgorged families suffering the after-effects of too much Christmas spirit.

Connor watched the straining waistbands and strained tempers with a slightly mocking smile. If Cindy hadn't died that might have been them; staggering back from in-laws, eager to return to their own little cottage.

He quelled the thought. Cindy was gone and he'd moved on. He'd had his chance of playing happy families and it was gone; vanished like so much morning mist. It had been finally crushed with the caravan which had been his last reminder.

He sipped his coffee and turned his attention to Luke who was watching the car park carefully.

The travellers' leader was at least six foot four and weathered from outdoor living. His dark hair was pulled back in a ponytail and a shadow of dark stubble coloured his jaw line.

Connor rather liked him. He ran a tight operation but a fair one and he didn't ask questions or expect more than you could give.

Connor thought Luke was probably as stubborn as he was, but it couldn't be easy keeping fifty or more strong-willed gypsies in order.

"That one," Luke said quietly.

A car and caravan were reversing badly into a parking space. The 'van wasn't huge, but it was bigger than the one Connor had lost. The car was a large, ancient Volvo.

"Why?" Connor asked.

Luke glanced sharply at him.

"A quest for knowledge," Connor said, "not a disagreement." He'd seen Luke arrive back with 'acquired' vans a couple of times over the past year, but he'd never had cause to go out on a trip before.

"Old car, careless family, three kids not strapped in on the back seat, lunch time, bloody awful parking on the end of the row." Luke sat back, watching him.

Connor frowned; it seemed to be some sort of test. He wandered what he got if he passed. "All right. Careless, so they might not lock the car and it's old so it won't be a problem to get into it even if they do. I get that bit. Lunchtime means they may have stopped for a while. The parking means we can get to the caravan easier. I don't get the kids bit." Even if he had, he probably wouldn't have admitted as much. Luke had to be the leader; the master to his pupil.

"Three spoilt and uncontrolled brats mean lots of bickering, lots of attention needed elsewhere, lots of keeping them happy. No chance they'll be noticing us by the car."

They watched the family slowly cross the car park with frequent pauses and loud discussions as the children dashed off ahead and were shouted back. Luke's assessment was uncannily accurate.

"Some people shouldn't bloody have kids," Luke said.

"If they run off in front of a lorry again like that, they won't," Connor said, raising a smile from his companion.

They waited while the family disappeared into the toilets and then re-appeared to join the cafeteria queue.

"Showtime." Luke grinned at Connor and threw him a set of keys. "Bring the truck over."

Connor followed Luke across the car park, striding through the puddles without hesitation, his mind occupied with what he was about to do. For the first time since his new life began, he was going to steal.

At least, thanks to the havoc on the roads caused by last night's storm, there were no police at the service station.

All the same, the two of them were taking no chances.

Connor reversed the pickup over to where Luke had let himself into the Volvo having unhitched the 'van. Working quickly, Luke let off the handbrake and rolled the car forward and Connor reversed the truck into the vacated space. He dashed round the back to replace the number plate on the caravan while Luke attached the caravan to the truck's tow bar.

Within minutes they had finished. Luke leapt into the cab beside Connor. "Not even locked," he said in disgust. "Now, off we go and keep it nice and steady. Take the first exit off the motorway."

Connor did as he was told, keeping a steady fifty and then turning off onto a smaller road at the first chance. Sitting in a layby were

Terry and Val, an elderly couple in their own beat-up Volvo.

The caravan was swapped again, gaining another number plate in the process. Just in case anyone had been watching, Luke also switched all the plates on the truck too.

"See you at home," Luke said as he and Connor returned to the truck. They set off leaving Terry and Val to idle along; just an ordinary couple taking their caravan home.

"Slick," Connor said, genuinely impressed.

"Don't do it often, never the same place twice in succession and so far I've been bloody lucky."

Connor waited. It sounded like a lesson and he wasn't sure it was finished. There were unspoken words in the air.

"I don't take risks, Con. I get the impression you don't either. Some of the youngsters, well, they don't pay attention. They're careless, forever needing telling when to stop."

"I noticed." They'd had three arrested before Christmas because they'd got greedy.

"This storm makes things bad. People'll want to replace stuff. Charlie would have been around to knock sense into them but ... well, I'd like you to watch my back, make sure the youngsters are responsible."

"Really?" Connor glanced at his passenger in surprise. He knew he'd gained a reputation as unapproachable when he first joined, which was what he wanted. Luke, like others, had misread grief for anger and given him a wide berth though sometimes even he had trouble telling the difference. It looked like Luke had changed his mind.

Could he do this? Did he care enough about the people he spent his life with now to make sure they stayed out of jail?

He'd been detached so long, hiding inside, that he honestly didn't know.

"I can't guarantee I'll be any good," he told Luke.

"They'll listen to you," Luke said, "and I trust you to say 'enough' at the right time."

"And if they don't listen?"

"They respect you. They'll listen."

Connor nodded slowly. He seemed to have made more of an impression than he'd realised.

"What'll you be doing?"

"I've got a bloody council to deal with, remember?"

*

Daniel paused on the bank steps and watched the stream of humanity gushing down the High Street.

Fractious families, tired and fraught from Christmas and New Year, fought their way into over-crowded, over-heated shops in search of bargains they couldn't afford.

Frantically flashing Christmas lights in store windows were overshadowed by the pointless giant 'Sale' posters that shoppers rarely paused to read.

Daniel closed his eyes, briefly letting the noise wash over him. He should have stayed in bed; would have done had James not been so enthusiastic about his new purchase.

"Meet me in town, outside Starbucks, and I'll show you."

So Daniel had got up unreasonably early, driven a circuitous route in to avoid all the storm damage from the night before, sat in a queue of cars to get into the multi-storey, stood in another queue in the bank to put all his Christmas cheques in and was resigned to the fact that his best friend had probably just got a new jumper.

Taking a deep breath, he plunged in amongst the crowds and fought his way towards the Eastgate shopping centre.

A sound stopped him as he passed Marks and Spencer. Rising

sweet and clear over the yelled conversations around him came the call of a flute.

It stirred memories – forgotten for a twelve-month period and yet always there, buried deep.

He pushed his way to the entrance, out of the main flow, until he stood two paces from the old man with the wooden flute.

He could remember standing listening in this very spot, hand in hand with his mother on their own forays to the January sales. The music was entrancing, soft and sweet and yet lost almost as soon as he walked away. Not a tune he had ever been able to hold to but one which rooted him to this spot, at this time of year, for eternity.

Daniel shook his head – stupid thought. How could the man be playing the same tune, year in, year out? After a full year, how would he even know what the man played last time anyway?

Except he'd been so sure.

Daniel pushed the thought away, half annoyed with himself but mainly amused at the tricks memory could play.

Completing the ritual, he reached in his pocket as he did every year, pulled out a handful of coins and threw them into the flute case.

The old man nodded his head slightly in acknowledgement, the notes continuing to ripple from the wooden flute he played.

Daniel paused, held by the tune.

Same man, same flute, every January for all the years he could remember – why not the same tune?

The eyes watching him were bright blue, laughter crinkling the corners. Shoulder-length white hair and a close-cropped beard of the same colour framed a weather-beaten face. Daniel had a sudden feeling that his thoughts were being read.

He turned away, remembering James as he did. He glanced at his watch; he was going to be late.

"Thank you," he said over his shoulder. "It's beautiful."

He dodged his way across the High Street and into the shopping centre which was, if anything, even more crowded.

Heavy bags whacked his shins and stray elbows punched into exposed areas. He nearly flattened one old lady who stopped right in front of him as she left Boots and he narrowly avoided standing on at least two toddlers but eventually he was out of the far end into Eastgate.

He made it to outside Starbucks just in time to see James arrive ... on a bicycle.

"You're mad. It's bad enough walking today."

"Don't you like it?" James pushed it towards him. "Twenty-one gears, adjustable handlebars, carbon fibre—"

"It's brilliant," Daniel laughed. "It must have cost a bomb."

"Used my Christmas present money and my Christmas bonus from nice Mr Tesco." The two of them worked evenings and holidays at the superstore to supplement their small allowances whilst at college completing 'A' levels. "Worth every penny."

"I saved mine." Daniel preferred to borrow his mum's car if he wanted to get anywhere.

"For next year?"

"Fingers crossed."

"Got any interviews yet?"

"Nottingham University."

"And your dad's OK with it now?"

Daniel knew he'd paused too long, but the question had come out of the blue.

"Still not sure?"

"No." Daniel waved a hand as James opened his mouth. "He's asked Phil to take over but," he shrugged, "We don't go there, OK, so don't ruin a nice day."

"You're right. The sun is out, the sky is blue, trees everywhere are lying down, we're being crushed by handbag-waving maniacs and your dad's going to kill you shortly. What could be better?"

Daniel laughed.

"Better," James said. A dozen years of friendship meant they knew each other inside out. Daniel supposed they complemented each other. James was tall, blonde and handsome and wore his heart firmly on his sleeve. Quick to laugh, quick to flare up, quick to forgive. Daniel was shorter, darker and quieter which didn't mean he wasn't involved in the scrapes. He was the one who thought through the consequences, looked before they leapt and saved James from the flak.

By now, confronted with a disagreement about his career choice, James would have had an almighty row with his own dad, won the right to do what he wanted and forgotten it.

That wasn't Daniel's way, nor was it his father's. Mr Calver had quietly and dogmatically assumed Daniel would be taking over the family shop. Daniel had other plans that he was pursuing just as assiduously. His father's disappointment hung heavy between them.

"Coffee?" James asked, disturbing Daniel's reverie.

"Peace? Space to breathe?" Daniel countered.

"I think the café in the park was open when I came through."

It was and a few hardy patrons sat outside enjoying the crisp January air as they watched the ducks on the small lake.

Two hundred yards away the back of the old manor loomed, the park spreading out round it.

The trees in the avenue from town were stark and bare at this time of year, though they all still stood upright after the night's excitements. Beyond the lake, the children's playground was nearly deserted.

"Here," James dumped a tray on the table in front of Daniel. "Two coffees, two bacon butties."

"Thanks, you're a star."

"Mass of fiery gas that shines a lot?"

Daniel considered his friend. "Yes, sounds about right."

"Hey, Dan, lighten up. Too heavy today, yes?"

"I'm sorry. There was an old man playing outside Marks and Spencers."

"Yeah, he's there every year."

"I know. I suppose it got me to thinking how time moves on."

"Oh God, you sound like my Grandad on Christmas day."

Daniel smiled. "Not like that really, just like ... oh, I don't know. I've stood and watched him every year for seventeen years and if I don't get out now I'll still be watching him for another seventeen."

"Your dad has agreed to let you go. You've applied now and everything," James said, suddenly serious and hitting straight to the root of Daniel's mood.

"But I'd like to be able to come back too, you know. Like the old man – gone most of the time but grounded here. If we part badly, dad and I, well ..."

"You can come and stay with me."

"I know."

"Not the same," James said for him. "I realise that. What's more important, Dan; going away or coming back?"

Daniel looked out across the park, the places he'd grown up; the swings he'd outgrown at nine, the duck pond he'd fallen in one New Year's Eve, the Manor he'd spent several school trips looking round. But that was the point; they were places limited by a child's vision and now he could see further.

"Going away," he said. "I want to see the world."

"Then you do what it takes to go."

They sat in companionable silence watching people feed the ducks and geese on the lake for a while and then took turns on the bike chasing each other up and down the long drive through the park.

By the time they went their separate ways Daniel was feeling much happier. Time with James usually had that effect. Even when they ended up in trouble it was worth it for the release of tension it gave him.

"Come 'round tomorrow," James said as he left. "We ought to check we've done all the homework before college starts."

"Ruin the day, why don't you," Daniel shouted after the cycling figure. He headed for the car park with a spring in his step. The crowds were less, walking was easier, and he moved through the town at speed.

Only as he passed Marks and Spencer did he slow. The old man was still there but had paused in his playing. He smiled up as Daniel passed.

Daniel grinned back. "Lovely tunes," he said and continued towards the car park. He almost added that he'd decided to go though he wasn't sure what prompted the thought.

Only as he reached the limit of hearing did he think the old man responded. Of course he hadn't, for what Daniel heard was 'Thank you, Daniel' and that was plainly impossible.

*

When Marshall and his sergeant arrived back at the station, they found Helen Lovell hovering around outside his office.

"Anything I can do, sir?" He really must get the constable to drop the 'sir'; she'd been on his team long enough to know it wasn't necessary.

"Well, you could check how the search is going on up at West Cross. Also, you could check the system and see if there are any similar cases, particularly the use of albino as a calling card. Mark, track down Calver's Hardware store and we might pay it a visit. We need to go out to The Highwayman and see if we can find out what Mr Knight was doing out there last night and I think we ought to speak to Curtis Yates. I want a cause of death from Liza and I'd be interested to know about Mr Knight's record as he seems to have been in trouble enough for his mum to consider it a usual occurrence to have police turning up on her doorstep." Marshall opened up his office. "Apart from all that and making sure various flying objects from last night are cleared from the roads, it should be a quiet day! Anything else to report from last night that could add to the workload?" he called over his shoulder as he went in.

"Another gypsy spree."

"That's uniform's problem."

"Well ..."

Marshall heard the hesitation and retraced his steps. "What?"

"Chief's talking about 'organised crime' and moving it to CID."

"Organised crime? That's paedophile rings and drug smugglers not a bunch of Irish conmen." He paused. "What do you mean, 'the chief's talking about'?"

"He wanted you in a briefing first thing and you were out, so I had to go. It has got a bit out of hand, sir."

"I thought the council were moving them on?"

"They're fighting it, I hear. Something about the landowner giving them the land to stay on as a permanent camp thing."

"And did he?"

"God knows."

Marshall sighed. "Sod it; where are they, then?"

"Out by where we were last night," Mark said, "possibly even the same farm."

"Right by where a man was found dead, you mean?"

"Careful, John, that could be construed as prejudice."

"Did I say anything? But add that to the list of things to do; another line of enquiry."

The phone on Helen's desk rang and she picked it up, listening without interruption to the person on the other end.

"Tell me that's good news," Marshall said. The look on her face suggested the opposite.

"'fraid not. You're needed at the tree on the West Cross road."

"Yes?"

"Yes, contractors have just got to it. When the roots came up, they brought a body with them."

CHAPTER 2

"So what do we know, Helen?" Marshall asked as Mark drove the three of them out of town. "Have we any details?"

"No. Body found lodged among the tree roots. That's it."

"From what I remember having had to detour round it this morning, it's a massive tree."

"So?" Mark said, taking his eyes briefly off the road.

"So, it's probably hundreds of years old. I think we should have called the museum to get an archaeologist out here for anything found in the roots."

"They did say 'body' not 'skeleton' on the phone," Helen said.

It was a body and a fresh one at that. Entwined with the huge display of waving roots that flailed the air hung a man. Various limbs twisted at painful angles and his neck had obviously snapped.

Caught beside him, almost within reach of his left hand, was a wheelbarrow. A saw had jammed with its teeth lodged in the grotesquely swinging right foot.

"Bugger me," Mark said, "the prat was gathering logs from a falling tree."

"Looks that way." Marshall never ceased to wonder at the stupidity of some people. He looked round. Down the hill he could see the sprawl of caravans that must be the traveller's camp and, just beyond, the flutter of yellow tape and a small white pavilion marked out the ditch Philip Knight's body had been recovered from.

"I don't like it," he said, "two bodies this close."

"No call about this one," Mark said.

"Wasn't technically a call about the last one," Helen added. "There could still be a woman out there too, you know."

"I bloody hope not." Marshall didn't want the sort of panic that the discovery of three bodies would produce. Two was going to be bad enough once the media got their claws into it.

"So where now?" Mark asked.

"The farm, I think." A large sprawl of a house loomed at the end of the field they stood in. "I can't imagine why they're not already here busy-bodying." In his experience it was a very unusual person who could see the police out of the window and not come to investigate. He had an awful feeling that the reason for the lack of presence was swinging grotesquely in the breeze.

Marshall picked his way round the huge scar in the muddy earth which had once rooted the fallen oak. "Helen, tell uniform to set up a proper diversion. We can't move the tree until we've got the body. Mark, come and see if the farmer's in."

They entered the garden of the farmhouse through the back gate into the field. Outhouses and barns huddled to the right of the large, red-brick house.

Marshall tried the back door, knocking loudly on the battered wood.

After several moments a lady in her mid forties opened the door. She had short, dark hair shading towards grey, a fading bruise on her jaw and a fresher one on her cheek. She had also been crying.

"Detective Inspector Marshall, Fenwick CID," Marshall began, at which point she collapsed against him, sobbing wildly.

"Shall we go in?" He guided her back into a traditional farmhouse kitchen.

The distraught woman clung to him as he led her to the armchair in the corner. "Madam, I wondered …" He stopped. What was the point; she wasn't hearing any of this.

"Cup of tea?" Mark suggested.

"If you think it'll help." Marshall had seen his sergeant pull this trick before with victims.

"The tea doesn't. The ordinariness does."

Marshall crouched beside the crying woman, supporting her grief while Mark began making tea. While he worked, he kept up a stream of inconsequential conversation taking farming as his theme. He talked about the Aga and the china and the pine dresser, then the time he had stayed in Devon and tractors on vertical hills in Wales. As the tears subsided, Marshall joined in adding his own memories of watching sheep trials in Yorkshire, and cream teas in Cornwall.

By the time the tea was made, the woman was almost calm though she still clung to Marshall. He disengaged himself gently so he could help her drink from the earthenware mug.

Once she had, he took a deep breath. He had to try again.

"Madam, I'm with the police. We're dealing with your fallen tree. Could I ask your name?"

Wide blue eyes watched him damply, but she managed, "Eileen Faulkner."

"Thank you, Eileen. Are you on your own here?"

"Yes." He heard the catch in her voice and looked to Mark who shrugged.

"You've got to ask; I'll find some tissues."

Marshall tried to come at it obliquely. "Are you usually alone, Eileen?"

"No." It was as if she knew that saying too much at once would re-open the floodgates.

"Who's normally with you?"

"Tom and Zoe." She paused and then it all rushed out in a barely coherent stream. "They went. He went and then Zoe went and they didn't come back and she wouldn't stay and she said to tell the police because he went and she went after him but I couldn't because he said then she might not come back and I knew she'd come back but she hasn't and the tree fell and I was so scared and I didn't know what to do." The end was lost in a fresh outpouring of tears.

Marshall tipped her chin up firmly so he could get through to her. "Are you saying your daughter is missing, Eileen?"

She nodded between sobs. "And Tom."

"Oh fuck," Mark said quietly. "I'll go and get them looking a bit closer. He was obvious stuck in the air like that but ..." He left the sentence unfinished and dashed from the house.

"I'm sorry, Eileen," Marshall said. "I think we've found Tom. We'll set up a search for your girl." With a heavy heart he wrapped an arm round her and held her while she sobbed. "Could you tell me what colour hair she has?"

"Black," she managed. "Long and black."

*

Zoe looked round the small hotel room. It was a basic double with ensuite but she wasn't paying for luxury, just a place to lay her head for a couple of nights while she sorted travel arrangements. She imagined all the rooms looked the same; cheap and cheerful. Cream walls held prints of beach scenes and the burgundy curtains matched the striped bedspread.

Dumping an armful of brochures on the double bed, she felt the pressure on her lift.

She'd done it; walked away in one piece. No-one had come looking for her while she fought the shoppers in town. If her luck held just a day or so longer, she'd be out of the country. Then she could write to her mum, promise to come home once she'd learnt to deal with the inner demons.

For now, she just needed to escape.

She put the small kettle on and pulled the striped curtains closed. The view of the busy ring road and McDonalds was uninspiring.

With a cup of tea in one hand she stretched out on the bed. Her feet ached pleasantly from walking for hours and her shoulders were sore from the unaccustomed burden, but it had gone well.

She ticked off a mental list.

She'd replaced the clothes she'd left with the sleeping girl when she crept out of the sheepfold at dawn. She'd also found a small tent that would strap to her backpack and a new mobile phone so her mother couldn't track her. It had a camera and internet access. This was most important because the bank manager had been sympathetic to changing her details so she could pick up statements on the web wherever she went. She had been pleased to find she had nearly five thousand pounds in her account. Three years of paying in every single penny she earned on Saturdays had paid off.

Zoe sighed and closed her eyes. Had she really been planning this day for three years? Was it only three years? Some nights it had felt like a lifetime; nights of listening to her mum sobbing and begging which had gone on forever.

Well, no more. The oak had seen to that.

And her mother had cried for him.

Zoe sat up, annoyed with herself.

"I'm moving on," she said aloud, "time to forget mum." That was easier said than done but the distance would help.

She turned over the magazines: Australia, India, America, Canada, Africa. The world was hers to choose from. All sights she'd never seen on their annual trips to campsites in France.

A flutter of excitement tickled her stomach; this was real.

She slid from the bed and indulged in a long shower. She could feel seventeen years of a different person washing away. Today she was no longer cowed or scared.

Today she was free.

Once she was dressed again, Zoe emptied her knapsack and retrieved her most valued treasure from its blanketing of clothes.

The ancient flute was a family heirloom and had passed to Zoe after generations of use by long-forgotten relatives. It had a beautifully carved wooden case showing what she thought of as the pied piper. An old man, playing a flute, danced though woodland while animals peered out at him or scampered along behind. Closest to him ran a hare and fox while a bird flew, glided almost, overhead. The animals were beautifully carved. There was real life and love in the picture and Zoe paused each time she played to run her fingers reverently across the wood.

The flute was as well made and its tone was soft and low, flowing richly from the wood. Music had always been Zoe's escape; something unsullied by her father and his fists.

She played from the heart. Today, she started with Mason's Apron and the Hullichan Jig for the joy of being on the road at last and then a slower air of her own composition written for her mother, though today she played it for the oak. One day, perhaps, she would share the regrets in the piece with her mum. She tried another tune, experimental and wild in free time suggested by the storm of the previous night. It needed polishing but she was pleased with the flow of it.

After working on the tune for a while she finished with some old favourites, jigs and reels, waltzes and polkas.

The knock on the door came as she finished playing.

Zoe buried the flute back in the bottom of her rucksack. Surely she hadn't disturbed anyone with the music.

The knock came again.

Warily, Zoe opened the door and then pulled it wide in surprise. "You!"

The huge dog grinned up at her, his tail waving madly, his auburn-haired mistress beside him. "But ..." But she'd left the girl asleep half a dozen miles and several hours away.

"I thought I should return these." The girl was back in her assortment of long skirts and jumpers. She held out Zoe's neatly folded jeans and sweatshirt.

"You shouldn't have. I replaced them. You can keep them."

"Thanks."

The two of them stared awkwardly at each other.

"How the hell did you find me?" Zoe blurted out eventually.

"Oh, it wasn't easy," the girl said, "but Merlin's good at tracking people down."

"That good?" Zoe couldn't believe it. She'd been in half the shops in town and then caught a bus out to the Travelodge.

"It's a gift and the music helped."

"Well, thanks, but you shouldn't have bothered." Zoe began to close the door. The last thing she needed was someone who could tell her mum where she was and the girl's explanation didn't inspire trust.

"OK," the girl and dog turned to go. "See you around."

"I hope not," Zoe muttered as she shut the door with a satisfying click. "That is one weird girl," she said to the empty room, "let's hope she knows how to keep her mouth shut."

The peace brought by the music had slipped away.

*

"Doctor's given her something to help her sleep," Helen Lovell said as she reappeared in the kitchen. At Eileen Faulkner's suggestion, the police were using the farm as a base while they searched, and half a dozen officers stood round the scrubbed pine table. "Any sign of the girl?"

Marshall shook his head. "Only the father in the tree so far. They're getting him down now so Liza can have a look at him."

Dr Liza Trent was standing by the sink holding a coffee, watching the work in the field beyond the garden.

Huge lights had been set up and the waving roots sent grotesque shadows dancing across the late afternoon. Already the sky was darkening, what little winter sun there had been was dying away behind more clouds.

"So, where's the girl?" Helen asked.

"Out there last night she could have been hit by anything," Mark said. "She could even be under the tree or after the other one–" He shrugged.

"Any news on our other victim, Liza?" Marshall joined her at the sink. "I realise we didn't give you a lot of time."

"Not a lot? No time at all is more like it. I managed a preliminary inspection and so far I can see nothing amiss, no marks at all." She turned away from her scrutiny of outside. "I think this one will provide rather more scope and probably be just as difficult to say for certain. Too much is as bad as too little."

"Sorry," Marshall said absently. "The two don't fit, do they?"

"The bodies don't," Mark said.

"Meaning?"

"Two women missing, one for each death? Perhaps the deaths were merely unfortunate side effects of the abductions."

"As soon as it's light we'll get a search party going if we haven't found anything in the tree," Marshall said. "Start from the farm and work out."

"The travellers might help," PC Kite suggested. He was one of those who'd been fighting the lighting rig the night before and Marshall felt a little sorry for inflicting yet another sleepless night on the man.

"What do you mean?"

"They're camped down in Faulkner's bottom field. I know they're a bunch of rascals when it comes to other people's property but I'm sure they'd help look for the girl or girls. Her dad did let them stay here after all."

"Well, we can but ask," Marshall said. The idea had possibilities and he liked to keep suspects where he could see them. "We'll pop in later; ask them to keep an eye out."

Another young constable stuck his head round the door. "He's down, sir. Is the doctor here?"

"Liza?"

"On my way, John." She carefully washed her mug and upended it on the draining board before she left.

"Sir," Helen joined Marshall at the table. "I'd say Mrs Faulkner's been hit."

"I saw the bruises on her face, Helen. I did wonder... and it's John."

"I saw the bruises everywhere else, sir ... John, while the doctor was examining her." They'd called in the local GP to give Mrs Faulkner something to help her settle.

Marshall raised an eyebrow. "Bad?"

"I'd say so."

"Any chance she got them trying to get her husband down from the tree?"

"The one on her face is the only fresh one as far as I can see."

"No chance," Doctor Gillespie said. He had followed Helen into the kitchen and now stood behind Marshall. "I'm afraid Mrs Faulkner 'fell' regularly."

"Fell?" Marshall raised an eyebrow.

"Her story, not mine, Inspector." Mrs Faulkner's doctor was tall and stooped, his eyes magnified by thick lenses. "She would never admit to the abuse."

"What the fuck was she crying for?" Helen said, voicing Marshall's thoughts.

He smiled slightly. His young constable was usually more refined.

"Sorry, sir," she said, "but surely she should be pleased he's gone."

Marshall nodded. He couldn't imagine Helen ever letting anyone hit her. He never gave it much thought but there was a certain detached efficiency to Helen Lovell. Earlier he had taken Mark to deal with a possible distressed wife leaving Helen to organise the crime scene because that was the way they worked best. Only her gender had dictated that she go upstairs to help Dr Gillespie.

He liked Helen; she was tough and clever and intuitive, but she was too cold for victims. How could you explain to someone so self-possessed that Eileen Faulkner would have loved her bully of a husband and probably saw herself to blame for the beatings.

"I don't know," he settled for saying. "I never have understood domestic violence."

"So it might," Mark said, "be more than just trees or murderers that hit the daughter if she went out."

"Anything's possible, Mark."

"I know," Mark said, "just sometimes I wish it wasn't. There are some victims who deserve every tree root they get."

*

"They're still there," Connor said, watching the blaze of lights round the felled oak.

"Ominous," Luke said, looking the other way to the second splay of lights below them. "I don't like it."

They'd been alarmed by the police activity earlier, fearing a swoop on the stolen caravan, but the cars had sped past and up the hill. All afternoon and on into the evening police flocked round the stricken tree, unrolling tape and erecting tents to match the one which had been present since first light.

"That means a body," Terry had said, watching it go up.

"No," Luke said, "it means a crime scene."

"What else could it be?"

"Buried treasure," Connor had suggested though in his heart he knew otherwise.

"Terry's right," Luke said, now standing beside Connor outside the purloined caravan. "It has to be a body."

"Fresh one, old one, more than one?"

"Let's hope it's more than four months old." Anything before the travellers had arrived at the beginning of a golden September.

"The older the better," Connor agreed. He wouldn't wish the grief of fresh death on any man. It must have shown in his voice.

"Sorry, Con, this must bring back bad memories for you."

"Some." More than Luke could know. Echoes of grief buried too deep for him to recognise the tremors as the prelude of the earthquake to come. "I'm moving on."

"We'll know if they come down. I doubt they'll bother us if it's an old corpse."

As if on cue the shout came from the gate.

"Visitor, Luke."

The two men picked their way round the rebuilt camp by the light of the lamps hanging on each van. The gentle hum of the generators filled the night.

A man stood by the watchers at the field entrance.

Dressed in black, a deeper shadow against the tree-lined dark of the lane, the stranger leant against the gate.

Connor shivered. Something about the man jarred. Maybe just the way he – an outsider – seemed at ease while the two youngsters from the camp were hesitant and nervous, jumping at Luke's approach.

"Who is he?" Luke asked.

"I'm Raven," the man said softly. "I've come to beg a place to camp for the night." He indicated a rucksack almost hidden in the gloom at his feet. "I have my own tent and can bring food to the pot and payment for anything I might need."

The voice was cultured and smooth, raising chills across Connor's neck. Normally he took time to know people. It disturbed him, such instant and abrupt dislike. Deeper even than that; with no reason, this strange man with his odd name scared Connor.

Something of the feeling must have communicated itself to Luke too because he paused before saying, "You're welcome here, Raven. Come in."

As the man bent to retrieve his pack, a car pulled up in the road outside and two men got out.

"Police," Luke hissed.

Connor didn't need to be told; even without uniform there was no mistaking their profession.

The two men approached confidently. One was tall, about forty, his hair showing brown in the lights of the car. The other was shorter, older, greyer.

After Raven, they gave off an air of comforting familiarity that Connor found disconcertingly reassuring. The police were not people he should welcome.

"What can we do for you?" Luke demanded, moving to block the entrance.

Connor joined him, noticing Raven stepping up on Luke's other side.

Solidarity or curiosity?

"Detective Inspector Marshall, Detective Sergeant Sherbourne, Fenwick CID. We were wondering if we could ask for your assistance?"

"Assistance?" That was unexpected. Connor heard Luke's amazement and stepped in following memories of his own.

"Help with your inquiries, you mean?" He'd heard it all when Cindy went. Perhaps this was too close for comfort.

"Possibly," the Inspector said, "but actually we have a missing girl, possibly two; vanished in last night's storm. They may be lying hurt somewhere. We wondered if you'd keep an eye out and help with a search tomorrow."

"Missing girls? By all means," Luke said, relief evident. "Of course we'll help."

"Thank you." The policemen turned away.

"What have you found?" It was Raven, his voice low and compelling.

"I don't think that's any of your business at present, sir," the Inspector said.

Raven laughed. "It will be."

"What do you mean by that?" The Inspector came back, closer.

"See a crime, pick on a traveller." Connor heard the bitter truth in Raven's words. He wondered what this strange man had been accused of and wished he hadn't brought it here, tonight.

"That's not the way we do things in Fenwick," Inspector Marshall said. "I'll bid you a good night."

The two of them climbed back into their car and drove away, leaving the three men standing in the field entrance.

"A missing girl," Luke said eventually as the noise of the engine faded, "that's bad. Who knows what she might meet."

Connor found his gaze drawn to their new guest to find his gaze returned.

"Who knows, indeed," Raven said.

*

"Hostile," Mark commented as they drove away.

"Unsurprising really. If they are behind all the recent thefts, then they hardly want us snooping around and if they aren't then they're going to feel picked on."

"Misunderstood."

"That as well."

They drove up the hill in silence.

"It's wrong," Marshall said as they reached the tree blocking the way. "He's on the wrong side of the tree. If he was out collecting firewood, surely he'd have been under the branches, not in the roots. And why the shovel?" The men getting the body out had found a spade lodged underneath the wheelbarrow.

"I had an idea," Mark said as they pulled up and got out.

"Go on."

"What if he had something buried under the tree which he realised the roots were about to bring up. He'd have to get in amongst the roots, dig round and saw them up to get at whatever it was."

"What sort of thing?"

"Don't know, but I might look him up on the computer, see if he might be the sort of person to bury secrets."

"I like it," Marshall said. "It would explain why the daughter missed him too. She wouldn't have expected him in the hole."

"So where is she?"

"It would help if the mother was more coherent. I'd like to know if the girl left before or after the tree fell."

"Surely we'd know if she was under it," Mark said. They stood and looked at the brilliantly lit tree where it sprawled in front of them.

Marshall shook his head. "It's a bloody big tree, Mark. If she was looking round this side for her dad." He shook his head again as if he could dislodge the idea. "We just won't know until we move the tree. And if she isn't, why isn't she home safe? I can't see anything but disaster in this one."

Liza Trent was waiting for them when they returned to the light and warmth of the farmhouse kitchen.

"What have we got, Doctor?" Marshall said.

"Initially, I'd say I can't see anything that isn't tree damage. He's fairly badly broken so I'm not going to be definite until I've had a close look inside, but it all looks ... natural, if you'll excuse the pun."

"One less problem, then," Mark said. "Just the girl."

Marshall set about making more coffee. "I'm not sure it helps much, Mark. We seem to have two men dead from natural causes and, coincidentally, reports of two missing girls. It's all a bit steep to believe they simply happened to die like that. And what on earth were the two of them doing out in the middle of that storm? I want to see what's under that tree but then I think I'm going to treat the deaths as mightily suspicious until someone tells me not to or something starts to make sense." It was going to be another long night while they waited for the contractors to safely and carefully move the tree.

And at the end of it?

He wasn't sure what to hope for. If she wasn't under the oak, then she might be alive but that meant he wouldn't get much in the way of sleep until they found her. And what about the other girl? Did she even exist at all?

Remembering the violence of the storm, finding anyone alive seemed a vain hope. Perhaps it would be better to find her sooner rather than later.

"I hate these cases," Mark said, echoing Marshall's thoughts, "too much effort with too little hope."

"Always some hope," Marshall said, automatically.

Mark didn't answer; he didn't need to.

Rather than spend an evening listening to the sawing and hammering from the tree, Marshall took Mark down into West Cross to visit The Highwayman. "We'll have a drink and maybe ask a few questions about Mr Knight's visit last night." Hickson had supplied them with a photograph of the victim earlier.

"We don't know that he was murdered, John."

"We do know that he was in the middle of a field in the middle of January in a hurricane. Asking a few questions won't hurt and we're not doing anything else except wait at the moment."

The Highwayman was a small country pub without any of the canned music or fruit machines of the city centre variety. A log fire burned in a huge hearth to one side of the bar and massive wooden beams separated the lounge into smaller, cosy corners.

Marshall ordered two pints and perched on a stool at the bar. There were very few people in, and the landlord was happy to stand and chat to the two policemen, sipping his own pint as he did.

"Last night? Quite crowded really for a Thursday. I think all the gyppos were down here rather than getting blown around the field. I don't blame them, not the sort of life I'd want, camping out in all weathers."

"Did you see this man?" Marshall put Philip Knight's picture on the bar. "His mum believes he was coming out here last night."

The landlord looked at the picture and then shrewdly at Marshall. "Something to do with all those tents and tapes you've got up at Faulkner's farm, would he?"

"It's possible," Marshall hedged. "Did you see him last night?"

"Yeah, he's a bit of a regular. Comes in with a friend of his from time to time and then comes and makes trouble on Sundays in the village when the hunt goes out."

"And last night?"

"He was a bit odd to tell the truth. I thought he'd be off on his soap box about blasted hunting again, but he was with some of the travellers going on about some bird dancing on the hills."

"A what?"

"Says he saw some naked woman with long white hair dancing up on the hill and had anyone else seen her. I thought he was pissed though he must have drunk elsewhere because he only had a couple here. He was trying to get people to go along and see if they could find her but I'm not sure he had any takers with the weather like it was last night.

"So you think he went up the hill?"

"No idea, left after closing time with his friend, could have gone anywhere."

"Thanks," Marshall handed over some more money. "Have one on us." The two of them made their way to the armchairs by the fire with their drinks.

"Well," Mark said, "that explains what he was doing on the hill. Unfortunately, it suggests this other woman may be real so we've got to find two of them."

"Oh, come on, Mark. Dancing naked on top of a hill? Midsummer, possibly, but January?"

"Perhaps she was trying to lure him out there."

"Why on earth would she do that? And why him?"

"I don't know – to kill him?"

Marshall considered that one while he finished his pint. It made an odd kind of sense. The woman had lured Philip Knight out onto the hill, played dead to get him to go close and then killed him. It didn't really explain why she'd let him phone the police or how she'd managed to kill him. Unless Liza could find a cause of death then he decided it didn't hold an awful lot of water as a theory and Marshall could think of easier ways to attract men than dancing naked on hillsides in hurricanes.

He put it to the back of his head. "I think we might talk to this friend of his, though. What did his mum call him?"

"Curtis something or other."

"Yes, him. He might know if Philip went up that hill to look for naked ladies last night. Perhaps he went with him."

*

That night Daniel had the most vivid dream he could ever remember.

Sleeping at all had seemed unlikely when he went to bed. The evening's argument had replayed itself over and over in his head.

"Philip's dead," his mother had said, almost as soon as he'd arrived in. "They found him in a ditch last night."

"What? How?"

"Don't know; the police aren't saying anything."

Daniel couldn't believe it. "He wasn't chasing hunters again, was he?" His cousin had some fairly strong beliefs and some rather dangerous ways of going about showing them.

"Don't think so. His mum said he just went to the pub last night."

While Daniel tried taking this in, his father had taken a deep breath and Daniel suddenly saw a chasm opening before him.

"You'll have to stay now, Daniel. I'll need you to take the shop on." His father said it as if there could be no possible argument.

"I'm sorry," Daniel tried to hold his temper in, "but I've got an interview at Nottingham and–"

"Philip's dead. You can't go now." His father's voice rose several degrees.

"You can find someone else, dad. I want to–"

"I don't want to find someone else. I built this for you," his father had shouted; something he rarely did.

"Then you shouldn't have bothered." Daniel couldn't ever recall being so angry. Why should Philip's death ruin his life too? "Who said this is what I want? Why would I wish to spend my whole life stuck behind a counter in Fenwick?"

"So I'm small minded, with no vision?"

The pain in his father's eyes was awful but Daniel wasn't going to let guilt rob him of a future. He bit back his first sour agreement with his father. "You're not me. I need to live my life."

"Please stop," his mother's whispered plea had halted them both momentarily. "Please don't row. I can't stand it. Phil's gone and now–"

"I'm sorry, Mum." He genuinely was. "I simply want to get a degree and do something with my life. I hoped you might be happy for me."

"And who do you think will pay for this new life of yours? You don't want the shop, just the money it will give you." His dad wouldn't let it go.

"I'll get a job, pay my own way." The injustice stung; when had he ever expected anything?

"Tesco, I suppose." Daniel nearly laughed; he couldn't win. Admission that he did pay his own way, but his dad had never forgiven him for taking work elsewhere despite Daniel's reasonable argument that Tesco was open evenings and Sundays - all the times when he wasn't at college, but their store was closed.

"Tesco or any bloody where. I'm leaving home this summer whether I get into uni or not. I can't stay here and be treated like a fucking child." He gasped for breath as if he'd been running but had to finish it. "I'm eighteen, dad, with my own life, my own needs. If I stay here, I'll always be a child with my life mapped out by you. I'm me. I've got my own fucking life and I'm going to live it. I don't want to die like Phil with nothing done."

He'd thought about slamming out of the house, going to James', but had contented himself with storming up to his room and banging the door.

He was too wound up to sleep at first but, as his mind replayed the scene, he felt as if a weight had been lifted from him.

He'd never been one to defy his parents, but it felt so good to stand up for himself.

He never swore at them or shouted either and he felt a bit bad about that but the anxiety and suspense gnawing inside had gone.

He'd told them; finally made his stand.

He had to go.

Sleep came surprisingly quickly – faster than in weeks – and, with it, the dream.

He was standing on a road which stretched away into unimaginable distances. It passed fields on either side and ran straight towards distant woods and mist-topped hills.

The sky above was blue and cloudless; a light breeze brushed his cheeks.

All around was music, sweet and clear.

Beside the road a rustic bench appeared. The old musician from the town centre sat on it, playing. It was from his wooden flute that the music sprang, filling the world.

"I remembered the tune," Daniel said in wonder. "It is the same." He was sure of it here, in this strange place. The man stopped playing though the music continued.

"For some," he said.

"What is it?"

"Moving on music. A traveller's tune."

"It's beautiful. Did you play it for me?"

"For those who can hear. Especially for those who can recall."

"Who are you?"

"Merely a traveller who plays tunes." The old man smiled, his blue eyes twinkling.

"In my dreams?"

"If your dreams are of travelling, why not?"

"But," Daniel didn't know how to argue with the calm assurance of the man. "You don't know me."

"Do I not, Daniel?"

"I ... but ..." Daniel gave up. "Where does the road go?"

"It's your road."

"But you're on it."

"I walk many roads. Sometimes I stop to point the way."

"Do you always speak in riddles?"

The man laughed and, after a moment, Daniel joined in. In the way of dreams, it felt right and the sound added to the music, becoming part of the tune and the fabric of the place. The joy of the road filled him.

"I allow my music to speak plain," the man said. "May your road rise to meet you." He lifted his flute to his lips again and the tune took flight, soaring high and swooping low as the road did.

Still smiling, Daniel stepped out on to the road.

It slid along, carrying him past fields of waving wheat, golden rapeseed and carpets of pale-blue linseed. The sun shone in an azure sky and sweet scents filled his lungs.

Ahead, the darkness of a wood approached, looming across the silver ribbon he travelled.

He became aware that he was slowing.

A figure stood on the path ahead of him.

Cloaked in black, with the hood pulled up to hide the features, Daniel wasn't sure whether it was man, woman or monster he faced.

The music faded as he stopped, and a sense of foreboding grew. The darkness under the branches hid dire secrets. The creature was a sentinel of evil, barring his path to the future.

Chills skittered down his spine and he clenched his fists.

Above, grey clouds obscured the blue and an icy wind blew from between the giant trunks which reared larger.

Daniel took an involuntary step back.

As he did the figure stepped forwards, looming taller.

Doubt wormed its way into Daniel's heart. How could he take the road? The music was almost gone and dread lurked beneath the trees.

The wind gusted, blowing the hood from the man in the road. Black hair framed a pale face, stern and forbidding.

The eyes held Daniel; deep as night, bottomless pits.

The man raised a hand and Daniel stumbled back, his feet tripping him.

As he fell, a sudden chord of ear-shattering violence rose around him and a giant animal leapt above. Growling horribly, a wolfhound flew at the figure ahead.

Daniel's head hit the road, knocking consciousness from him. As he fell into darkness, the music billowed up, accompanied by the harsh bass of the dog's rumbling snarl.

He must have sunk into a deep sleep because it was getting light when his mobile phone woke him. Its shrill tone cut through the music still ringing in his head.

"Hello," he muttered, still half asleep. "Who is it?"

"Dan," James said, "they've stolen my fucking bike."

CHAPTER 3

4th January

Zoe was waiting for her breakfast to arrive the next morning in the Little Chef when Lacewing slipped into the seat opposite her.

"Good morning."

"Are you following me?" Zoe glanced round. The wolfhound sat patiently on the grass outside the front door.

"You look like someone who needs a friend."

"Well I don't." Less than two days from home and she'd already managed to pick up a weirdo. "I'm not sure I can say it much plainer. Leave me alone."

"I've got a friend you should meet," Lacewing said as if Zoe hadn't spoken.

Zoe tightened her hands round the mug of coffee she was holding, anger bubbling inside. Why did no-one ever pay any attention to what she wanted? All the times she'd told her mother to go and the stupid woman had just carried on making the tea or ironing as if Zoe wasn't there.

And her dad ...

She blocked the memories, unwilling to remember.

"Go away," she said through gritted teeth. "Why don't you listen?"

Something in her tone must have got through to the strange girl. The wild green eyes were suddenly and disconcertingly focused, their gaze drilling into Zoe.

"I do listen. I can hear your soul and the music you play. You need a friend."

"No, I need to escape."

There was a pause while Zoe's full English breakfast arrived.

"He plays the flute, like you do," Lacewing said.

"What? Who does?" Zoe paused, a forkful partway to her mouth. "How do you know what I play?"

"You don't listen much either, do you? I told you; I followed your music to find you."

"But ..."

"My friend plays too. You'd like him."

"If he's anything like you, I shall probably want to strangle him," Zoe said, giving up on being remotely polite. This odd girl didn't seem to take any notice however rude she was. At least she was being honest.

"Look, I promise I'll go away, if you want me to, once you've met him." Lacewing grinned, showing a neat row of white teeth. "Otherwise I may just stick with you – to be friendly, you know."

Zoe did know and it wasn't a thought which appealed. She could try losing Lacewing but, after yesterday, she wasn't sure that was at all possible.

"All right, I'll meet your friend," she said, "but that's it."

"You'll like him." It sounded like a threat.

After breakfast Zoe retrieved her bag from her room and settled her debt.

She'd decided last night that she would go west. Her limited history suggested this was an age-old flight instinct; to follow the setting sun, first to Ireland and then across the deep blue to the Americas. Canada sounded good but, for today, she was going to book a trip to the Emerald Isle.

Or perhaps not.

It looked like she'd just agreed to go and meet some flute-playing oddball.

Lacewing and the wolfhound, Merlin, escorted her towards the town centre.

They walked, the crisp winter air filling their lungs.

Zoe relaxed. Perhaps she ought to walk to Ireland. The exercise made her feel good. It always had. She'd walked the boundaries of the farm regularly in a bid to get out of the house.

She lengthened her stride to a comfortable walking pace, letting the anger flow away.

"You're happy now." Lacewing fell into step beside her.

"Walking ... well, it just ..."

"I know."

And Zoe realised that she did. Lacewing's step was firm, her head up, her eyes fixed on the distant skyline.

"You can listen to the world out here," Lacewing said.

Zoe raised an eyebrow. On the farm she could but they were walking along the main road into the centre. Cars, lorries, and buses charged past, filling the air with noise.

"The life of the town," Lacewing said, "but you have to focus deeper and wider. Look." She pointed across the road. "Wagtails." Two small, black and white birds were bouncing along the kerb.

"And there." Above a magpie flew in a straight line towards the Travelodge they had just left.

"That's seeing, not hearing," Zoe pointed out.

"It's a start." Lacewing paused, watching the cars, her head on one side. "That one." A small red Ford shot past. "He's in a bad mood, late for work, hates the world this morning."

Zoe laughed. "It's gone nine and he's in a suit so it's a safe bet he's late for work and in a bad mood because of it. To be honest, if he fights the rush hour traffic every morning, then he's bound to hate it." She continued walking. "I'm not stupid, you know."

After a moment Lacewing said, in a more remote voice, "He's late because his wife spilled coffee on his suit, and he had to hit her to teach her not to do that."

Zoe paused, her good mood slipping away, then she forced herself to keep walking. "Now you're making things up and that's just pointless," she said, her voice tight.

"It's true."

Zoe whirled, bringing her fists up as she did. Lacewing was right behind her and she found herself nose-to-nose with the girl.

"It's no fucking joke. You've no idea what you're talking about."

In the silence the traffic receded. Zoe could hear her heart thudding in her ears, blood surging upwards in angry waves.

As they stood there, Lacewing saying nothing, Zoe felt the anger slide away. The watchful expression in the other's face struck her. There was none of her mother's fear. Lacewing looked almost as if she was trying out responses in her head to see which might best fit the situation.

Cross with herself now as well – she was supposed to be leaving the violent parts of her past behind – Zoe turned away.

"I'm sorry," Lacewing finally said behind her.

"Whatever."

"Running doesn't always help."

Zoe stopped a second time, turning more slowly.

"Just who the bloody hell are you? What do you want of me?"

Merlin walked forwards to nudge his head against her hand.

Zoe looked down, startled, and then uncurled her fingers to stroke the soft fur.

"We're friends," Lacewing said. "Trust me."

*

James was incandescent, stomping up and down his bedroom, whirling his hands so fast that Daniel was surprised he hadn't knocked more off the shelves.

"Two days, two fucking days and they fucking took it."

"Who? You keep saying 'they' took it like you know who." Daniel had run through all the possible suspects from college on the way over, but he couldn't imagine anyone wanting to deprive James of a brand-new bike. They knew some idiots but no-one who was an outright thief.

"The gyppos. Who do you think?"

"I think the papers just blame everything on—"

"I saw them, Dan. They made a hell of a racket getting into the shed."

"I'm surprised you didn't go down." In, all guns blazing, that was James' way.

"Of course I did, but I had to get dressed first. By the time I got there they were off on my fucking bike."

"How could you know it was—"

"They have a look, Dan."

Daniel gave up trying to convince his friend otherwise. "Have you told the police?"

"Like they're going to do anything."

"I think–"

"Yes, I told the bloody police. Dad insisted. It took them forty-five minutes to get anyone here." James continued his pacing.

"What did they say?"

"They'll do their best."

"Well, that's good, I suppose–"

"Which means 'bye bye bike'."

James threw himself so violently on the bed Daniel expected it to collapse under him.

"I'm sorry." It sounded inadequate. "I suppose you don't really feel like checking homework."

"I'm going to go and get my damn bike back. You're going to drive seeing as I now have no bloody transport."

Daniel frowned; he should have expected that. "Well, we could go and just look I suppose. There's no harm in looking. Then we could point the police in the right direction."

James sat up, a glint in his eye. "OK, we'll 'look'."

Daniel wasn't fooled for a moment but if he drove slowly then he would have time to get James to cool down before he rushed in and did anything stupid.

"In fact," Daniel said, "we may be in luck. There was something on the breakfast news this morning about a missing girl out West Cross way and a big search. So, there might be lots of people milling about near the gypsies' camp and we can blend in."

"What missing girl?" James was momentarily sidetracked.

"Don't know. Teenager, disappeared in the storm. I think they said her dad had been found under a tree or something and the police are concerned for her safety."

"Shit." James gave a half smile. "I suppose it's only a bike but it would be good to get it back."

"I know. We'll go and look."

"Maybe," James offered, "while we look we can keep an eye out for this girl too. What's she look like, did they say?"

"I think they said dark hair?"

"That's it? Some detective you'd make. We better get an Advertiser on the way; they've probably got a picture."

The paper had a full colour photograph of Zoe Faulkner on the front. She had masses of black curls and bright blue eyes which looked too large for the slim face. Daniel thought she looked like a wild animal cornered on the page; something in her stance which suggested she was poised for flight.

"Pretty," he said, looking back at the road.

"Seventeen," James said, reading aloud. "They say she is believed to have gone out to find her dad and never came back."

"Probably got blown away." Daniel wished the words back as soon as they'd been spoken; it wasn't a laughing matter.

"Hopefully."

"Hopefully?"

"Better fate than some of the things you read in the papers that happen to missing girls. There's an awful lot of perverts out there."

"I suppose."

James scanned the rest of the brief article. "Says here there's a possible second girl missing too. No picture of her, police not released any details."

"Not good," Dan said, "not good at all."

They drove through Manor Estate in silence and then turned out past Five Oaks Junction. Not that it deserved the name any longer; three of the five had blown down in the hurricane of '87.

"Perhaps the gyppos steal people as well as bikes," James said suddenly.

"If it was them you saw."

"All right, all right, I got the message, Dan. Just looking. But if we look for the girls too, we could be heroes."

This obviously fired his imagination. "We'll creep into the caravan and smuggle them out and then you can drive away while I act as decoy and ride off on my bike in the other direction."

"While being chased by a giant ball?"

"What?"

"All sounded a bit 'Indiana Jones and the Last Caravan'."

"James Bond if you don't mind," James said, sounding much more cheerful than he had earlier. "I, of course, shall get the girl."

"That's not fair. You're getting the bike."

"Watch it!" James yelled, dragging Daniel's attention back to the view ahead.

He slammed on the brakes to avoid the figure standing with his back to them in the middle of the road ahead.

The car slalomed to a halt, tyres screeching and burning rubber.

"Fuck, sorry mate." Daniel drew a deep breath.

"No problem. Bloody stupid place to stand."

Daniel opened his mouth to agree and then all the words drained from him as the figure turned.

"Him." Flashes of his dream exploded in his head.

"What? Dan, you OK?"

"I dreamt about him last night."

"Bloody hell."

"I had a dream about a road, and he was standing in my way."

"You mean you predicted this?" James looked awestruck. "Wow, Dan that's–"

"No, not like that." Though, had it been meant as a warning? "He was ... he ... I don't know. It sounds silly now, but he felt evil. It really, really scared me and then this dog attacked him, and I blacked out."

"So who is he?"

"I have no idea."

Dan attempted to control his trembling hands. The double shock of a near accident and sudden recognition had left him shaken.

While they sat there, the man lifted a hand to the two of them and then unhurriedly walked from the road into a farm entrance and away across the field it opened into.

*

Marshall yawned as he stood outside the farmhouse. He was getting too old for nights dozing in armchairs.

"No sign," Mark said, his voice flat. Marshall understood. Despite a sleepless night watching a tree coming down, the work was just about to start.

The road was clear now, the wood stacked in neat ranks beside the hedge.

"What time did you tell them?"

"Nine. We'll get all the bodies that uniform can spare."

"No calls? Sightings? Either girl?"

"No, but it's early days. It was on the local radio this morning and the Advertiser are running it, front page."

Marshall stared round at the fields gradually appearing as the early morning mist dissolved in the rare January sunshine. "How far would she get, Mark?"

"Personally, back as far as the kitchen would have seemed the best bet."

"So why didn't she?" He didn't expect an answer.

They stood side by side, leaning on the garden gate, judging the landscape of the farm set out before them. The grassy field was bounded by overgrown hedgerows, oaks looming at intervals. It sloped away sharply downhill to the tree-lined brook that ran, swollen and sluggish, across the lower fields. The tent where Philip Knight's body had been recovered was looking grubby and bedraggled at the bottom of the hill. Small stone-built huts littered the landscape and the circled caravans of the traveller camp were emerging as the sun rose.

There looked to be a dozen or more caravans, a couple of large trucks and several cars, some of which had seen better days. Plastic tables and chairs stood between vehicles and washing lines stretched to nearby trees.

"What do we actually know about that lot?" Marshall pointed downhill.

"Nothing much. Arrived September time. No trouble until late November then one of them – Charlie Monaghan – was nicked for GBH. Got into a fight in a pub, knifed a bloke. Since then there's been trouble with theft; youngsters mainly. Council want to serve eviction notices, but the travellers claim they've got permission to be there from the landowner."

"Would that be our corpse?"

"I expect so."

"Convenient for the council."

"I'm sure they arranged the storm specially," Mark said. "So far the guy in charge down there seems to be fairly reasonable and civil."

"Which might not last if his main argument is dead." Marshall turned his back on the view. "None of that remotely suggests they'd know where the girl is."

"So we don't search the camp?"

"Unfortunately, we currently have no reason to though I'd like to know what Mr Knight was talking to them about and see if they know anything about a naked dancer."

After a moment's silence Mark said, "You think she's dead in a ditch somewhere, don't you?"

"Tell me you don't, Mark. We'll find her within two hundred yards."

"Or not at all."

Which would be worse.

Uniformed officers arrived in two large vans at quarter to nine, piling out into the lane bringing warmth and high spirits to the cold January day.

Joining them, though hanging back in wary clumps, came a group of travellers. That they had come at all was a triumph; helping the police was not something that Marshall imagined would have been top of any traveller's list.

"Thank you for attending." He raised his voice to quell the conversation. "As you are aware, we are looking for a missing girl. Zoe Faulkner was last seen here about thirty-six hours ago. She left the house in the early hours of the morning of the third of January, possibly at about the time the tree came down. She is approximately five foot four with long, curly black hair and blue eyes. She may well be hurt. We are also looking for a second woman with white hair who may have vanished at about the same time. Again, there is the possibility she may be harmed. I'd like you to spread out and will civilians stay within calling range of police officers at all time as all officers are trained in first aid. Please concentrate your search below the hilltop at present as our scene-of-crime officers are investigating possible evidence there." Despite watching closely, he saw no signs that this statement meant anything to his audience.

Marshall left Mark to organise the lines, watching them as they slowly strung out across the hill in different directions.

Helen joined him. "Mrs Faulkner's awake, sir. John, would you like to talk to her?"

"Not particularly, Helen, but I suppose I better. Is she calmer?"

"A little."

Eileen Faulkner was still in bed, wrapped in a fluffy pink dressing gown, her eyes hollow and red-rimmed.

"Is there someone we can call for you?" Marshall perched on the edge of the bed.

"Zoe always had her mobile with her."

It wasn't what he'd meant but it was news that might help. He grabbed the phone from beside the bed. "Give me her number." He dialled as she recited. There was no answer and he hadn't really expected any, but he left the phone ringing and used his own mobile to get hold of his sergeant.

"Mark, I've got her mobile ringing. It might help. Tell the searchers to listen as well as look."

"Now, is there anyone I can call to be with you?" He turned back to the pale woman in the bed.

"I want Zoe."

"We're doing our best, Mrs Faulkner."

"She said she was going to find her dad."

"So you said. Have you any—"

"Why would she do that?"

"Do what?"

"Find her dad. She hated her dad. She said he was evil."

"We all say things—"

"She said I was weak and stupid."

"Mrs Faulkner–"

"Why didn't she come back? I begged her not to go." Her voice had become ragged and upset again, tears gathering in the raw eyes.

"We're trying to find her," Marshall said helplessly; it sounded so useless. He dreaded what he might have to tell her if they did find the girl.

Marshall's phone rang. He left the bedroom to answer it, grateful for the chance to escape.

"John, it's Liza." The doctor sounded bright and brisk despite the lack of sleep she must have had. "Thought you ought to know. Your body from the tree was murdered. The wound was hidden by the way the tree root smashed him up, but it's quite clear to be seen now that I've got him on the table. Hit repeatedly round the head with a blunt instrument at some point before the tree went over. Though not much before, say between midnight and two."

"What sort of blunt instrument?"

"I'd suggest getting forensic to have a close look at that spade you found."

"Will do, thanks Liza."

"I'm sorry, John, doesn't exactly make your job any easier. Any sign of the girl?"

"I think your news just made that less likely. Any news on our first victim?"

"That one's got me stumped to be honest, John. No visible cause of death at all. Everything looks in perfect working order so, by rights, he shouldn't be dead at all. Looks like his heart simply stopped."

"That happens even to the young."

"Oh yes, granted, but I don't like it. I've sent his stomach contents for analysis in case and you may be interested in the hair."

"What hair?"

"I found a couple of long white hairs on his jacket. I've sent them off to Hickson too."

"So, this other woman might exist after all?"

"Ask Hickson, but it looks likely."

"Bugger, I was sort of assuming she didn't." He put the phone back in his pocket.

So, Tom Faulkner had been murdered. What did that make Zoe - witness or suspect? Either way he could now think of a wealth of reasons why she wouldn't have come home.

*

Connor walked slowly; his eyes fixed on the ground. They'd made it, in their ragged line, almost all the way back down the hill to the camp. There'd been no sign of any girl though – short of a body – Connor wasn't sure precisely what he was looking for.

Two hours ago, he'd assumed that every dip in the grass could be a footprint, every bent twig a clue but now each clump of grass looked the same as the last.

He plodded on, watching the floor so closely that he nearly walked into the stone wall. It was one of the small sheds for animals to shelter in.

He looked to his left where the shorter of the two policemen from the night before walked.

"Should I check inside?"

"Carefully." The man came to join him and the two of them peered through the entrance. The low January sun fell clear through the window hole and cast rays of light amidst the dancing dust. More shafts speared down from where the slates had vanished from the roof.

"No-one in here." Connor was relieved. He didn't want to be the one to find a body; not again.

The policeman – a sergeant if he remembered right – crouched down, peering at the door post near the earth floor.

"Something's been in here. Keep back, could you, sir."

"What do you mean?" Connor tried to work out what could convince the man of a presence whilst not entering the building. Then he paused and bent lower; a flash of something purple caught his eye. "What's that?"

"Looks like purple wool, sir, caught on the stone."

"Was that what she was wearing?"

The policeman flipped his phone open, ignoring Connor's question.

"John, I've got traces of something. No idea what or if it's connected to the girl. Can you send SOCO down the hill and see if the mum can tell us what she was wearing."

"What are we looking for?" The reply sounded tinny and faint.

"Purple wool."

"You don't know?" Connor said accusingly.

"Her mother is upset. She has already lost her husband."

"I don't think he was much of a loss."

"Really?" The Sergeant looked properly at Connor. "Why 'not a loss' would you say?"

"He was rude and foul mouthed the times he came down for the rent."

"You paid him rent?"

"Luke paid, for all of us. Not much but it gave us a legit arrangement, so the council were scuppered; that's what Luke said."

"Right, and you are?"

"Connor." No surnames, nothing offered unless absolutely necessary. He could see the sergeant filing away the information about the deceased for future reference.

"Well, Connor, I'm Mark and I appreciate your help. If you could back out, we'll continue the line in a moment and let SOCO take a look in here."

Once outside Mark bowed his line slightly. "I'd like those closest to concentrate on the route to the gate out to the road." It made sense; whoever had sheltered here hadn't come down the hill so perhaps they'd come from the road.

Slowly the line arrived at the five barred gate, closing the entrance to the field. There were clear sets of human footprints in the frozen mud around the gate and beside them ...

"Shit, look at that," Connor said, pointing further from the gate. Huge pawprints sank deep into the mud.

The sergeant, Mark, looked from the gate to the prints and back. Then he walked through and examined the other side of the gate. There were more prints on the other side.

"I don't know what it was," he admitted, "but it leapt the gate."

"Chasing the person?" Connor said. He looked round, seeing the same thought in several pairs of eyes – travellers and police. Already people were formulating 'beast' stories in their heads.

"We have no way of knowing that, Connor," Mark said firmly. "I think we should move back so we don't contaminate the evidence."

With repeated persuasion the policeman continued them on their way down the hill and stopped to wait for the other men that were just arriving.

*

"Mother says no purple wool." Marshall said.

"We've got a bigger problem. Expect 'Beast of Fenwick snatched girl' stories all over tomorrow's papers." Mark pointed out the marks in the mud.

"What is it?"

"Large dog, I'd say," Craig Hickson said cheerfully. Marshall had never known him to be thrown by anything, no matter how bizarre. The small, balding man now stooped over the prints. "Yeah, quite a size but definitely dog."

"When?" Marshall asked.

"Before the rain stopped. There's damage to the prints from water falling. Probably some point during the storm. Difficult to be more accurate, I'm afraid."

"And the human prints?"

"Around the same time, possibly. Sorry, John, that's the best guess I can give you on that."

"OK, let's have a look at this hut thing."

Marshall pulled his sergeant back as they headed for the sheepfold.

"Just heard from Liza. This one is murder. Had his head bashed in."

Mark stopped. "So, what does that mean for the search?"

"It makes it less certain she's dead."

"Do you suppose she did it?"

"No idea. We really need to get more sense out of the mother. If she didn't then she's running, possibly because she knows who did do it."

"Or has been taken by them."

"Don't know why they wouldn't just kill her too."

"If they only intended to kill him, for a specific reason, then they wouldn't have done her. Some people are very specific." Mark shrugged. "Or perhaps the intention was always to kidnap the girl and the father just got in the way."

"Too many variables, Mark. And to cap it all, Liza says there were white hairs on our Mr Knight too."

"And then there's this animal."

Marshall threw up his hands and continued walking. "I give up. We need to eliminate possibilities. All we seem to be doing at present is adding to the list."

Hickson was poking about on the floor of the hut under where the roof was least damaged.

"There's more than just wool, John. I'd say the dog came in here."

"Sensible creature," Marshall said.

"There's traces of the wool where something rubbed against the stones." He showed Marshall several small evidence bags. "I've collected some of the dog hair too."

"So, there was a person in here with the dog?"

"I'd say so. Probably a purple knitted top of some sort."

"Zoe's mother says she doesn't have anything like that. Can you get fingerprints?"

"I'll try. Can't promise."

Hickson suddenly dived at another place on the floor and carefully picked something up. "Interesting. This isn't dog hair."

"Human?"

"I'd say so."

"White," Marshall suggested with a sinking feeling.

"No."

"Zoe's is black," Mark pointed out.

"Well, we've got a problem then," Hickson said. "This is a quite beautiful shade of red."

"Red?" Marshall said, incredulous.

"Red." Hickson poked about the floor a bit further and collected something else. "This one's black," he said, waving the evidence bag at Marshall.

Mark rolled his eyes. "Where does the redhead come into this?"

"God knows," Marshall said.

"Sir!" A young PC stuck his head through the doorway. "We've reached the limits of the gypsy camp. Should we go further?"

Marshall pushed his way past, back into the light.

"Do any of them claim to have seen anything?"

"Not that I've heard, sir."

"Mark?"

"No, John, nothing suspicious and I can't imagine so many would have turned up today if they were involved."

"And we'd need warrants for the caravans."

He thought while the others waited for a decision.

"Currently they're helping and relatively friendly. You and I both know, Mark, that if we start searching the camp, we're going to find a few things that shouldn't be there and that's not our priority today. So let's leave it unless we have a damn good reason to go in. I'll interview later but, for now, finding Zoe takes precedence and we may need their continued cooperation. Take them across the field and along down the stream."

"Will do," Mark said.

"Actually, no, I'll do it. You go and use your charm and understanding and see if you can get a coherent statement from Mrs Faulkner. Times and details, please, Mark."

"Coward."

Marshall laughed shortly. "I know my team, that's all. You're the best person for the job."

While Mark strode off up the hill, Marshall began re-ordering the searchers' line along both sides of the stream.

*

Daniel peered through the hedge he was crouched behind, trying to get a clear view. His trainers were caked in mud after the tramp across the field from where they'd left the car in the lane and he was beginning to wish he'd brought gloves with him.

James squatted beside him.

"Can you see anyone?" Daniel asked.

"Two or three dogs chained to caravans but that's all."

"Dogs? Where?" After the strange man in the road, Daniel was still a little shaken and talk of dogs put him in mind of the dream again. "Anything huge?"

"No, small mongrel things. Why?"

"I just didn't want to get bitten."

Daniel became aware that James was now looking at him searchingly.

"That dream I had, there was a huge dog in it too. Attacked the man."

"Did you eat too much cheese before bed last night, mate?"

"I had a huge row with dad before bed." Daniel looked away, studying the gap in the foliage. "Phil's dead and dad—" He shrugged.

"Oh shit. Dan, I'm sorry. And here's me going on about my bloody bike. Why didn't you say something?"

"Oh, I don't know. I ought to be sad, Phil's gone, but I'm just bloody furious with him."

"What happened?"

"No idea really. Mum said he was found in a ditch but then dad got unreasonable and I never stopped to ask." He still couldn't find any tears for the cousin he'd known from infancy. "I'll talk to mum about it later."

"I suppose your dad wants you in the shop now."

"Yeah, now his son-substitute has gone. Trust Phil, he never could get anything right."

"Come on, Dan—"

"I know, but his timing was always lousy. The number of times the police got him because he'd just wait that bit too long, do one more stupid bit of ... every bloody time we ever went out together we missed the damn bus. He never thought of others, only the perishing animals."

"Dan–"

"He was probably in a fucking ditch trying to protect a rare species of flaming beetle."

"Dan–"

"Ruined every bloody Boxing Day trying to save foxes from the hunt and–"

"Dan," James shook his shoulder, "Come on. Your dad can't force you to stay, whatever happened to Phil."

"Too bloody right. I told him – I'm going. Final, end of story."

"No going back?" James said quietly.

Dan's anger drained away. "I really don't know. I hope not for mum's sake, but he just wasn't listening."

"We don't have to do this, you know. Shall we go? I could come and face him with you."

Daniel looked back at his friend, touched. "What? Go and mope? No, Jay, let's see if we can find your bike now we're here. If we find it, we won't exactly have to go far to find a policeman."

They could see the line of people making its slow way down the hill, half of them in the trademark fluorescent jackets.

James squeezed his shoulder, gave a grateful smile and then led the way along the hedge towards the gate through into the travellers' camp.

They had to climb the gate as it was chained shut.

Once in, they found themselves round the side of the circle of caravans. A dog tied to the nearest barked violently at them and they slipped back, following the hedge line towards the stream.

They passed the back of one flat bed lorry with gas cylinders piled on it and a couple of large, fire-blackened oil drums. Then they had to duck under a set of washing lines, stretched from the next caravan to a nearby tree. Large polybins of water stood by the steps to the door and two bikes leant against the back. James peered and crept slightly closer and then pulled back.

"No, too old."

They moved on. The next caravan also had several bikes sprawled in the mud round it.

"There," James hissed, pointing. "That's mine."

It looked dirtier than when Daniel had last seen it, but it was definitely the one he had ridden the day before.

"I'm going to get it," James said, starting forwards.

"James ... idiot." Daniel moved more hesitantly, trying to keep a watch all round as he went. They were moving among the circle of caravans, out into the open where they could be seen. The dog began again, raising its voice in protest at their intrusion.

"Oy!" The shout came from their left. "Who are you?"

Two youths, barely older than Daniel, had come out of a caravan further round the circle.

"What do you think you're doing?"

James stopped creeping and stood up straight. "I'm here for my bike. The one you lot stole."

"Who said?"

"I can fucking see it. It's there." James pointed.

The younger of the two lads looked worried and Daniel thought he may be on the verge of telling them to take the bike but the older strode towards James, fists raised.

"No way, that's my bike."

"It bloody isn't." James lifted his own fists.

"James. Come away. We'll tell the police." Dan didn't fancy a fight.

"That's my–"

"And he's bigger than you," and not slow to show aggression, "and god knows how many more of them there are."

"I'm not afraid," James said.

"I never said you were, but the police can do it."

"Your friend speaks sense." James and Daniel whirled towards the new voice. The strange man they'd almost run down in the road stood behind them.

"That's my fucking bike," James said, though he was sounding more wary now they were obviously outnumbered.

"I promise to look into the matter for you," the dark-haired man said. "If it is yours then it can be returned."

Daniel repeated his own argument as a third youth joined the first two. "James, you can't take on all of them. We ought to tell the police."

"They have missing girls to find," the man said. "I am Raven, and I give you my word that I will sort this for you. Why don't you return tomorrow and all will be arranged."

Daniel frowned but Raven seemed reasonable and there was none of the unreasoning fear he'd felt in the dream. There was a current of danger here, but Daniel thought it came from the situation rather than the man. "James," he said.

"All right, but we'll be back tomorrow, and we'll have the bike or the police'll be here."

"Thank you." Raven smiled at them and at the lads watching.

Moving carefully, trying not to run, James and Daniel began to walk away.

Behind them one of the lads said, "You had no right."

"Ssh," Raven said. "Do you want the police here, now? We're not ready. What's the loss of one bike?"

Daniel glanced back to find Raven still watching them. The man raised a hand as he had done in the road earlier before moving away.

"Well," James said as they climbed over the gate and headed for the car. "One chance, that's all he gets. Stupid name too."

"We could still tell the police."

"Do you think they care? He's right; they've got these girls to find."

"Should we help?" Their visions of rescuing a maiden in distress had faded in the light of reality.

They paused in the lane beside the car.

"We could do," James said and then, more positively, "Yes, come on."

"Where?" Daniel climbed on to the field gate to observe the land.

"Well, they're obviously moving out from that farm up there."

"And they can't have found her or they would have stopped."

James pointed downhill. "I don't know, what's that down there? Looks like another police thing."

"But there are still people all over the place," Dan said.

"Yeah, guess you're right. I wonder what that is then?"

"Didn't you say her dad was found dead?"

"Oh right, that'll be it." James nodded. "So, she sets off from the farm. Now, if you were on a farm and in a storm, why would you go out?"

"Check on the animals."

James nodded, caught up in the puzzle. "Excellent idea. So where are the animals?"

"Up there, I imagine, close to the farm in winter."

"Oh," James deflated. "Bugger, not such a good idea. They'd have found her already."

Daniel looked round for further inspiration. As he glanced up the long slope of the road, he had a sudden vivid picture of a girl striding in brilliant sunshine, long hair swinging and a rucksack on her back. She marched down the road towards them.

With the vision came a snatch of familiar music.

"Hey!" He lurched forwards, falling from the gate to land in a painful heap in the long grass. He leapt up but there was no sign of any girl.

He stared hard down the road, but it stayed resolutely empty.

"Dan? What is it?"

"Running away."

"What?"

Daniel was suddenly sure, on no foundation whatsoever. "She was running away. She wasn't in the fields at all, she was on the road." He paused, certainty draining. Why would the sun be shining, she left at night.

"Why would she run away?" James said, echoing his own doubts.

"I don't know, it was just an idea that came to me."

"You didn't dream it, did you?" James got down slowly from his perch atop the gate. "Are you sure you're all right, Dan?" He sounded genuinely concerned.

"Yes ... no ... I'm not sure. I just thought I saw her in the road, and I was certain she'd run. I don't know what happened."

"I think we'll go," James said. "And I want you to tell me all about this dream and what you saw. You're starting to worry me."

Daniel didn't argue; he was starting to worry himself too.

CHAPTER 4

Zoe saw the paper at the garage on Lacey Road as they took the main route through Manor Estate. The petrol station on the end of the row of shops had queues of motorists at the pumps and Lacewing strode past unheeding but the display of pictures caught Zoe's eye.

She peered at her photograph staring back at her from the front of the Advertiser. It was one her mother had taken last year during the summer trip to France.

"I can't go into town," she said and then louder as Lacewing kept walking. "I'm not going."

"Why not?" The other girl came back to where she had stopped.

"This." Zoe pointed at the papers lined up in their plastic boxes. "They're looking for me."

"Why?"

"God knows. It's not as if anyone cares." Zoe turned away to hide the lie; her mother did care, in her own way, just not enough to be strong.

"It says here that your dad was crushed by a tree."

"Best thing that ever happened to him." And then, just when they were free, her mum had cried for him and Zoe had hit her, repeating the cycle. Except she wasn't going to be her dad, so she had run.

And now they were looking for her, to chain her to her mother's needs.

"I'm not going back," she said.

"Running doesn't always help," Lacewing said.

"So you said before and, believe me, you couldn't be more wrong. I'm sorry but I can't meet this friend of yours. Everyone who reads the local paper will know who I am now. I need to get away."

Lacewing watched her in silence, the green eyes not entirely focused as if she was listening to music only she could hear. "I shall ask him to come to you," she said after a long moment.

"I'm not waiting around here to be found." Zoe settled the pack more firmly on her shoulders and faced back the way they had come. "I'm sorry but I have to go."

"I understand," the strange girl said softly. "A shame you do not."

Zoe didn't stop to ask what she meant. She simply strode back along Lacey Road towards the bypass.

She had gone barely five paces when she became aware of the dog's silent pacing beside her.

"Merlin will keep you safe," Lacewing yelled from behind her. "I'll be as quick as I can."

Zoe glanced back to see Lacewing sprinting off in the other direction.

She felt strangely lonely as she marched on, the giant dog matching her step for step.

*

Mark carried a tray of tea and biscuits up to the bedroom.

"Here you go," he said cheerfully as he entered, "best thing for coping with shock and grief."

Helen gave him a grateful smile from where she sat in a chair by the window. Eileen Faulkner gazed at him blearily through bloodshot eyes.

"Right, the good news is that, so far, we haven't found your daughter."

"Good ..."

"Not under any trees or in any ditches, not hurt or suffering anywhere. So, we're going with no news being good news so far." He placed a mug of tea on the bedside table and offered her a chocolate digestive. "Come on, you have to eat. Can't get Zoe back here to discover you've wasted away to nothing."

Reluctantly she took a biscuit and nibbled at it while he talked.

"So," Mark continued, "I need you to do two things for me to help us. First, I want you to think back and remember everything that happened when Zoe left to see if that gives us a clue to where she's gone."

"And the second thing?" She sounded small and lost.

"I'm afraid we need you to officially identify your husband's body."

"I couldn't."

"Is there anyone else who can do it?"

"Pete, he's our shepherd. He worked with Tom all the time."

"That's fine, I shall ask him. Now," Mark pulled the plush stool from the dressing table over to beside the bed, "let's see what you can remember."

Helen pulled her chair up to the other side of the double bed while Mark got his notebook out.

"All right," Eileen stared at him expectantly. Helen rolled her eyes at him.

Mark sighed, wished he'd chosen a more comfortable seat and

began, his pencil poised.

"Can you tell me what happened ... shall we say, when the storm first started?"

"Tom shut the animals in. He was worried about them." Her voice became stronger as she spoke of normal things.

"That makes sense. Did he do that alone?"

"It was late. Pete had gone home. He finishes when it gets dark."

"So Tom shut the animals in. Did he do anything else outside?"

"Well," she looked furtive suddenly.

"What else did your husband do, Eileen?"

"He said he ought to dig the box up."

"Which box was this, Eileen?"

"The gypsy's box."

Mark looked up from his writing, surprised. "Let me get this clear, the travellers in your field have given—"

"Oh no, not them." She sounded animated for the first time. "There was an old man, came here years ago."

"And he gave—"

"He gave Tom's…" she paused, obviously trying to work out a relationship.

"Ancestor," suggested Mark, unwilling to get side-tracked.

She nodded gratefully. "Yes, he gave Tom's ancestor this box for luck and the flute. I think it was a thank you for something and the family buried it and planted the oak to mark the spot." She was livelier now the conversation had moved away from the immediate cause of grief.

Mark glanced at Helen, unsure what to make of this. The constable shrugged slightly, indicating her own confusion.

"So you had a box and a flute, and they were buried by the oak?"

"The box, Zoe plays the flute now though her granddad used to.

He said it would bring the family prosperity and wealth."

"What was in the box?"

"I don't know. I never asked."

Mark paused again; this wasn't getting them anywhere and he wasn't sure any of it was relevant.

"Did it bring you wealth?" Helen asked, leaning forwards in her chair.

"Of course." Eileen sounded as if she thought they were stupid for having to ask. "No BSE, no foot and mouth, no blue tongue. Best price for our lamb and beef and milk and we sold a couple of fields for the new estate at West Cross. We've done really well."

"Surely that would all have happened anyway," Helen said, sounding unconvinced.

"Maybe. Tom wasn't taking any chances. We kept it buried but when the tree started to fall, he said he had to get it safe."

"So did he re-bury it?" Mark said.

"I don't know. He never came back." For the first time she managed to handle this fact without dissolving into tears.

"So your daughter went to find him?"

"Yes, she said to call the police and tell them she'd gone after dad."

"But you didn't call the police."

"No." She seemed surprised by this lack of action.

"Why not, Eileen?"

"I ..." She frowned. "Zoe was going to come back. She wouldn't leave me."

"But she didn't come back," Mark pressed.

"No."

"And you still didn't call."

"No. Why didn't I?" She pushed herself upright to stare at him. "I was going to and ... I know." Relief lit the blue eyes. "He said not to.

I'd forgotten. Why would I forget that?"

"He? Who?"

"The gypsy."

"What gypsy?" Mark thought there were a good sight too many gypsies in this case.

"A young man, dark haired, I think. He came after Zoe was gone, I think. I let him come in from the storm and he said it would be okay. That's odd, why would I forget him?"

"You have been under a lot of stress, Mrs Faulkner," Mark reassured her, "our brains sometimes lose bits of memories in that situation. Was he one of the travellers from your bottom field?"

"Oh no, I don't think so, I'd never seen him before at all."

"Is this the same gypsy who gave the family the box?" Mark asked.

"Oh no, I don't think so, that was years and years ago." She paused; her eyes distant as she worked out dates. "Nearly two hundred, I think."

"Would you recognise the man who came here if you saw him again?" Helen asked.

"I ... well, I might do. He had dark hair."

Mark took a deep breath and moved on. "So, apart from this gypsy, did you see anyone else after Zoe left?"

"Luke came to pay the rent. Oh no, I think that might have been earlier."

"Before Zoe went?"

"Yes, maybe. It might have been before Tom went or ... no, I'm not sure."

"And Luke is?"

"One of the gypsies. From the field. I think he might be in charge."

Mark stretched, pulling the kinks out of his back. The stool was nowhere near as comfortable as it looked.

"Can you give us any idea of times, Eileen?" He didn't hold out much hope and she shook her head hesitantly.

"Anything I've missed, Helen?"

"Clothes."

"Oh yes. Could you tell us what Zoe might be wearing?"

"Her winter coat and hat and gloves. It's winter and the storm—"

"I realise that. I was meaning more sort of underneath her coat."

"I don't know. She just wears jeans and things most of the time."

"Ok, thank you, Eileen."

He caught Helen's eye and she mouthed 'abuse?' at him.

Mark hesitated. The abuser, as far as they knew, was dead. He saw little point in raking over painful memories. On the other hand, the doctor had said this was murder and the abuse gave Eileen Faulkner a powerful motive.

"Did you go outside at all after your husband?" Mark said, trying to come at the subject obliquely. "To find him or to talk to him?"

"Oh no, he said to stay indoors."

"He? Who?" Mark was worried that another spurious gypsy was about to materialise.

"Tom said. He said it wasn't safe out." She paused as if struck afresh by the words. "He was right, wasn't he?"

"So," Mark said to Marshall over lunch, "it was a bit like Piccadilly Circus here that night."

They were in the kitchen eating soup provided by a Mrs Jenkins. She was a small, homely woman, almost as big round as she was tall. She'd arrived mid-morning, bustled in cheerfully and told them she was from the 'farm across the valley' and 'here to look after poor Eileen'. As she had then proceeded to supply coffee, soup, sandwiches and cake to any policeman or searcher who came through the door, Marshall had encouraged her to stay.

"Quite an achievement considering the weather," Marshall said. "We need to talk to this Pete guy to see if he'll do an identification for us."

"I think he joined the search this morning; leathery looking old fellow."

"How about this Luke character who came to pay rent?"

"I think he's one of the travellers. One of them mentioned the rent thing to me this morning."

"So there could have been a row about amount," Marshall said, pushing his bowl away where it was immediately pounced on by Mrs Jenkins.

"Or this mysterious box."

"If it exists."

"Why would she make it up?" Mark said.

"We haven't found any box."

"Maybe it's valuable and whoever killed him took it."

"And the daughter?" Marshall said.

"Perhaps she killed him and took it."

"So, instead of waiting for one day when he's out on the farm and taking the box, you think she waited until the middle of a storm and then killed him while he was digging it up. It doesn't really ring true, Mark."

"'spose not."

They contemplated their coffee for a while until Mrs Jenkins placed large slabs of chocolate cake down in front of them.

"Then there's this other gypsy," Mark said eventually, "the one she can't really remember. And someone with long red hair stayed in that shed with a large dog. And Philip Knight, or someone using his phone, wandered up the hill to make a phone call." Hickson had confirmed this earlier. "And there may or may not have been a white-haired female dancing naked somewhere up here." Mark shook his head. "Do you suppose it's something in the water?"

"Do you know, I'd almost be tempted to say that someone was out to muddy the waters," Marshall said.

"But?"

"Oh, I don't know, common sense perhaps. Who in their right mind would organise that many people to mess us about in that sort of weather?"

"Someone who knew it'd work?"

"That is not a reassuring thought." Marshall slammed his cup down. "No, Mark, we're going to find this girl and catch a murderer, no matter who thinks they can screw this up. Let's make sure we get this right."

Marshall's mobile rang. It was the station.

"John, we've got a possible sighting out at the Little Chef on the ring-road. Sounds a genuine call."

"I'll take it. I'm tired of looking under hedges."

"Come on, Mark," he said snapping the phone shut, "possible witness. We might be going somewhere."

*

Tanya Small had dyed blonde hair pulled back in a ponytail under her hat, nicotine-stained fingers and a lukewarm IQ.

"She came in for breakfast," she said, stabbing a finger at Zoe's portrait. "Her and another girl."

"You waited until lunchtime to phone?"

"I didn't know it was her then, did I? I went out for a fag at lunchtime and saw the paper in McDonalds."

"Don't you sell papers here?"

"Not local ones, people travelling don't want them, just national."

"So, she was here for breakfast?" Marshall steered the conversation back to Zoe. "With someone?"

"Well, not to start with. The other girl came later."

"But they were friends?"

"Nah, arguing."

"Do you know what about?"

"Well, not really," Tanya said reluctantly. "Just this girl," she tapped the photo again, "was telling the other one to leave her alone."

"Really?"

"Well, yeah, but she wouldn't go and then she followed her out and she had this massive dog so she had to go with her."

"You're saying you think Zoe was being taken against her will," Marshall said, floundering his way through the pronouns.

"Well, yeah, for definite," Tanya said, her eyes sparkling with the excitement of it. "Dragging her along she was."

"This other girl was using force?"

"Well, I'd say, 'cos the dog was huge and had lots of teeth."

Marshall suppressed a smile. "Could you describe the second girl for me?"

"Well, long orange hair, all the way down her back so she shouldn't have been in purple 'cos Cosmopolitan says they clash something chronic. I read up on fashion 'cos I'm going to be a model one day, and she was so out of fashion. Knitwear was last season and skirts should be short and ..."

"Thank you, Tanya. If I send a police sketch artist out do you think you could put together a picture?"

"She needed a makeover and ..."

"Just what you saw," Marshall said forcefully.

They left the young waitress and wannabe model sulking.

"Purple wool? Large dog? Red hair?" Mark said as they crossed the small car park.

"My thoughts exactly and I'm going to risk another hunch." Marshall walked past their car and into the Travelodge facing them. "Who breakfasts at a Little Chef?"

"Someone staying nearby."

The woman on reception was petite and nearing retirement age. Eyes of the same steely grey as her hair judged the two men as they entered.

Marshall allowed his badge to be taken for a close examination before he showed Zoe's picture.

"Did this girl stay here overnight?"

"I have no idea, Inspector. I came on at two today."

"Perhaps you could check your records for a Zoe Faulkner? She's missing and we believe she may have been here overnight."

She watched him carefully while thinking it over and then glanced through the forms piled in front of her.

"Room 203."

"Could we have a look at it please?"

"If you must." She took a key from the wooden pigeonholes behind her and led them up two flights of stairs and through a pair of fire-doors.

As they paused outside the door, they could hear a phone ringing inside.

"Has someone else taken this room?" Marshall said.

"No, else I wouldn't have allowed you in."

He took the key from her and let them into the room. It was resolutely empty, the phone louder now they were within.

"Find it, Mark."

The two men scoured the room and found the mobile phone stuffed at the back of a drawer. Marshall picked it up and pressed answer. "Hello? Hello?" He raised an eyebrow at Mark's enquiring glance. "It's odd. I can hear noises but there's no-one on the line. Cover your ears." He raised the phone to his lips. "Hello! Is anyone there?"

There was a pause and then a familiar voice said, "Zoe? Zoe, is that you?"

Marshall sighed and closed his eyes. "No, Helen, but it does look like we've managed to locate her phone. Do apologise to Mrs Faulkner, I'd totally forgotten that I'd left her phone off the hook all this time."

He shut the phone and turned on Mark who was trying not to laugh out loud.

"What?"

"Excellent piece of detecting there, John. You managed to find yourself."

"Ha ha. Doesn't find the girl for us, does it?"

"I know, I know. It just struck me as funny. So, now where?"

"I wish I knew. Back to the farm, I suppose."

As they headed down Lacey Road, Marshall spotted a familiar name and slammed the brakes on. Pulling the car into a convenient space, he pointed the shop out to Mark. "Calver's Hardware. Isn't that where Philip Knight worked?"

"The point being?" But Mark was already taking his seatbelt off.

"I know, but you never know what might come up and we're passing."

The shop was nestled between a hairdresser and a baker, its window full of assorted pots, pans and electrical items. "Don't get places like this anymore," Mark commented, pushing open the door. "Surprised the superstores haven't put him out of business."

The interior of the shop was crammed with shelves and stands covered in a huge variety of electrical and DIY oddments. At the back of the store was a counter. The wall behind it was a massive rack of small boxes that Marshall was sure would hold screws, nails, washers and other assorted treasures in any size you cared to mention. A balding man of medium height stood behind the counter watching the two policemen narrowly.

"Can I help you," he said eventually as they reached the counter.

"Mr Calver? I'm Detective Inspector Marshall and this is Detective Sergeant Sherbourne of Fenwick CID. We're investigating the death of Philip Knight. I believe he worked here."

"He was my nephew. He helped out when he could."

Marshall frowned. "His mother suggested he was expecting to take over as manager here shortly."

"It was a possibility. My son showed no interest, but I am hopeful that will change."

"So it wasn't definite? His mother suggested he was taking accountancy courses because–"

"We were covering all eventualities in case Dan didn't see what was best. I wanted the shop to stay in the family."

"Dan being?"

"My son, Inspector."

"And now Mr Knight is dead your son will get the shop?"

"I hope so." Mr Calver frowned. "Dan was quite annoyed."

"About what?"

"Over the shop, Inspector."

"Right." Marshall made a mental note of that. "So, do you have any ideas, Mr Calver, why your nephew might have been out at West

Cross two nights ago?"

"It'll be something to do with animals, Inspector. It usually was with Philip."

"Animal rights?"

"Every time. West Cross, you say? That's normally the hunt. He was out there on Boxing Day trying to get himself trampled to death."

"You think there might be people who wished him dead? Maybe among the hunt?"

"I expect so. He went and rescued the quarry on Boxing Day or so he claimed. I doubt that made him very popular."

Marshall checked Mark was making notes. "Can you think of anyone else who might wish your nephew harm?"

"He was always in trouble over one thing or another. Had a mate, Curtis something or other, who he did these things with. He'd know."

"Well, thank you, Mr Calver, you've been most helpful." Marshall glanced round. "Your son not here today?"

"No," Mr Calver said, his mouth snapping shut on the word. "I've no idea where he is."

"No love lost there," Mark said as they headed for the car.

"Sets up nephew in business to get son interested," Marshall said, "not a ploy designed to breed family harmony."

"Do you suppose he was a bit too convincing about it? Son does away with rival to gain inheritance? Or is that all a bit Agatha Christie?"

"Possible," Marshall said. "I think we need to talk to Dan Calver and then there's this hunt thing. I think it's high time we paid Curtis Yates a visit as well."

"What if Liza says its natural causes? She hasn't found anything wrong yet."

"Apart from the fact that he was laid out like an effigy in a ditch? Nothing will convince me that was 'natural', Mark."

"Okay, okay, where first?"

"The son, I think. He actually has a motive and I'm fed up of vanishing females. At least this is concrete and I can understand it."

*

"We'll go and talk to the old man," James said. Daniel had given him a detailed account of the dream and the strange vision on the road.

"What?" Daniel narrowly avoided the car in front as it eased to a halt at the traffic lights on Lacey Road.

"This old man said your name."

"Well, I thought he did."

"And then he's in your dream. So, we'll go and ask him about it."

"I think I might feel a bit daft," Daniel said.

"Why?"

"Oh, come on, Jay. Hello sir, I dreamt about you last night, did you know?"

"What's the worst he can do? Look at you oddly and say 'no'."

Daniel drove a short way in silence. "I think," he eventually admitted, "I'm more worried about if he says anything else."

"You need to confront him."

Daniel blinked, hit by a surge of déjà vu; James had been saying the same thing for weeks about university and facing up to his dad. Now he'd actually done that, he had to admit he felt better so perhaps James was right about this too.

"All right. We'll go and see if he's outside Marks and Spencers again."

"Excellent." James grinned. "This could be fun."

"It could be a waste of time."

"I'll pay for the car park and buy you a coffee. Okay?"

"Okay."

The town centre was still crowded with January shoppers hopefully looking for bargains.

"Barmy," James said. "January sale means they've got thirty-one days; the clue being in the name. Yet here they all are, piling in in the first week."

"My mum used to."

"And mine. Doesn't mean it's not stupid." James dragged him across the street. "Look, there he is."

The old musician wasn't playing. He was being harangued by a young woman. She was in her early twenties with long auburn hair falling almost to her waist. She had a long, belted cardigan of heathery purples, blues and greens and an ankle length skirt of complementary shades.

"You've got to come," she was saying as they approached. "She won't come into town."

"But I'm expecting visitors," the old man said, looking up to meet Daniel's eye. "Ah, here they are."

"I ... er ... hello." Daniel could think of nothing to say; he hadn't thought that he might be expected.

James had no such inhibitions.

"Are you messing with Dan's head because I'm worried about him and you should stop."

"An admirable sentiment for a friend. You would be James."

"So?" James said, refusing to be thrown off his stride.

"So I am not messing with your friend. I played a tune he recognised, and it led him to a certain place where conversations can happen."

James put his head on one side, his eyes narrowing. "So you're saying you were in his dream?"

"In a way."

"Who are you?" the girl demanded. "What do you want because we should be going? There's a girl who needs us."

"I saw a girl," Dan said, for no particular reason, "on the road earlier except she wasn't really there. How did that happen?"

"Really?" The old man stood up. "Sometimes the music opens channels in people. Tell me about it."

"Well, we went to get James' bike back and then we were going to help search for the missing girl but I thought I saw her on the road and not in the field except the sun was shining." Daniel stopped, aware of their gazes and how mad what he was saying must sound. "I'm sorry, that wasn't clear but–"

"True sight," the girl said, "not bad for one tune."

"What?"

"Lacewing," she said, offering her hand. "I think you could help me. We need to get out to the ring road and fast. Did you come in a car?"

"What?" Daniel said again, unsure whether he should be pleased they hadn't laughed at him or worried that they thought his day's experiences were normal.

"Sorry, I thought I said it clearly. Are you simple or something?"

"No, I'm bloody not."

"Then you need to get Gwion and me out along Lacey Road and fast. Come on."

"But–"

"Oh, come on, Dan." James grabbed his arm. "Follow us," he instructed the others.

"What are you doing?" Daniel said.

"Having an adventure."

"We don't know anything about them." Except that they popped up in his dreams and knew what he was going to do before he did it; none of which was remotely reassuring.

"You dreamt about them," James said, as if following his train of thought.

"That doesn't mean I want to get to know them."

James let go of his arm and took a step back. "All right, sorry," he held his hands up. "Your call, Dan."

"There's a damsel in distress," the girl said, "and I don't mean me."

"Come on, Daniel." The musician laid a light hand on his arm. "I set you on this road, allow me to walk with you a while."

"Oh for ... if you've all finished. Come on." Daniel set off back the way they'd come. "Let's have an adventure then, James. I just hope I can get us out of whatever mess you've got us into this time."

James laughed so Daniel added over his shoulder, "and you owe me a coffee."

*

The woman was short and mousy and obviously intimidated by Luke in the close confines of his caravan. The traveller wished Fenwick Council had employed someone he could respect rather than this wishy-washy woman who had no strength of character. God knows what they were thinking of sending a woman out. She nodded eagerly over all his arguments to the point where Luke started making things up just to see if he could push her into showing a backbone. She tactfully skirted round the issue of thefts in the town and failed entirely to blame them except in the most general way. Then she moved on to the possibility of them moving on.

"We've been living here for months now, and paying rent, so you can't do anything," Luke said.

"Well, obviously up to now but with Mr Faulkner's death the land passes to someone else."

Luke paused and then tried, "He may well have left the land to us."

"I ... er ...I think we need to see what his will says."

"Oh, for fuck's sake woman, as if he would have left the land to us. He'll have left it to his wife but I may have a talk with her."

"I'm not sure it calls for swearing, Luke. If I can help with the liaison ..."

"Yeah, right. I think I'd prefer you to stay as far away from her as possible, you're hardly going to be encouraging her to let a 'bunch of bloody thieves' stay on her land."

"I work closely–"

"Bullshit. You've sat here and nodded and forgotten every word I've said the second you step outside." He couldn't imagine she'd ever taken any of his points back to the council, let alone argued for them on his behalf. "You and your bloody welfare assessment which is political speak for working out how easy it will be to throw us out of our home."

"I'm not sure this is getting us anywhere." She clutched her hands together.

"Finally, something we agree on."

"Maybe I should come back when I've spoken to Mrs Faulkner."

The knock on the door startled her to silence and she glanced from Luke to the door and back like a rabbit caught in the headlights.

Luke frowned. He'd told them not to interrupt him. On the other hand, this conversation was going nowhere.

"Come in," he ordered.

The stranger, Raven, stood in the doorway. He looked at Luke and then the woman.

"Sorry, I didn't realise you had company."

Luke took a fleeting look out of the window. Terry still lounged in the seat by the steps to keep people away.

"Really?" He was very unsure about this man. Raven had a disconcerting air of confidence and suppressed violence that made Luke uncomfortable.

"We had a ... an incident. I thought you should know."

At least the man seemed to be discrete.

"That's all right," Luke said, relenting a little. "This is Miss Shaw and she was just leaving."

"A friend?"

Luke gave a harsh laugh. "You have got to be joking."

"I try," she began, "to be a friend to the travellers that–"

"Bollocks you do," Luke said. "Friends don't help hand out eviction notices."

"Or deprive people of their homes," Raven agreed, his own voice noticeably cooler. "So, you're the council."

Miss Shaw shrunk even further into herself. "I haven't handed out any notices yet. I'm just trying to help."

"I've seen your sort of help before," Raven said. "No heart, no soul, just paperwork and working to rule. All we want is a home. We're not hurting anyone here."

Luke nodded, impressed despite his misgivings. They could have been his words.

"I've told her that. I don't think she's listening."

"She ought to." Raven loomed closer. Luke stood, concerned as to the man's intentions but Raven simply leant across the table so he was nose to nose with the woman. "This is our home. Believe me, we'll fight to stay."

"I've already told her that too," Luke said quietly. Not quite as threateningly and he had, at least, had the right to say it. Raven had been here barely twelve hours.

"Sorry, merely backing you up." The dark man drew back to stand at Luke's shoulder.

Luke was reminded of Charlie; always loyal and too eager to rush in. Was Raven angling for a position of trust here? Luke stifled a sigh; he didn't need another over-zealous deputy.

"I think you get the idea, Miss Shaw," he said.

She nodded, wide-eyed.

"I don't think there's anything more to say."

She still sat there, nodding vaguely.

"So fuck off," Luke said without any real malice. "Don't come back."

"Oh, right, yes, well, it's been nice to meet you. I do hope we can sort this out to everyone's best–"

"Goodbye." Luke opened the door and almost pushed her through it. He slammed it behind her.

"What a waste of space and she has no legs to stand on until we know who owns this land now." He turned on Raven. "When I say I'm not to be disturbed I don't appreciate people barging in here, particularly not some arrogant twat who only waltzed in last night."

"No offence meant." Raven sat himself down at the small table. "I feel quite strongly about people being deprived of their home."

"Obviously."

"And you want this to be your home, don't you?" Raven said softly.

Luke hesitated. He'd been on the road all his life, forever moving on but recently he'd felt the urge to settle, get to know a place and put down some roots. Fenwick was a good place and he did feel at home here. The possibility presented by Tom Faulkner had been too good an opportunity to miss. "It would be nice to stay here," he said, "for a while."

"Why should you be moved on?" Raven looked him in the eye; black eyes that Luke felt could swallow a man. "You have a right to say where you live."

It spoke to Luke's heart, to desires he couldn't articulate. "I do," he said and then stronger, "of course I fucking do."

Raven grinned.

A second knock came on the caravan door.

"Sorry, Luke," Connor said as he stuck his head round the door. "Police."

The three of them descended into the early afternoon sun. Already the temperature had dropped to near freezing.

"I take it you didn't find any girl," Luke said as they headed for where the policemen waited politely at the gate. Around them travellers were gathering, leaving the warmth of fires and caravans to come and see what the police wanted.

"No," Connor said, "totally vanished. We might want to warn people; there was some sort of large animal roaming round up there."

"Really?" Raven sounded amused.

"Yes, really," Connor snapped. "I saw the prints myself."

"Okay," Luke touched Connor's arm briefly. "I'll tell people. What do the police want?"

Connor shrugged. "Interviews, I think."

It was the Inspector again, wrapped up against the cold in a thick overcoat, with several officers grouped behind.

"I'm sorry to disturb you, sir," he said civilly.

"Luke," Luke told him.

"I wanted to thank you all for your help this morning." He raised his voice to the assembled crowd. "I am going to have to ask for further aid. I would like you all to speak to one of my officers." He indicated the group standing behind him. "We need to know if you saw anything at all which might help us either during the night of the storm or since."

"In relation to the girl?" Luke said.

"Anything, anything at all, sir. We now have evidence to suggest Mr Faulkner's death was not natural, so any information you can give us about–"

"Murder? You think he was killed?" Around him, Luke could feel the travellers almost physically drawing into themselves; no-one wanted to be caught up in such an investigation.

"Yes, sir. Can you think of anyone who might want him dead?"

"That stupid bitch from the council. He was getting in the way of her eviction."

"You expect us–" one of the policemen began.

"No, I don't," Luke said.

"Of course not," Raven added. "Why would the police actually consider someone with a motive when they can blame the travellers, the outsiders? Won't look to their own."

"As I said last night," Marshall said, "that's not the way we do things here. If this is someone you believe had motive then we will investigate. Can you give me a name?"

"Miss Shaw. She's Traveller Liaison Officer."

Marshall impressed Luke by actually writing the name down. "Now we would like to interview people." He looked round. "Where would be best?"

Luke approved; no marching in as if he owned the place. Bit of a shame this man was a policeman because he actually seemed to have his head screwed on; doing his best to not see anything he shouldn't – at least while he was worried about a murder.

Luke glared round the travellers, hoping his glance conveyed everything he wanted about what they should say and do. "You can use my caravan," he said.

Out of the corner of his eye he saw several travellers fade away; off to remove anything that might be seen as the police crossed the camp.

"Thank you, sir. That's most kind."

'Unexpected' hovered the unspoken word. Luke smiled; one up to him.

"Connor, organise everyone. I think the police can probably manage two at a time." His wasn't the biggest caravan but it had room for several people. "If you don't mind the cold, you could do a couple more outside." He caught Terry's eye. The old man raised his hand in a small salute.

"I'll sort a couple of tables," Terry said.

"Make it four at a time, Con," Luke said. "If that suits?" He looked to the inspector.

"Admirably," Marshall said. "We're much obliged."

Luke nodded; they were and he wouldn't forget it. "This way." He set off confident that, by now, there'd be nothing for anyone to see.

*

Marshall sat back as the latest pair of interviewees left the caravan. There were some benefits to rank; he and Mark were in the warm.

"What you get so far?"

His sergeant moved from where he was sitting on the bed to join Marshall at the small bench-table.

"All very similar. They were mostly up and saw the oak go down because a branch had fallen on one of the caravans."

"Yes, the bloke called Connor."

"I spoke to him briefly this morning. He said Faulkner wasn't much of a loss."

"General opinion seems to be that the victim was a loud bully," Marshall said.

"Yes, anyone give you more on this rent thing?"

"No, Luke paid it. No-one could tell me how much though they were agreed that it wasn't a lot. I think we need to talk to him about it."

"What do you make of him?" Mark said.

"Bit of an enigma. I get the impression he rules this lot with a rod of iron, but he isn't the usual loud-mouthed, anti-police yob."

"Or he's intelligent enough not to show it. One bloke I spoke to suggested he'd been on the receiving end of Luke's fists."

Marshall frowned. "Intelligent and violent? That makes him dangerous."

"Do you suppose Mr Faulkner found that out the hard way?"

"Let's ask him. Go find him, Mark. We'll do this one together."

While Mark was gone, Marshall investigated the caravan. He was careful not to open any shut doors or cupboards, but he'd been invited in so anything on display was fair game. Anything that might give him an insight into the owner's character would be useful. There were more books than he expected; most of those he'd interviewed so far had been illiterate. There was even the odd fiction classic as well as several ordnance survey maps.

The small sink held some dirty crockery but only what might have been used for breakfast by a couple of people. A guitar case was stowed in one corner, a plectrum among the loose change in a small dish by the bed.

There was nothing incriminating to be seen. Marshall sat back down, slightly disappointed. This case was offering no breaks at all.

Mark arrived back with Luke. "I've told Connor that we'll see him next."

Marshall smiled his thanks. "Do sit down, Luke." He waited until the two of them had slid into the bench seat opposite him.

"So, you're in charge around here?"

"As much as anyone can be."

"I think you don't have many problems."

Luke raised an eyebrow. "If you say so." He smiled slightly. "I didn't have much success keeping Charlie in line or with the little thieving shits some of my companions call children."

Marshall was impressed; take the fight to the enemy. It was something he would do himself.

"We are not currently interested in investigating thefts. I would like to catch a murderer and find a missing girl."

Luke relaxed. "So how can I help you? I can assure you that no-one has confessed killing him to me."

"What did you think of the victim? I believe you probably had the most to do with him."

"He was an evil bastard and, if I was the sort of person to go 'round killing people, then he's the type I'd have willingly strung up." Luke's voice was flat and cold.

"Would you care to explain that?" Mark said as Marshall sat, momentarily lost for words.

"Have you talked to his wife?"

"About what?" Marshall hedged, surprised by where the conversation was heading. Wife beaters didn't normally brag about what they did behind closed doors.

Luke leant back in the seat. "Not giving anything away, Inspector?

The day we arrived, I walked up to the farm to offer something for using the land. Just to be neighbourly, you understand. There was no answer to the doorbell, but I could hear a woman crying so I went 'round the back. The kitchen door wasn't locked so I let myself in. It's not something I usually do uninvited but ..." he paused, his eyes looking in at the memory. "I don't like hearing a woman crying and begging like that, you understand?"

"I believe so," Marshall said.

"They were upstairs, and he was using a belt. So I stopped him." His tone left little doubt as to how he'd done so. "So there he is, flat on his back when the silly bitch throws herself across him, starts begging me not to hurt him. I told her she should report him but no, he was her ... oh, god knows, so fucking stupid." Luke took a deep breath and settled, calm again almost immediately. He leant forward, bringing his face close to Marshall's. "I told him I would quite happily beat him to a pulp and she said what could they do for us to stop me. So, I said we'd be staying as long as I wanted, and I'd pay him a fiver a week in rent."

"A fiver?"

"Yes," Luke bit the word off. "I told him if he wanted more, I'd quite happily pay her more while he was in hospital or gaol."

"Blackmail?" Mark said.

"If you like," Luke kept his gaze on Marshall. "I'm not totally heartless, Inspector. I told him that if I had any evidence at all that he'd been hitting her again while we were here then I would personally ..." Luke paused.

"Kill him?" Marshall supplied.

"Drag him to the nearest police station?" Luke suggested, leaning back.

"Really?"

Luke grinned, the gesture lighting his face. "Unlikely, more along the lines of beating the crap out of him but somebody just did his wife a favour and killed the bastard so not a wise thing to admit."

"I believe you were up there on the night he died?"

"I took the rent up. That's all I did, I promise you. I didn't stop to string him up in his tree."

"I believe he came down here for rent usually," Mark said.

"It was a 'game', Sergeant, though not a particularly nice one. I tried to get up to the farm on a Wednesday before he got down here. That way I could try and check on his wife and the girl. I knew really when he'd been at them because he was down here, dragging me out of bed he was so early. This week he was very late, so I went up."

"Do you think he hit his daughter too?"

"I'm not sure. I never saw evidence but then I rarely saw her. She was out a lot; college, Saturday job, getting out of the house. Didn't blame her."

"So who do you think killed him?" Marshall said.

"I'd like to say I thought his wife had suddenly seen the light, but the stupid cow was never going to get it. It could probably have been just about anyone else that ever met him."

"And what about Zoe? Did you see her when you went to take rent the last time?"

"No. He was outside messing with the Oak. I gave him the money and left. Not the sort of person I fancied spending a lot of time with."

"So you've no idea where she might be?"

"Anywhere out of reach of his fists would be sensible."

"You never use your fists?" Mark said.

Luke laughed. "You've spoken to everyone. You answer that. Plain and simple, I've never hit a woman and I don't let anyone here do so. I've hit men and they've hit back but not often either way. I'm not saying I'm a fucking angel but there are things you just don't do … ever."

"I couldn't agree more," Marshall said. He didn't let his emotions get the better of him in cases but he couldn't help hoping Luke wasn't his culprit. The traveller had an integrity Marshall respected.

"Can I ask you about that evening," Marshall pulled out a picture of Philip Knight. "I believe some of the travellers were in The Highwayman. Did you see this man?"

Luke took the photo and then laughed. "Him? Mad as a bloody hatter, Inspector, or pissed more like."

"Why do you say that?"

"Claimed to have seen some woman prancing about the fields here with no clothes on. Said he was going to find her."

"Did you see him after you left the pub?"

"No, he was still there when we left and trying to persuade his mate to go climbing the hill with him. His mate wasn't up for it as far as I could tell."

Marshall smiled. "I don't suppose there were any naked women up here that night?"

"In that weather?"

"No, I suppose not."

"To be honest, Inspector, there could have been legions of them but I, for one, wasn't going to go outside my caravan to see if I could find them." Luke paused. "Do you think this man had something to do with Mr Faulkner's death, then? I didn't see him out here but then I wasn't looking and I doubt I'd have heard anything with the wind howling as it was."

"I'm afraid this man was also found dead just down the hill from you on the same night."

Luke frowned. "I really can't help you there, Inspector. He was fine when we left the pub."

"Never mind. Thank you for your time and the caravan. Could you ask Connor to step in?"

"Sure. Do you want to see Raven too?"

"Raven?"

"Strange bloke. Turned up last night. Not sure what to make of him."

"Yes, after Connor."

Luke left the caravan, letting in a chill blast of air as he went.

"Well?" Marshall prompted.

"I rather like him," Mark said, "and I get the impression he knows nothing of Mr Knight, but I wouldn't put it past him to have done for our other victim."

"Unfortunately, I'd have to agree."

CHAPTER 5

Zoe stood, irresolute, on the junction of Lacey Road with the ring road watching the lights change from green to red and back to green.

Running away had seemed so simple and she'd spent so long saving and planning. For one brief, glorious moment two days ago it had seemed she could stay and then everything had changed.

Now all her plans lay in tatters, blown to smithereens by a photograph. Once she'd seen it, she could hardly miss them. Every newsagent, post office and corner store for the length of Lacey Road seemed to be plastered with her face. The Advertiser decked every store front.

She couldn't risk a travel agent or the station. Even hitchhiking might be a bad idea until she got away from town.

And what if they didn't find her? Would her face soon be all over every paper and television screen?

She wanted to scream in frustration.

"How am I going to get anywhere?" she asked Merlin. The dog sat patiently beside her, trusting brown eyes never straying far from her face. She absently stroked his head; it was calming. "I'm not going to give mum the satisfaction of going back."

She peered back the way they had walked but no familiar figure approached. "I wonder where your mistress went to. She said you found me, but can she find you? And now I'm talking to a dog ... oh, fuck, why did she have to tell the papers?" She looked back down at her attentive listener. "Motorway, I think, Merlin. Lots of people charging past who won't have seen my picture. I may be able to get a lift. Not sure they'll be keen on you but it's about six miles out so I'd appreciate the company on the walk. Coming?"

She set off across the lights, now showing red, heading towards the roundabout which would take her out to the motorway. Merlin fell into step beside her as she tramped along the verge.

"Thanks," she said. He gave her hand a brief lick in response.

*

"There," said Lacewing, pointing suddenly.

Ahead of the queue a slim figure with a large dog had crossed the lights they were waiting at.

"You didn't mention a dog," Daniel said. His mother's Fiesta was only just going to fit a fifth person in it. There was no way the huge animal was going to climb in too.

"It's my dog," Lacewing said unhelpfully.

"It's too big for the bloody car."

"That's all right. He'll follow. He's good at it."

"She's heading along the bypass," James said.

"We can pick her up," Lacewing told them.

"It's a dual carriageway. I'm not supposed to stop," Daniel said. "Why not?"

"Law, police, highway code, that sort of thing."

"It'll be okay just to pick her up." Lacewing sounded totally unconcerned.

"I ..."

"Trust me."

Daniel sighed and inched towards the lights which had turned red again. "What am I doing?" he said aloud. All because of some stupid dream he was picking up random strange girls. He hoped the next one wasn't as bossy.

It took three more rounds of the lights but eventually Daniel turned left and headed after the retreating figure. Only as he pulled up alongside did realisation belatedly hit him.

"It's the missing girl, the one out of the paper."

"Bugger me," James said while Lacewing said, sounding smug, "Well, obviously. You said you saw her."

"But it was ... well ..."

"No it wasn't. It was a connection." She pulled open the door to confront the startled girl as Daniel pulled to a halt. "I told you he'd come to you. Get in."

"What?" Her eyes flicked to Daniel.

"Oh, please do. I have no idea what's going on, but Lacewing tells me you're a damsel in distress."

"Get in child," Gwion ordered, "we have somewhere safe we can take you."

"I don't know you," Zoe said.

"I don't know them either," Daniel said, "but they seem harmless. I think it's one of those days - like a dream. Just go with it."

"We won't hurt you," James said. "That's a promise. They'll have me to deal with if they try."

"Merlin won't fit ..."

"Merlin, follow," Lacewing glanced at Gwion, "Where?"

"We'll go to the library."

"Library, Merlin. Find David."

The huge dog loped off along the verge.

Lacewing smiled. "He'll find us. Get in, Zoe. We're blocking the road and Daniel's very worried about it."

With a last look after the disappearing dog, Zoe slid into the car, cramming herself and a large rucksack into the back with Lacewing and Gwion.

"So where now?" Daniel said, pulling away.

"Smith Foundation, Museum Street," Gwion answered. "David's expecting us."

Daniel wished people would stop anticipating his movements.

*

Connor entered the caravan with some misgivings. It was too soon since he'd last done this and the memories weren't pleasant.

"Sit down, please." Marshall waved to the seat opposite.

Connor slid in beside the sergeant. He'd sat here for breakfast with Luke this morning. A quick glance told him the dishes were still piled in the sink.

"We're interviewing everyone," Marshall started. Connor recognised the 'policeman putting witness at their ease' tactic from last time. It didn't take long to progress to 'policeman grilling the witness' and then 'policeman harassing a suspect'. He blinked and realised he'd missed what the inspector was saying.

"Sorry, miles away, could you repeat that?" Not a good start.

"I just said that I believe you had a near miss the night of the storm."

"Yes." Six inches closer and he wouldn't be having this conversation. "A tree came down."

"Crushed your caravan?"

"Yes." Connor waited for the inevitable question about stolen caravans.

"Staying here with Luke now I believe?"

Connor thought he managed not to betray his surprise. "For the moment. He's a good man."

"Unlike Tom Faulkner?" the sergeant suggested.

"I didn't really know him."

"You said earlier that he was no great loss." He had; he ought to be more careful with his words.

"He came down here on a Wednesday morning. Must have been on his way to do milking or something because he was usually here before anyone was up and he made a right racket getting Luke up to demand his rent. He seemed determined to annoy us all."

"Why would that be?"

"Because we were on his land," Connor hedged, unsure how much they knew.

"And he wasn't happy with that?"

"People usually aren't."

"So it would be nothing to do with his wife beating?"

Connor sighed; why couldn't they be up front? "You know about that? So you know why he wasn't happy. Luke knew what he was so he had to let us stay."

"Luke told you?"

"Of course; we're a family. He shares important things with us. He asked us to keep an eye out."

"No-one saw fit to share this information with us," Mark said.

Connor laughed. "Of course not."

"Go on."

"First, it's Luke's to tell. Second, you'd go and arrest his wife and we're of the opinion he deserved what she did."

"You think Mrs Faulkner did it?"

"Who else?" The abused only ever took so much.

"Luke doesn't think so," Marshall said

"Oh." Connor stopped, surprised. "Well, I suppose he's the only one who's ever properly met her so he's probably more accurate than the rest of us."

"So you never met the wife? How about the daughter?"

"Saw her out walking a couple of times at a distance. She always looked lonely though I've no reason to suppose she was."

"Did you see her or her father on the night of the storm?"

"Only thing I saw – vividly and rather closer than I wanted – was a tree branch."

"How about since?"

"No, sorry Inspector, I can't help."

"How about this man?" Marshall slid a photo across the table. It showed a young, dark-haired man that Connor vaguely recognised. He searched his memory for the last time he'd seen the face.

"I think he was in The Highwayman the other night." The face came back, along with its drunken idiocies ringing round the crowded pub.

"Can you remember anything about him?"

"He'd had too much to drink, going on about ... oh, some stupid story about naked ladies dancing for him or some such thing. I didn't pay too much attention."

"Do you think he had a link to Mr Faulkner?"

"I have absolutely no idea. I'd never seen him before."

"And have you seen him since."

"No, Inspector."

"Thank you. I think that will be all for now."

Marshall watched the young man leave.

"Something off about him; not what I'd call a typical traveller."

"Naughty, John, stereotyping not allowed. Very non-PC," Mark said.

"So what did you make of him?"

"Someone I interviewed said he'd only been with them a year. Joined them when his wife died. Walked away from home, job, family, everything."

"Am I allowed to say, 'I told you so'?"

"Not a killer though."

"Anyone can be a killer, Mark, but I have to admit he seems unlikely. Everyone says he was definitely asleep in bed when the tree fell on him though that doesn't stop him being up and about earlier."

"We're not getting anywhere, are we?" Mark said.

"Nowhere. Might as well see the last of them while we're here."

"Raven."

"Bloody stupid name," Marshall said, "bound to be hiding something. Bring him in."

Marshall's mobile rang as Mark was leaving.

"We've got a problem," Helen said on the other end of the line.

"Just the one?"

"Sir?"

"Oh, don't mind me. Just going nowhere fast. Go on, what problem?"

"I've just had some council woman here talking to Mrs Faulkner. She was asking about wills. You know, who owned the land now the farmer is dead."

"Why?"

"Because his arrangement with the travellers is no longer valid and it is up to the new landowner whether they have permission to be there."

"That makes sense though she could have waited a little before dashing in." Even the most insensitive councillors he'd met before had had more tact. "I assume Mrs Faulkner is landowner now?"

"Oh yes, all legal."

"So, what's the problem?"

"She went totally off the deep end. This neighbour of hers who makes the superb cakes has managed to convince her that it must have been the travellers who killed her husband. So, she is demanding they go; had an absolute screaming fit over it."

"Well, it is a possibility, Helen. Understandable, I'd say." And fairly predictable from what he knew of the woman.

"Granted but this Miss Shaw has gone away promising a section sixty-one."

"Miss Shaw? I think she was poking her nose in down here as well earlier. Bugger. All right, thanks, Helen. I'll see if I can track her down once I finish here and talk her out of it."

"Problem?" Mark had arrived back, a tall, dark-haired man looming behind him.

"Tell you later." He didn't want that sort of news travelling.

He'd only been involved in a section sixty-one twice before. The first had resulted in every traveller vanishing in under twenty-four hours, never to be seen again. If he wasn't careful, he'd lose possible murderers before he was anywhere close to catching them. Though that may well be preferable to the other option which had involved a full-scale riot and dig-in lasting nearly a fortnight.

He realised Mark and the traveller, Raven, had sat themselves down and were waiting for him to begin.

"I'm asking everybody about the night of the storm," Marshall said.

"I wasn't here. I only arrived last night." It sounded like a challenge.

"You weren't in the area at all?"

"Why would I wander around in a storm?" Which didn't answer the question.

"You tell me. Where were you if not here?"

"I can't say. I just travel. I could have been anywhere."

"I'd like you to try a bit harder to remember," Marshall said coldly. He didn't like the arrogance of the man's attitude at all.

"I don't think so." The traveller was unperturbed by Marshall. "I can't force memories." He seemed amused by the statement.

"I–"

"Am I a suspect?"

Getting closer with every word, Marshall thought, but he simply shook his head. "Not at present, sir, but we're looking to gather all the information we can about that night. Do you remember seeing the murdered man or his missing daughter?"

"Hand on heart, Inspector, I saw neither."

That, at least, had the ring of truth about it.

Marshall showed the man Philip Knight's picture. "How about this man?"

"No, well…" Raven hesitated.

"Have you seen him?" Marshall pressed.

"No, I think not but I thought it was someone else. I'm sure I saw someone who looked very like him just today. Maybe a relative. A young man was poking around here earlier today."

"Really?" Marshall waited, encouraging elaboration.

"There were two young men and one looked very like that picture. It's probably nothing. I think his friend called him Dan. He was a bit preoccupied, I felt. In fact, he nearly ran me down in the road."

"But not the man in the photograph?"

"No, not him."

"He's hiding something," Mark said as he shut the door behind Raven's departing form, "but whether it's a murder?" He shrugged.

"Maybe. I'm not convinced that he doesn't know anything."

"What about this 'Dan' he says he saw? A little convenient?"

"You know me, Mark, I don't like coincidences. Dan Calver just made it to the top of my list of people I want to see. I'd like to know what he was doing out here where his cousin's body was found."

"So, what now?" Mark asked. Outside lamps were being lit against the early dark of the January day. "Call it a day?"

"One last thing. We need to track down a Miss Shaw from the council and convince her that giving a set of murder suspects twenty-four hours to bugger off is not the way we usually work."

"Oh God," said Mark.

*

Daniel pulled into the crowded expanse of the Pay and Display car park in Church Street. "This is as close as I can get you."

"Space over there," James said, pointing.

"Are we stopping?" Daniel wasn't sure he wanted further involvement; this was already too weird.

"Of course." James had a look in his eyes that Daniel recognised; it was normally associated with a rapid descent into mayhem and trouble.

"I'd appreciate the company," Zoe said from the back. "Well ... of normal people."

Daniel nodded and reversed the car into the empty space.

"How long should I pay for?"

"I'll do it." Lacewing leapt from the car and strode over to a machine. She stood and stared at it for a moment and Daniel got the funniest feeling she was talking to it. Then she removed a small piece of white paper that she brought back and handed to Daniel. It allowed him twenty-four hours parking.

"How did you do that?"

She looked him in the eye for a long moment and then turned away. "Come on, let's go."

Daniel fell into step beside James, Zoe on his other side. "She didn't put any money in, I'm sure of it."

"She had a whole breakfast she didn't pay for this morning," Zoe said, "and no-one noticed."

"Who is she?"

"No idea. Calls herself Lacewing. I met her the night of the storm and I can't get rid of her. She said I had to meet a friend of hers who plays the flute."

"That's him. Gwion." Daniel indicated the old man striding ahead of them, deep in conversation with Lacewing.

"You know him?"

"No, he just appears in Daniel's dreams," James said cheerfully.

"Really?"

"Well yes, I suppose."

"And Dan had a vision of you," James continued, regardless of the daggers Daniel was looking at him, "out on the road by your farm."

"Really?" Zoe said again, looking at Daniel in amazement.

"I ... er ... I thought I saw you. You had that rucksack with you." He could feel colour flooding his cheeks. "I don't know what happened. It just did. Gwion says it's something to do with a tune he played and being in my dream."

"I just wanted to get away," Zoe said sadly.

"Er ..." Daniel paused, unsure how to broach the subject. "Do you know your dad is dead?"

"Best news I've ever had."

Daniel and James glanced at each other.

"That's a funny thing to say," James said.

"Oh yes, hilarious." There was no mistaking the bitterness in the tone.

"No, I meant–"

"Do me a favour and butt out." She lengthened her stride to join Lacewing and Gwion.

"She's odd," James said.

"No." Daniel saw deeper than the bravado. "She's hurt. I wonder what he did to her."

They rounded the corner into Museum Street in silence and stopped in incredulity. The ancient building that was the Smith Foundation Library dominated the street, its massive wooden doors standing open at the top of the stone steps. Sprawled across the doorway like a giant hearthrug lay the huge wolfhound, its tongue hanging out in a cheerful grin.

"That's not possible," Daniel said.

"Dogs can move fast." James didn't sound too sure.

"Not that fast and all the way across town."

"Merlin always finds his way." Lacewing looked pleased by their bemusement.

"Shall we go in?" Gwion led the way up the stairs, patting the dogs head as he passed.

Feeling even less sure about the sanity of proceeding, Daniel followed.

The Smith Foundation Library smelled of age and leather. Dark shelves of heavy wood towered in rows behind the modern desk with its beeping computer.

A slim girl, not much older than Daniel, was sitting on a high stool behind the desk, her fingers tapping away at the keyboard. She had wheat blond hair pulled back in a ponytail and a crease mark between her eyebrows from frowning at the screen.

She looked up as the group of them entered, her frown deepening slightly before her face cleared and she smiled.

"Hello, how can I help you?"

"We're looking for David, child. Who are you?" Gwion said.

"Jenny Williams." Daniel nearly applauded her for keeping calm in the face of such a patronising tone. "I help out on the desk sometimes when David has jobs to do in the back office."

"We know David," Lacewing said. "We'll go through. You ought to go home."

"I beg your pardon?"

Gwion smiled gently, looked the girl straight in the eye and patted her hand. "It's all right. David knows we're here. You run along. It'll be fine. I'm sure he said to expect us."

"He said to expect you," the young girl said as if reciting a line. "Go through to the office and I'll shut up shop and get home."

"Shut ... What's going on?" Daniel demanded, watching in amazement as the girl started closing down the computer.

"We're finding Zoe somewhere safe," Lacewing said, "and I want to know what you can see. So come on and stop complaining."

She grabbed his arm and dragged him away from the desk.

The office at the back of the library was an odd place. It looked more like a sitting room of a stately home to Zoe with its huge fireplace and wealth of comfortable armchairs. A large leather-topped table stood to one side amidst a scattering of books and other, stranger, objects. Behind the desk a doorway led through into a garden.

Ahead of her, Daniel paused and then turned to look back through the library, a frown creasing his forehead. Zoe found herself considering him intently; he seemed friendly, genuinely concerned about her. It was that care in him that had prompted her to ask them to stay. She wouldn't class herself as the helpless female who needed a young man to help her but something about Daniel was reassuring.

"James," the object of her scrutiny said, "where have we parked?"

His friend gaped at him. "Dan? We're in the—"

"No, I mean point to it, from here."

"What? Well, we came in ..." James went through the same process of turning and frowning. Zoe worked it out with them and suddenly realised what was upsetting the dark-haired young man.

"Behind that wall," she said before James could speak.

"About where that garden seems to be?"

"I'd say so."

"I'm not seeing things then." He sounded relieved. She didn't blame him - if his friend was to be believed, he had been seeing a lot of impossible things recently.

"Definitely a garden," she said, offering a smile. She moved past him to take a closer look. "It looks a nice place." It did; peaceful and sunny and impossible.

"Well?" Lacewing joined her, the wild green of her eyes twinkling in amusement.

"What is it?" Zoe wasn't going to give the girl the satisfaction of denying the evidence of her own eyes.

"It is not Church Street car park," James pointed out. "Is it a projection of some sort on to the wall?"

"Step through," Lacewing invited, obviously enjoying their confusion.

Zoe glared at her, hesitated and then decided she'd risk walking into an illusion. Making a big movement of it, she stepped over the sill and into the scene beyond. Despite her assumption that she would walk into the wall, nothing shocking happened. She simply stepped down on to the manicured lawn. A smell of fresh grass and rose blossoms filled her lungs.

"It's not even winter," she said accusingly.

"It's a special place," Gwion said. "Come back in and we'll tell you about it. Then you can explore if you like."

Zoe stepped back through the doorway with reluctance. Something in her needed the peace she felt in the garden.

"So where's our car?" Daniel said.

"Church Street car park." Lacewing said. "If you go back out the way you came in, you'll find all as you left it. Only through this door is the world ... different, shall we say."

"Where's David?" Gwion occupied a chair next to the roaring fire. "I fancy a talk with someone nearer my own age."

"Who's in my library?" The voice came from the doorway and Zoe whirled round to find a man standing in the garden behind her. Greying hair flopped across his forehead, a smile creasing the unlined face.

"Gwion, you old rascal," he said, his smile broadening, "and Lacewing." He stepped through into the office and crossed towards where Gwion sat. "Only two? What have you done with the fiddler?"

*

Marshall didn't have to look far for Annabel Shaw. As he and Mark strode into the CID office in late afternoon, the Chief Inspector stuck his head out of his inner sanctum at the far end of the long office.

"John, the very person. Have you got a minute?"

Marshall changed direction mid-step and followed his superior.

A small non-descript woman perched on the edge of a chair beside Chief Inspector Edwards' desk. "This is Miss Shaw. She's with the council."

"I've heard of her."

"She has a request from a Mrs Faulkner to remove the travellers from her lands. I believe this is out where you've been working."

"Mrs Faulkner is wife to the man we found hanging in the tree, sir."

"The man was being blackmailed by the travellers for the use of the land," Miss Shaw said, showing more personality than Marshall had given her credit for. "She thinks they may have murdered her husband and, understandably, would like them moved."

"There is the chance though, Miss Shaw, that Mrs Faulkner is right, so I'd prefer my suspects not to be scattered to the four corners of the earth just yet."

"Is there evidence that they're involved, John?" The Chief Inspector said.

"No real evidence to point to any one person at all yet," Marshall had to admit.

"Motive?"

"They weren't really happy with the deceased's treatment of his wife."

"But they'd known about that for months," Miss Shaw pointed out, showing herself remarkably well-informed. "It was the cause of the blackmail I believe."

"So, you're arguing they can't have killed him? A moment ago, the possibility they had was reason to—"

"Mrs Faulkner's belief that trespassers on her land may have been involved in her husband's murder and daughter's disappearance and her consequent distress are reasons enough, Inspector."

"Anyone with better motive or opportunity, John?" Chief Inspector Edwards prompted as Marshall glared at the woman.

"Well," Marshall was determined to score some points in this exchange. "It has been suggested to me that Miss Shaw has one of the best motives."

"Me?" She stood up ramrod straight, her whole posture one of outrage.

"Miss Shaw wishes the travellers gone. The only thing standing in her way was Mr Faulkner."

"Well ... I ... really ... I ..."

"Be serious, John," Edwards said.

Marshall hesitated momentarily but then annoyance got the better of common sense; he really wasn't happy about the way Miss Shaw was about to balls up his investigation.

"I am being serious, sir. I believe the traveller's concerns are as genuine as Mrs Faulkner's and should merit as much investigation. I was, myself, surprised at the speed with which Miss Shaw visited Mrs Faulkner to encourage the travellers' removal. I was given her name earlier today by the travellers and I intended to search her out before leaving tonight." That wasn't a lie; he was glad he'd made a note of the name now. "I wonder if you can tell me where you were between midnight and two on Wednesday morning."

"I was in bed, Inspector."

"Can anyone verify that?"

"Well," her mouth dropped open as she grasped that he was serious about his questions. "No, I sleep alone."

"And can you give me your opinion of the victim?"

"Well, obviously I didn't think he was a very nice man."

"Not nice? The man was a wife beater."

"I realise that," her voice rose as she appreciated the corner he was backing her into. "I have to admit I felt very uneasy in his company."

"Did he ever behave inappropriately towards you?"

"John," Edwards said warningly.

"All right," Marshall made a point of noting everything down. "Don't leave town, Miss Shaw. I may wish to talk to you again."

She stood, dumbstruck, while Marshall finished writing. Then she rallied.

"The section sixty-one, Chief Inspector?"

"Come back in the morning, please. I'd like to get up to speed on the current situation before we make any decisions."

"You were a bit hard on her, John," Edwards said as Miss Shaw slammed the door on her way out.

"She's trying to deprive me of over half my suspects. They'll vanish."

"Surely they would have already vanished if they'd done it."

"Possibly," Marshall admitted, "but I'd prefer to be sure."

"Without better evidence than you currently seem to have against them, I don't think we can stop this eviction. Sorry, John."

*

David made them all coffee.

Daniel and James took the opportunity to have a look at some of the strange objects in glass cases around the walls. Zoe trailed along with them, the three of them feeling out of place.

In front of the fire Lacewing, Gwion, and David were involved in the sort of discussion old friends engage in. Plenty of 'Do you remember' and 'What have you been up to' and a disregard for others present.

Daniel got the impression that, for the moment, any thoughts of keeping Zoe safe had taken second place and the three of them might as well not have been present.

"So," James said as they stood nervously by the desk, uncertain of what to do next. "You don't want to go home?"

Daniel fully expected the slim girl with them to tell James to piss off, but she surprised him by shrugging.

"Why should I?"

"They've got loads of police out looking for you. We saw them today, lines of them."

"You and another girl, the papers said," Daniel added. "I suppose they meant Lacewing."

"They were looking for her too?" She was momentarily thrown.

"I suppose." James shrugged. "The hill was crawling with police."

"What were you doing there?" She scowled at James.

"Those gypsies stole my bike. We went to get it back."

"They're all right," she was immediately on the defensive, "they had one up on my dad."

"Is that a good thing?" Her tone of voice suggested it was.

"You bet."

"You didn't like your dad much," James said, rushing in where someone more tactful may have kept quiet.

Zoe snorted. "I hated the bastard."

"What did he do?" Daniel asked softly as James was momentarily silenced by the ferocity of the reply.

"What business is it of yours?"

"None." Daniel held up his hands. "Just sometimes it helps to talk."

"For God's sake. Everyone's suddenly a fucking expert on what's best for me. Well, let me tell you," she prodded him hard in the chest, "I know what's best and getting as far away from home as I bloody can is it."

"But he's dead." Daniel dared to argue.

"I wish he was." Her voice rose. "I wish to hell he was, but he isn't. He's in me; his blood is inside me and I have to get away."

"But," James said unwisely, "if that's so then you just take him with you."

Zoe thumped him.

It was a good blow, delivered with the force and precision of a closed fist wielded with power. It sent James' head snapping back and drew blood from his nose.

"Zoe! Stop!" Lacewing leapt to her feet and the dog, which had been snoring in contented bliss before the leaping flames, materialised between Zoe and James, a low rumble growling deep in his chest.

"Fuck," Zoe said, clutching her hand. She turned and ran, heading for the doorway to the impossible garden.

"Zoe!" Lacewing called after her, but David was already moving.

"I'll stay with her, keep her safe." He followed Zoe's retreating figure.

"Sorry," James said, holding a handkerchief to his nose. "I didn't mean to annoy her. I just pointed out–"

"Leave it, Jay." Daniel steered his friend to an armchair. "I don't think anyone was blaming you." He glanced round.

"No," Lacewing agreed. "I thought she was going to hit me earlier. I think it's been boiling inside of her for a while."

"So what do you want with her?" Daniel said.

"To help her."

"Will she be all right out there?" Daniel looked towards the doorway Zoe had charged through.

"David will take care of her."

"Why do you want to help?" James demanded.

"She has ... something. Akin to what Daniel has but deeper," Gwion said.

"And the music," Lacewing added. "Don't forget the music."

"Is that supposed to help?" James said while Daniel wondered what he was supposed to have. He didn't feel any kinship to Zoe outside of a desire to get away from home. He wasn't sure why these odd people would want to help either of them with their need to get away.

"I'm sorry, James, you couldn't begin to understand," Gwion said.

"That's it? Sorry, you won't understand? Well I'm not sure what the hell we're doing here." James stood up. "Thanks for the coffee. Come on, Dan, let's go home."

"By all means go but we need to talk to Daniel about—" Gwion began.

"Then you don't talk to my friend like he's a moron," Daniel said. "James and I are a team." There was no way he wanted to be left alone with a bunch of weirdoes. He needed James.

Gwion and Lacewing looked at each other, hesitating.

Daniel stood up. "Fine! I drive you round. I rescue some mad girl who then punches my friend. And you sit there and insult us. If you can't give us some respect then—"

"Sorry," Lacewing smiled properly for the first time since they'd met her. It made her suddenly beautiful. "I'd forgotten about the fires of youth. Two of you in two days questioning and unwilling." She held out her hand to James. "Be welcome, James." She sounded less strange and much, much older.

James blinked then shook the proffered hand and sat back down.

"So, what happened to Dan earlier; the dream and seeing that girl before we saw her if you know what I mean? It really freaked us out."

Dan smiled slightly to himself, quite happy to let James do the talking. He'd been 'freaked out' most definitely but James provided a safety net; he could listen to the questions and answers and pretend it was something happening to someone else.

"Your friend has a touch of the old blood. The travelling tune I played set him on a path." Gwion frowned. "Most do not remember the dream, just the tune and the desire to move on."

"The dog was in the dream," Daniel said. "Merlin."

Gwion and Lacewing exchanged glances again; too many secrets. "Yes," Gwion said slowly, "that is interesting, as is the later vision of Zoe. It suggests a deeper calling than I knew. I only meant to confirm a desire, set your feet to a path."

"So what have you done to him?" James demanded.

"Opened channels to his heritage. Many of the old blood have the true sight."

"Meaning?" James pushed.

"Seeing what is and has been, sometimes even, what is to be."

Daniel felt a chill slide down his spine, even as James said, incredulous; "Telling the future? You're joking."

"We can try it," Gwion suggested.

"Yeah, right. Have you got your crystal ball with you, Dan?"

Daniel laughed, his tension disappearing to be replaced by sheer disbelief. The man was cracked; had to be.

"Must have left it at home, Jay."

"I believe David has a tarot of mine," Gwion said, unperturbed, "I gave it to him many years ago for safe keeping."

"That tarot's yours?" Lacewing sounded surprised. "I think he keeps it in his desk." She rooted around in a drawer and retrieved a highly decorated pack of cards. "But these work for me too and I don't see the future."

"So sure?" Gwion said. "I merely wish to demonstrate a foretelling not a reading." He handed the pack to a startled James. "Shuffle these, young man."

James frowned but did as he was told.

"Stop when you feel like it."

James gave the cards another shuffle and cut for good measure.

"Now, Daniel, tell me what card your friend will turn over."

"But I don't even know–"

"Concentrate, look within and then speak."

Daniel closed his eyes, trying to remember if he knew anything about tarot cards outside of James Bond. He couldn't even remember which film. Unbidden in his mind an image rose of a man hanging in a tree.

"Death," he said.

James looked at him, looked at Gwion and then grinned. Daniel recognised the mischief in the look. "And now," James said, "you're about to do some sort of trick. Well, sorry mister, you won't catch us. With a violent jerk he threw all the cards in the air, closed his eyes and held out his hands. He closed them on the first card that touched and handed it, still with closed eyes, to Daniel. "Here."

Daniel took it and turned it over. His heart plummeted.

"Shit," James said.

The card showed a figure robed and hooded in black bearing a scythe.

As they stared, open mouthed, the picture blurred and vanished to be replaced by that of a man bending amongst the roots of a toppling oak.

With anticipated finality, a spade was descending towards his head.

CHAPTER 6

Luke finished clearing away the plates from tea. Outside he could see someone had started a small bonfire and his people were gathering around it.

"Looks like someone needs us," he said. Connor sat behind him at the small table. The bonfire was a way to attract people; sometimes to celebrate but also when advice or support was needed. Luke guessed this was one of those times. He could also hazard why after an afternoon spent with the police here.

What he wasn't sure about was his own heart. Should they go or stay?

"Police won't want us leaving," Connor said having obviously followed his own train of thought to the same place.

"I'm not sure I want to leave. This is a good place."

"Some will want to though." Few were keen on so close a scrutiny by the law.

"How about you?" Luke handed Connor a beer. "Stay or go?"

"Part of me wants to go, as fast and as far as possible."

Luke raised an eyebrow, curious as to what had made his new second-in-command so wary of the police, but he contented himself with saying, "But?"

"I don't want to spend my life looking over my shoulder. Let's go, if we're going, when we can do so with no hint of suspicion."

"Sound advice."

"Possibly. We may have a problem."

"What?" Luke could think of several, most of whom were probably gathering outside to tell him how fast they should be getting out of there.

"I heard two of the lads earlier. Some boy was round today demanding a stolen bike back. He was threatening to tell the police. Raven told him to come back tomorrow for it. Our lads aren't too happy, but we can do without a fight with town youths if this one today has friends."

"I think Raven was trying to tell me earlier." In front of the council woman - that would have gone down well. "Right. Let's go and join the throng. See which way the wind's blowing." Most of the camp was lounging around the small fire now.

The two men took their beers and left the caravan. Luke moved amongst the men standing around in the firelight, exchanging greetings, slapping backs and moving on; getting a feel for the mood of the group.

He saw too many frowns, eyes clouded with worry in the flickering dark. Voices were generally muted and subdued though two or three of the younger groups were speaking loudly against the police and their right to move them on. Luke guessed that not all of it was alcohol-fuelled bravado and he could have problems come morning if he wasn't decisive now.

Once he'd ascertained the general mood, he moved closer to the fire and raised a hand, waiting for quiet. While the noise died, he looked round and noticed Raven. The man stood in the dark, outside the circle of light. He seemed to be watching the travellers as closely as Luke was. Luke shuddered; the man disturbed him for some reason that he couldn't put a finger on. Raven had been as eager as Luke to tell the council woman this was home; had acted, in fact, just like he would expect any one of the group to. Which was perhaps the problem; the man wasn't one of the group, no-one could be after so short a time. No-one who wasn't family and Raven hadn't claimed such privilege.

Luke turned to summon Connor forward. As he did so he thought he saw a girl amongst the trees behind Raven, tall and slim with long white hair, but when he looked back there was nobody there. He shook his head and beckoned Connor to stand with him as the chatter faded away.

"Who set the fire?" Those with concerns had first voice.

"I did." Raven pushed his way forward carrying his bag.

A murmur crested and ebbed away, and Luke could feel his own temper rising. This man really had no idea of etiquette. How dare he presume to call the camp together?

"You have concerns?" Luke said, allowing his anger to show a little; Raven needed to know he overstepped boundaries.

"Don't you?" Raven put his bag down at his feet. "But actually, I lit the fire merely because I wished company, to sit round the flames and tell tales to hold back the dark. We could play a tune or two and sing the old songs." He stared Luke in the eye. "I assumed we would be staying tonight."

A babble of voices rose; some agreeing, some arguing against.

Luke let it swell and die away. "Why would we stay?"

"This is our home now," someone yelled from the dark.

"We've settled," a second voice added.

"Police won't let us go," a third, perhaps wiser, said.

"Of course, you always do what the police tell you to," Raven said.

Luke kept a tight rein on his temper. This was a discussion the travellers needed to air even if the time had not been of his choosing. "We are not murderers," he said.

"You are thieves. There was a lad here today asking for a bike."

"You had no right to admit it was here or offer it back," Luke said. No right to interfere in his rule and authority.

"He'd already seen it. I stepped in to prevent a fight. With the police crawling all over the farm I didn't think it was a good idea if he suffered." The sheer reasonableness annoyed Luke further but he had to admit Raven was right.

"So what were you planning on doing when he comes back?"

Raven grinned, showing too many teeth. "That's up to you."

"Hide the bike," one of the younger crowd yelled, Luke couldn't tell who but several of the others cheered.

"If we leave," Terry shouted to make himself heard over the uproar, "then the problem goes and the police questioning about the murder does too."

"The police won't let us go while they're investigating a death," Connor said. His harsh words, said with authority, brought sudden quiet.

"They can't stop us," Terry argued. "If we go now then we'll be gone by dawn."

Luke sighed; here it was, decision time. He'd so wanted this to be home. He was tired of moving on. Unfortunately, Terry was right – if they were going, they should do so immediately. They could be miles away by the time the police came back. If they split up, joined other caravans, they'd never be found. But this was his group, his family, he didn't want them spread to the four corners of the country. Ignoring the expectant crowd, he tried to think; hesitant in leadership for the first time.

"What if that's what the police want?" Raven said.

"What?" Luke was thrown, his train of thought derailed.

"What if I told you that you'll be getting an eviction order in the morning? Twenty-four hours to leave."

"All the more reason to go," Connor said.

Several people nodded agreement but there were angry mutterings too.

"That is what the police want," Raven said, stoking the dissent. He seemed determined to play devil's advocate. Luke wondered what the strange man really wanted. "They have no right to tell you to go."

Luke didn't miss that 'you'; so much for the man attempting to be part of the group.

"The farmer let us stay," Terry said.

"The farmer's dead," Luke snapped.

"His wife should honour the agreement." Carl was a young man with a girlfriend in town, he wouldn't want to leave.

"His wife should be grateful." Another voice hurled from the back, unwisely.

"Grateful?" Luke's anger came flooding out as he whirled in the direction of the comment. "Grateful? Why? Did you have something to do with the death? Did any of us here? You speak words like that and we suggest to everyone that we were involved."

"So would leaving," Raven interjected as Luke drew breath.

Luke whipped back round. "And what the fuck do you want?"

Raven was unperturbed, his smile flickering out again. "I said. To tell tales, play tunes, sing songs. Like travellers always have." He reached into the bag at his feet and drew forth a fiddle case. "Play with me and let the cares of tomorrow wait."

"If we're going," Terry began.

"We're not," Luke raised his voice. "I'll not quit our home without good cause. I won't have the police thinking us killers and," he stepped to within two inches of Raven, bringing his face to almost touching, "I'll not take the unsupported word of a stranger that we're to be evicted tomorrow. Play you're fiddle if you want to. You won't play me."

He stepped away from the fire; Connor a heartbeat behind him.

"An eviction would mean they don't consider us suspects," Connor said as they pushed through a now-silent crowd. "We should probably go if that happens."

Luke nodded. "That's what my head tells me."

Beside the fire Raven ran his bow across the fiddle strings, his instrument crying a mournful tune.

"But I'll not do what that man says until I know what he's up to," Luke said. He glanced back at the fiddler and then turned away. "He's trouble; I just don't know what kind of trouble."

Luke stalked back to his caravan, leaving Raven to lead the singing and playing into the night.

*

Once she was past the initial lawns and sculptured flowerbeds, Zoe found herself amongst a maze of more overgrown hedges. She blundered on for a while until she found herself in the centre where a fountain tinkled merrily into an ornamental pond set amidst an oasis of green. A summer house stood on the opposite side of the cascading water. Zoe circled the pond, curiosity overcoming the desire to run.

Her hammering heart calmed a little, though the tears still hovered unshed. Only if she kept moving and exploring would she keep those at bay.

The summer house contained a single, sunlit room. A large desk filled one end and bookshelves lined the walls. A guitar stood on its stand in a corner, a music stand beside it, precariously situated amongst a pile of song books and folk tunes. Zoe peered at the bookshelves; rows of thrillers and fantasies.

She recognised the room suddenly, or its purpose at least. This was a bolt hole, somewhere that its owner could run to when they wanted to escape. Here they could play and read and forget the world. Her bedroom at home looked much the same and for as good a reason.

Feeling as if she was trespassing, Zoe crossed to the desk. Whoever came here also drew. A pencil drawing of a tree took up most of the surface. The detail in it took Zoe's breath away.

"That's mine." David, the supposed librarian, had followed her into the room. "All of this is." He had Zoe's rucksack which he put down just inside the door.

"The drawing's fantastic."

He joined her, looking down at the work. "I was an artist before I became a librarian." There was a tinge of regret to the voice that Zoe couldn't read.

"I ... why ..." She didn't know where to start, her head was so full of questions and regrets of her own. "I'm sorry about back there," she settled for. "Did I hurt him?" She hoped not. She hadn't wanted to hurt him like she hadn't wanted to hurt her mother. He'd offered to protect her, the first thing he'd ever said to her, and then she'd gone and thumped him.

"He'll be fine," David said. "Have a seat." There was a large armchair in the corner opposite the guitar, ideal for curling up in with a good book.

Zoe slumped down and closed her eyes; it had been a long and stressful day.

"No-one will find you here," David said. "No mother, no police, no-one you don't want."

Only her dad, because he was inside her and could make her thump people. She pushed the thought aside, trying to concentrate on other things.

"Is this really here?" She opened her eyes again, forcing the memories and images of her dad away.

"Yes. It's a long story."

"I'm not dreaming?"

"No, I'm real. This is all real." He waved a hand round him.

"Perhaps I got hit on the head. The oak hit me when it fell and I'm dreaming all this and ..."

David crouched in front of her, grasping her hands. "No, Zoe, don't. This is real." Gentle blue eyes looked into hers. "You should get some rest though. Sleep will heal."

"Some things never heal." Some wounds ran too deep. "Do you play the guitar too?" She clutched at topics to distract her mind from the usual painful channels.

"Yes." He stayed where he was, holding her hands in his. He felt substantial enough for all her doubts.

"I play flute," she said.

"So Lacewing said."

"It's in my bag."

"Would playing help you now?"

Zoe gave him a grateful smile. "It usually does." Her own escape.

He brought her the rucksack and then retrieved the flute for her. "Beautiful," he said after an initial intake of breath. "May I listen?"

Feeling self-conscious, Zoe began to play. Gradually she relaxed as the notes flew through her and became part of her. She played some old favourites and then some of her own compositions and then searched through the sheets by the music stand, trying any that looked good. 'Woodland Flowers' was one she'd not heard before, but it sprang easily from her fingers followed by 'Come by the Hills'. David surprised her by joining in, his mellow voice making the words haunting and particularly apt considering where she now stood.

"You've a nice voice," she said as the last echoes died away.

"I sing with Jenny sometimes. She has a folk club here once a month."

"She's lucky. No-one ever sang with me. We never did things together." Except hurt, she wanted to say, we suffered together but the words stuck in the lump in her throat. Despite their lack, David understood. Taking the flute from her unresisting fingers he laid it on the desk and then gathered her to him, letting her sob into his shoulder.

"Oh, child," he said, "I'm so sorry. Let it go. Let it all go."

*

"How did you do that?" Daniel demanded. He dropped the card to join all the others lying scattered across the carpet as if it scalded him.

"I did nothing," Gwion said.

"Who was the man in the tree?" James retrieved the card which now showed only the figure of death with his hood and scythe. Then he hit his forehead lightly. "Don't be stupid, James," he admonished himself. "It must be Zoe's dad. He was found in a tree."

"Was he hit by a spade then?" Daniel said. "The paper didn't say that."

"The police keep things to themselves," James said. "I read that once. They know they've got the right person because they know all the facts."

"Oh, great. So now we know it too. The police might think–"

"I don't think that's likely," Gwion said. "That was merely a demonstration of what you can do."

"But it's all to do with Zoe," Daniel said. "I saw her on the road and then I see her dad in the card. Why her?"

"There's a connection," Lacewing said. She looked to Gwion. "There must be some link."

Gwion studied Daniel; the sharp eyes almost seemed to be looking through him. "It may be simpler than that. I awoke his talent yesterday and I am concerned with Zoe. He may simply be reading my desires through the tune we shared."

"What?" Daniel said but James was quicker.

"Like crossed wires on a telephone?"

"Exactly." Gwion smiled.

"See," James pointed out, "I do understand."

Lacewing laughed. "A well-scored point. So tell us what it means."

"It means it's nothing to do with Dan. He's just listening in."

"I think your friend may be right," Gwion said after a quick exchange of glances with Lacewing. "I apologise for involving you. Take your own path with good heart." He stood, offering his hand. "I suggest you keep away from the travellers and from here for a little while and the link should fade."

Daniel and James stood slowly. They could hardly miss the dismissal but, now he had been let off the hook, Daniel was reluctant to go so meekly. Everyone shook hands and then they found themselves walking back through the library.

"It's bloody rude," James said. "Suggesting you can see things and have special blood and then just, 'oh, no, thank you and good night'."

"And keep away," Daniel added, refraining from pointing out that it had been James who had come to the conclusion it was nothing to do with them.

144

"No way," James said, "We've got to get my bike back. They're not going to stop me."

"We could do it the other way," Daniel said. "We do know a lot now."

"What do you mean?"

"We could tell the police."

"Go to the police?" James said. "We told that man we wouldn't, that we'd go back to get the bike."

"But we also now know where their missing girl is — or one of them. They might not care about your bike, but we have got some information they want."

"I don't think Zoe wants to be found," James said still unsure.

"I know." Daniel felt a bit sorry, but he was also annoyed with Gwion's casual dismissal of them and the way he felt they'd been messed about all day. "But that's not really fair on her mum and I'm not sure about these people." A sudden thought came to him. "How did Gwion know her dad had been hit on the head?"

"What?"

"Well, come on, do you really think I made that card do those things? He must have done it somehow and he knew her dad had been hit on the head with a spade. Now how would he know that — it's like you said about only certain people know all the facts."

"I never thought of that." James hesitated before the huge wooden doors of the library. "Do you suppose we ought to confront him?"

"No, I don't. I think we go tell the police."

Daniel pulled James out of the oak doors and dragged him down the steps.

*

"That was Helen," Mark Sherbourne put his mobile away. "I think she's getting a bit stir crazy."

Marshall looked up from the pile of paper on his desk. "Get a WPC out to be with Mrs Faulkner. I don't think she's going to give us much more that's useful so Helen can get back here for now." Trying to encourage empathy in his young constable by lengthy stays with distraught victims probably wasn't productive.

"What have you got there?" Mark said, joining Marshall in his office carrying a stack of files of his own.

"Reported sightings of our missing girl."

"Oh great." Mark rolled his eyes. "The world and his wife think they saw her, I suppose."

"About that. If these are to be believed then she visited every other shop in town yesterday before going out to the Travelodge."

"Why do people do that? It's not as if it's remotely helpful."

"There's one here from the bank which sounds genuine. Mr Long claims she came in and altered various bank account details so we need to talk to him." Marshall picked up another piece of paper. "And there's a lad in the Carphone Warehouse claims someone using Zoe's name bought a new mobile."

"Well that would explain why she left the other one in the bedroom. It does look awfully like someone covering their tracks."

"So what about the girl and the big dog? Is Zoe covering her tracks willingly or not?"

"Good question. Anything from forensics on the spade?"

"No prints but it matches the indents in the skull." Marshall sat back in his chair. "We're not getting anywhere and Zoe's suspicious behaviour is reason enough for the DCI to accept the section sixty-one claim. We've nothing concrete on the travellers at all."

"Do you think they'll go quietly?"

"It wouldn't surprise me to find they've already gone."

"Well," Mark dropped his own mountain of paperwork in front of Marshall, "you might find this interesting."

"Go on."

"I looked up on the computer to see if I could find any cases with similar MOs – you know, missing girl, albinos, bodies in ditches sort of thing." He tapped the files. "Found this little lot in a stack in the archive downstairs. All reports of bodies found on Hill Farm land in the last hundred and twenty years or so, all unsolved, all unexplained deaths."

"You are joking."

"Nope, half a dozen cases at random intervals and the last folder is interesting – set of copies of newspaper cuttings from about a hundred years before that all mentioning bodies found at Hill Farm from the local rag, obviously before the police force was big round here."

"How many?"

"Eleven bodies in the last two hundred years. All found on Hill Farm, all unexplained." Mark shrugged. "I haven't looked through in any detail, but I'll get round to it tomorrow and see if there are links to Philip Knight or Tom Faulkner."

"A two-hundred-year-old serial killer?"

"Yes, all right, I realise it's not particularly helpful, but you've got to admit it's strange."

"Granted." Marshall looked at the pile of folders. "What does S F mean on the front of this?"

"Don't know, I wondered that. I thought it was the initials of the officer in charge to start with but they've all got it on. I'll see if there's a case I've missed if you like, they may all be cross referenced to something."

Marshall sighed. "I hope not, really, we've got enough loose ends in this case already."

Marshall's phone rang. It was the front desk. "John, we've got two lads to see you. Claim they've come from the Smith Foundation. They say they've got information about Zoe Faulkner."

"I'll be right down." Marshall put the phone down slowly. "Smith Foundation," he said slowly, touching the letters on the front of the files. "Interesting. Come on, Mark."

Marshall studied the two young men who sat across the table from him.

Daniel Calver was about five foot ten with black hair and dark eyes. He looked wary, perched on the edge of his seat, his eyes flicking to take everything in. His friend, James Scafell, seemed more relaxed. The tall, blonde youth had done all the talking so far, his tone shading towards belligerent.

If he had to hazard a guess, Marshall would have said the pair of them had had experiences which meant they were wary of strangers and possibly confrontational.

"Shall we start at the beginning?" Marshall prompted.

"I suppose it started yesterday," James said, "when Dan saw Gwion outside Marks and Spencers and then he had this dream."

"James–"

"Well, it did, and then I had my bike stolen so we went to get it back and Dan thought he saw Zoe on the road and he fell off the fence so we went into town to see Gwion and he had Lacewing with him and she knew where Zoe was so we went to get her and then we all went to the Smith Foundation and there was this impossible garden and Zoe hit me and then–"

"James," Daniel said sharply, "I don't think you're making any sense to them."

"You have met Zoe Faulkner today?" Marshall said.

"Yes, we just left her at the Smith Foundation Library," James said, "with–"

"The place in Museum Street?" Marshall thought the story would probably be more coherent if he stepped in. Sometimes it helped to allow witnesses to talk but James Scafell seemed to be one of those who allowed his mouth to follow the stream of his consciousness.

"Yes, obviously the place in Museum Street," James said.

"She wanted to go there?"

"Not particularly," Daniel said, "but they promised to keep her safe."

"And who is 'they'?" Marshall held up his hand. "A little more than names, if you can. Gwion, Lacewing, I think you said. Who are these people?"

"Well," James was actually lost for words. "To be honest, we don't really know."

"Gwion plays the flute outside Marks and Spencers," Daniel said. "Does it every January but then goes so I suppose he is a gypsy. Lacewing was with Zoe, we thought she was the other girl you were looking for from the paper. Though she knew Gwion."

"Gypsy?" Mark said. "Not another bloody gypsy."

Marshall echoed the sentiment. "These people took Zoe to the Smith Foundation and are there with her now. Is anyone else there?"

"A bloke called David who they said was the librarian."

"I'll check what we've got on the place," Mark said, leaving the room.

"In your opinion of these people," Marshall continued, "do you think Zoe is in danger?"

The two lads looked at each other. "Well, they're bloody weird," James said, "and they have ... well." He stopped and then began again. "Look, as I was trying to tell you, we got into this because some odd things have been happening to Dan, dreams and such and this Gwion guy seemed to know what he was going to do before he did it and then there was this garden in the library which shouldn't have been there and he made pictures change on the tarot cards and," he shrugged, "to be honest we were a bit freaked out by it all. I'd say they can mess with people's heads and they seem to be fixed on Zoe and I don't like it."

"And you, Daniel?"

"I don't like it either," Daniel said quietly. "I don't like people getting in my head."

Marshall nodded. "Had you met Zoe Faulkner before today?"

"No." Both lads shook their heads.

"This Lacewing. Can you describe her for me?"

"Redhead," James said. "Hippy sort of, long hair, long skirt, long cardigan."

"Did she have a dog?" Marshall asked.

"Bloody massive thing," James agreed.

"That was odd too," Daniel said. "It wouldn't fit in the car, but it made it across town to the library on its own and was waiting for us like it knew where it was going."

"The car?" Marshall prompted.

"When we took Zoe to the library."

"So, let me get this clear. You found Zoe with these people and took them to the library because they wanted to go and you didn't think before that to tell anyone?"

"No," James said, "we went looking for Gwion because he was messing with Dan's head and he was with Lacewing and they asked–"

"Told," Daniel said.

"Told us to help them get a damsel in distress – that's what she said, a damsel in distress – so we were trying to help and then it was Zoe and she was with the dog but the dog didn't fit in the car so it just went to the library by itself."

"And then you just left Zoe there with these people who, you've just said, you think are 'weird'?"

"Well, I suppose so," James sounded slightly less sure of himself now. "They said we could go and we really weren't wanted. You could tell."

Marshall sat back in his chair and tried to think. If he'd heard it third hand, he'd have said someone was trying to pull his leg but the two boys opposite him didn't strike him as the type to come into a police station and tell a huge fabrication of lies for no reason. He could think of no reason at all for their tale except to convince him to go to The Smith Foundation Library, and why would they ask him to do that if the girl wasn't there?

He put the worries about the story to one side for a moment as Mark arrived back. "Any luck?"

"Man in charge at the library is called David though we don't have a surname," Mark said carefully. "As far as I can tell, and I haven't looked too deeply, the librarian at the Smith Foundation is always called David."

"What?" Marshall said, his train of thought derailed.

"A story for later," Mark was still being careful.

Marshall looked hard at his Sergeant who gave a non-committal shrug.

"Can we go now, then?" James said. "We've told you where she is."

"Actually, now you're here, I have been meaning to arrange to speak with Daniel," Marshall said. "Your name has arisen in connection with another unexplained death we're investigating – I believe Mr Knight was your cousin." He felt on safer ground with this one, away from stories of odd people in libraries.

"Phil, yes he is ... was ... I don't know what happened, mum didn't say."

"He was discovered in a ditch on Hill Farm on Wednesday night. Do you have any idea what he was doing there?"

"Me? No way, it was probably some animal or other. Save the vole or weasel or some beetle or something." The lighthearted response didn't altogether disguise the bitterness in the tone.

"You didn't believe in your cousin's causes?"

"He ruined every family get together and every family Christmas," Daniel said. "It just felt selfish to me."

"He often spent nights in fields and ditches?"

"Sometimes, and most Boxing Days."

"Any time, in fact, when he wasn't working in your father's store?"

"And regularly when he was supposed to be," Daniel said. "He wasn't amazingly good at attendance."

"And yet your dad was going to make him manager. That doesn't seem like a sensible thing to do."

"Well, dad wanted it kept in the family."

"But not you? I bet that annoyed you," Marshall watched Daniel closely, but it was James who reacted.

"You have got to be joking. Dan's off to uni, what does he want with a poxy hardware store?"

"I got the impression from Mr Calver that Daniel was rather angry about the shop, actually."

"He was angry–"

"Thank you, James, I'd like Daniel to tell me about it," Marshall said. "Had you fallen out with your cousin over the shop, Daniel?"

"No, of course I hadn't," Daniel said.

"And so you were out at Hill Farm today for totally innocent reasons?"

"Innocent?" Daniel flushed slightly and his chin came up. "We went to get James' bike back. The travellers have stolen it."

"Really? I was told you tried to run one of them down."

"What?" James leapt to his feet. "You have got to be joking. The idiot just wandered into the road. And it was him who said I could have my bike back tomorrow if we went and didn't tell you about it."

"Interesting," Marshall said. "I notice that you hadn't mentioned that so far. What else were you not mentioning?"

"We do actually have a report from Mr Scafell of a stolen bike," Mark said. "I checked them on the system just before and his name came up. Reported last night."

"See," James said, indignant. "And we went to see if we could get it back and to help search for your missing girls and we found the bike and we found the girl and you can't even be bothered to say thank you, just go on about Phil."

Marshall held up his hand. "I'm sorry, Mr Scafell, but I have to cover all eventualities. Could you tell me where you were on the night of the storm, Daniel?"

"I was in bed," Daniel said, "where any sane human being would have been."

"Can anyone verify that?"

"Mum and dad were in though they obviously don't actually sleep in the same room as me."

Marshall made a few notes. "Thank you, gentlemen, I think you should probably go home now. And despite your misgivings, I would like to thank you for the information about Zoe and be assured we will follow it up."

"And the bike?"

"Yes, Mr Scafell, and the bike. Please allow us to do our jobs."

"So, what do you think?" Marshall was back in his office.

"I think we've got a damn good reason now to take a search warrant to the travellers' camp," Mark said.

"For stolen goods, perhaps, but they've nothing to do with the girl's disappearance."

"Really, what about this flute-playing bloke?"

"And the murder?" Helen had joined them.

"I think we need to talk to the girl." Zoe's behaviour looked increasingly suspicious. "Let's go and see this library."

The Smith Foundation was shut; its massive oak doors creating an imposing barrier.

"Shall we try knocking?" Mark said as they stood beneath the still cheerfully glowing Christmas decorations of Museum Street.

"We can try." He knocked lightly on the door and tried the handle and then, when there was no response, tried hammering again, rather loudly.

"I suppose they've shut up for the day," Mark said.

"Probably."

"Shall we try getting in?"

"On what evidence, Mark? The word of a possible suspect in one murder case tells us that the possible suspect in another is holed up in a library with a cast of weird characters? I think we'll wait for the morning. Let's put a watch on the door and intercept whoever comes to open up in the morning – hopefully this David character – and then we might get somewhere." He turned away while Mark radioed in for a uniformed officer to keep watch. "What were you not telling me about this place?"

"There's a whole file on it in the archives. I put it on your desk. I only had a brief glance, but it seems to be a set of unsolved cases. The librarian seems to have been called David for hundreds of years."

"And does that help us at all?"

"Absolutely no idea," said Mark cheerfully, "just one more piece for the puzzle."

"Puzzle?" Marshall laughed, "This is definitely one of those where they forgot to provide a picture."

*

Luke wasn't sleeping; he was lying in his bed staring at the ceiling, listening to the last members of the party outside dispersing.

The singing and playing had been loud and boisterous led by Raven's driving fiddle. Luke could feel the pull of it tugging at him to go out and join in, but he wasn't going to dance to another's tune however well played; particularly not one where the musician wasn't to be trusted.

He had a glance out occasionally and once thought he glimpsed the white-haired girl again standing back amongst the trees, but he refused to be drawn outside.

Instead he lay on his bed and watched the firelight cast dancing shadows across the roof and went over the arguments – should they stay or go?

At five to two the decision was taken out of his hands by the arrival of Niall Murphy.

Luke knew Niall vaguely from family gatherings. He was a cousin several times removed. He was also the first on the scene if trouble was brewing.

The burly Irishman announced his presence with several loud blasts of his horn as he pulled into the field entrance.

Luke swung himself out of bed, hastily pulled on a pair of jeans and headed for the source of the commotion.

"Luke," Niall's foghorn of a voice encouraged more bleary eyed travellers from their caravans. "Hear you're fighting an eviction. I've put the word out. They'll be in from all quarters by morning. Tell me the lie of the land and I'll start the ditches." He swung an arm round Luke's shoulders in a crushing hug. "Family's coming, lad. Don't you worry."

CHAPTER 7

5ᵗʰ January

Marshall didn't sleep well. Visions of disaster kept him awake and dreams of fire in the dark and riots amongst the trees disturbed any sleep – dreams he thought he'd left behind in London.

Eventually, just after six, he gave up and decided to go back into work. Perhaps if he read through all the files on the unexplained deaths at Hill Farm it would take his mind off the forthcoming nightmare that would be the travellers' eviction.

Leaving Marion sleeping, he headed back to town.

Early as he was, Mark was there before him.

"Couldn't sleep," Mark said, "and unlikely to for days yet." He presented Marshall with freshly made coffee.

"Bad news this early?" Marshall threw his coat over a chair and perched on the edge of his Sergeant's desk. "What do I not want to know?"

"Travellers are still there."

"I doubt they've been served notice yet and I'd quite like to hang on to suspects as long as possible."

"Report from the incident room at the farm from last night says they started arriving at two making a hell of a racket."

"Arriving? Oh, crap."

"And they are still coming in."

"Digging in?" It was what they'd done last time. He could still remember the horror of crawling down hastily constructed tunnels to arrest the stubborn remainders who wouldn't move.

"I imagine so. Bit hard to tell in the dark."

"Bloody council idiot. We might as well give up on catching the murderer now. Every spare man is going to be fighting travellers for the foreseeable."

"Been there before I take it?"

"I spent two weeks fighting the bastards and six weeks off work with a smashed arm last time I got involved in a sixty-one." Fire and blood and screaming defiance had haunted his sleep for months after as well. He rubbed a hand across his eyes to dispel the unpleasant memories. "Well, we're not going to see anything there yet. Let's do something constructive and look through these files and then we'll go and drag Curtis Yates out of bed and visit the Smith Foundation Library.

The top file was slim and bore the title 'The Smith Foundation' in the elegant copperplate handwriting that Marshall recognised as belonging to his predecessor.

Inside, the first sheet simply contained a list of dates and the question 'How long has David been here?'. The other sheets in the file were lists of cases with their reference numbers. Marshall put a couple into his computer and discovered unsolved cases – a couple of missing people, a couple of thefts, a couple of unsolved deaths. At the back of the file were a few copies of news reports of odd happening and supernatural sightings in Fenwick.

And that was it.

Marshall passed the file to Mark who was seated on the other side of the desk looking through one of the unsolved death files. "What do you make of that, Mark?"

Mark flicked through the half dozen papers. "All these cases?"

"Unsolved, I think."

"You could be right; some of these names are what I've got here." Mark tapped the file of folders. "And we're supposed to think this 'David' character is to blame? Some sort of criminal mastermind who has escaped conviction?" Mark sounded profoundly sceptical.

"I've seen this sort of obsession before," Marshall said, "but it usually takes up several boxfuls of material while the officer tries to prove the case. Half a dozen pieces of paper ... it doesn't make sense. What was DI Cole trying to prove?"

"Perhaps all his evidence is in the case files of all these in this list. Perhaps this is just a reference."

"Possibly," Marshall didn't believe it. "The problem is that it isn't clear what he suspects so we could be dealing with some criminal Mr Big who now has his hooks in Zoe Faulkner so we need all the information we can gather or we might not and this could just be DI Cole's paranoid obsession. A hint one way or another would be nice without trawling through twenty unsolved cases."

"I'd be tempted to, well, take DI Cole with a pinch of salt at present," Mark said.

"Why?"

"Oh come on, John. We're the longest standing members of this department and we've barely been here six months. What station replaces its entire CID if there isn't a problem? Now I don't know what was wrong with DI Cole or his department, but I'd be inclined to meet this 'David' first and jump to character assassinating conclusions later."

Marshall nodded; the thought had crossed his own mind upon his arrival that there must have been something dodgy going on. His polite enquiries had met with just as polite non-committal answers about the age of CID and the need for fresh blood from which he'd deduced that the new broom of DCI Edwards had decided to sweep out the department. Perhaps though there was something more sinister to it.

"This file," Mark said, "doesn't convince me of anything. There's even a news report here on a ghost sighting. It's just garbage."

Marshall nodded. "Okay, we'll leave it and try talking to David instead." He kept to himself the thought that he might look into DI Cole and his 'retirement' when he had a minute. "Is there anything more useful in your files?"

"Interesting, but useful? No, probably not." He spread the top three out. "Ted Miller, aged sixty, farm hand, found dead just over twenty years ago. John Carpenter, aged forty-five, poacher, found dead fifty-five years ago. William Moore, aged thirty-five, son of the local landowner, found dead a hundred years ago. No cause of death found, and all had been talking before their death of seeing some woman dancing on the hill. All three described the woman as having white hair."

They sat in silence for a while as Mark finished looking through the other folders. "Less information as they go back in time but basically the same case in each," he said eventually. "The last folder just has some news reports in of men dying in unexplained circumstances out at Hill Farm. The earliest is from the beginning of the nineteenth century but it tells a similar story. Interestingly, the victim in that case was Thomas Faulkner, the farmer."

"Oh great, so we shouldn't really be worrying about the age of David when we seem to have a two-hundred-year-old albino serial killer," Marshall sighed. "It's fascinating and I really don't like coincidences but seriously, a two-hundred-year-old woman who dances on hill tops to lure men to lie down in fields and die? I ask you. They'll be replacing us next if we come out with solutions like that." He carefully stacked all the folders on the corner of his desk. "That got us nowhere. Let's go and get Curtis Yates out of bed. I fancy a chat with someone who may talk more sense than what we've just been reading."

Curtis Yates wasn't quite what Marshall was expecting from an animal rights protestor. He was thin and pasty with a look of someone who didn't get out much. The bags under his eyes spoke of too many sleepless nights. He lived in a one-bedroom flat above a newsagent on the outskirts of the town centre. Every spare inch was crammed with books and papers apart from one corner of the living room which was taken up by a state-of-the-art computer. This was surrounded by coffee cups and used plates, suggesting Curtis spent most of his time sitting in front of the screen. They had obviously drawn him away from a forum to answer the door.

Marshall moved a stack of magazines from a chair before sitting in it. "I believe you were a friend of Philip Knight."

"Yes, well, I suppose, I, well, yes."

Looking at the books and computer, Marshall guessed Curtis Yates didn't really have friends, just online associations. Mark was attempting to stifle a grin.

"I believe you were with him in The Highwayman on Tuesday night." Having met the man, Marshall was a bit surprised that Curtis had made it to a pub, but the young man nodded.

"Oh yes, we were trying some recruiting. Well, I was. I took along the leaflets and everything but Phil–"

"What about Phil?"

"He was being really odd. He was going on and on about seeing some woman on the hill. He just wanted to talk about her. He even told me to shut up when I tried to hand out leaflets."

"Was Mr Knight drunk?"

Curtis considered the question, his brows drawn down but then he shook his head. "I had a half and then an orange juice and then a coke so he must only have had three pints and he could take a lot more than that before he started being ... well, obnoxious."

"So who was he talking to about this woman?" Marshall asked.

"Just about everyone and I think they were all laughing at him really. It didn't do our cause any good at all. I told him that, going 'round talking rubbish when we were supposed to be convincing them about the hunting but he just wasn't listening. He was really very rude."

"Do you know when he'd seen this woman?"

"I don't think he'd seen any woman; he was just pissing about. He probably dreamt it. He said he'd seen it in the night for the past couple of nights, but I don't think he'd been out there then."

"So you didn't do any recruiting really? Then what happened?"

"We left and I came home."

"What time did you leave the pub, Mr Yates?" Mark had balanced himself a bit precariously on the arm of a chair covered in more books.

"Shortly after closing time." Curtis gave the questions some more considered thought. "I finished my drink after last orders and then tried to persuade Phil to come home and then I left so it was probably about twenty past eleven."

"You say you tried to persuade Phil. Does that mean he stayed at the pub?"

"No, he left the pub. He went up the hill. I told him it was stupid in that weather and that I wouldn't wait for him. I got drenched just standing by the car. But he said he was going to find this woman and he set off across the fields."

"So you just left him?" Mark said. "Wasn't that a bit mean? You didn't think of going after him?"

"I hadn't seen any woman. Besides, when Phil got an idea in his head then he was going to do it whatever anyone said. No-one could ever stop him. It was safer to leave him to it and get as far away as possible."

"That sounds like the voice of experience," Marshall said. He got the impression Curtis hadn't really liked Philip Knight all that much.

"He let all the dogs out last year, got us all in trouble with the police. I told him it was stupid."

Marshall smiled to himself. For all Curtis' wish to hand out pamphlets, he obviously drew the line at more active protests.

"I imagine it got you in trouble with the hunt too," Marshall said.

"Phil was always in trouble with the hunt. Every year."

"Including this year?"

"He saved the quarry this year," Curtis said with a touch of pride and grudging respect. "Rescued it from right in front of the horses."

"He grabbed the fox?" Mark said. "I'm surprised they didn't mow him down."

"Not a fox," Curtis said. "It was a hare, a white one. It was beautiful, they had no right to be hunting it."

"So he rescued this hare?" Marshall was impressed. For all he sounded fairly insufferable, Philip Knight had had guts.

"Yes, here." Curtis leapt up and began searching through a stack of paper on the computer desk. "I've got the maps here somewhere. I keep a record, organise routes and so on." He was suddenly animated, his fingers flicking through papers at speed. Half an inch of paper slipped sideways on to the floor unnoticed where it joined an already present heap. "Ah here, got it."

Curtis handed Marshall an aerial photo of the area around West Cross. There were several lines in different colours drawn on it. "The red line is the route the hunt took," Curtis explained. "The others were various groups of protestors. The letters show where incidents took place. Phil's group was the blue line and 'F' is where Phil grabbed the hare." Curtis tapped the photo showing a point where the blue line crossed the red one.

It made a warped kind of sense, Marshall decided, that 'F' also marked the ditch they'd found Philip Knight's body in.

"I think I'll borrow this," Marshall said, "it could be useful."

Curtis swelled with pride and proceeded to produce a whole set of pictures he'd taken of the hunt protest insisting that Marshall take them away with him.

"Were any of the hunters in The Highwayman last Tuesday?" Mark asked.

"We mainly spoke to the travellers. I didn't really look round the others in there."

"So there could have been someone who followed Philip up the hill?" Marshall said.

"In that weather?" Curtis' tone suggested he thought Marshall had taken leave of his senses. Marshall didn't argue the point.

"So, as far as you know, the only reason Philip Knight went up the hill was to find this woman?"

"Yes, he really didn't stop going on about her."

"And yet no-one else saw this woman as far as you are aware?"

"No, but," Curtis said with the air of a conjuror producing a rabbit from a hat, "I did find out about her."

Marshall, who had been about to stand up, settled down again. "You did? How?" So far, all forensics had managed was a couple of hairs off Philip's body. He made a mental note to check with Hickson about results on those.

"I looked online, Inspector. It seems over the last few hundred years there have been several sightings of a white-haired woman dancing above West Cross and it always leads to an unexplained death. So it's obvious."

"What is?"

"It's a banshee," Curtis explained in the tone of one having to convince a moron that two plus two equals four. "They herald death."

Marshall stood up. "Right, I see. I'll bear that in mind, Mr Yates."

He and Mark managed to keep straight faces all the way back to the car but only by avoiding catching each other's eye.

*

For the third day in a row, Daniel was woken by a call from James.

Unexpectedly he'd slept without dreams and felt refreshed. Perhaps the oddness of yesterday had been a lingering link with the old man after all. On balance he thought that was more relieving than otherwise.

Therefore, he greeted James breezily. "Someone stolen something else, mate?"

"No, I just need a lift to get it back."

"Can't we just leave it to the police; let them do it?"

"If we don't get it."

"That inspector said—"

"I'm going to try," James said belligerently. "That man yesterday,

Raven, said we could have it back today so I'm going to get it. Just say if you don't want to help."

"I'll pick you up in half an hour." Daniel wondered briefly whether to phone the police station and try and talk to the inspector, but he knew what the response would be to James' harebrained scheme. At least if he didn't phone them, he wouldn't be disobeying a direct order from a policeman when he went to help out.

"Where are you going?" His mum was hovering at the bottom of the stairs.

"Out." Then, relenting slightly, he added, "to see James."

"You ought to talk to your father. You can't avoid him forever."

"Avoid him? I'm not, mum, I was just busy yesterday and I don't want another row."

"He doesn't want to lose you. Neither of us do."

"I'm going to university, not Mars. You won't 'lose' me, mum, except if he slams the door behind me."

"The shop's been his life." No judgment in her voice; just hard fact. "Without Phil, well, it's just—"

He gave her a quick hug. "I know. But it isn't my life. I want to ... you know. I've got to go, James is waiting."

James was pacing up and down the pavement outside his parents' semi clutching a small toolbox.

"What's that for?"

"In case they've got it chained up or in pieces or something, so we can take it."

Daniel didn't think that was such a good idea, but he kept the words to himself. James wouldn't listen when his mind was made up.

"Okay, get in."

They drove for a while in silence, each preoccupied with their own thoughts.

"So," James said eventually, "did you have any more dreams?"

"No."

"What, nothing?"

"Nope."

"Well, I suppose that's a relief." James sounded disappointed.

"Sound like you mean it, why don't you."

"Well, 'my friend the prophet' sounded quite exciting. Imagine being able to predict the future."

"That's easy. I predict you're going to get a smack in the gob if you keep on about crystal balls."

"Aren't you curious though, about what they're doing?"

"Who?"

"Those people yesterday, and Zoe." James flushed slightly as he spoke. "She's in hiding and everything."

"Inspector Marshall will have got her by now."

"I suppose. I hope she's all right."

Daniel laughed. "You only met her once. Don't tell me you—"

"Bollocks. I just feel sorry for her, that's all."

"Yeah right. She punched you."

"So?"

Daniel gave up. He had to admit that the girl had been quite attractive, and he also felt sorry for her. There was a deep vulnerability and pain lurking beneath the brittle exterior.

"Let's just go get your bike back, Jay, and forget her. OK?"

The traffic in front of them gradually slowed as they reached West Cross.

James leant out of his window to try and peer ahead. "I think it's a caravan," he reported. "They shouldn't allow them on the roads; that's what my dad always says. Or they should only travel in the dead of night."

"Wouldn't go caravanning in the middle of winter, personally." Daniel checked his mirror. "There's another couple behind us in the queue."

They crawled up the long slow hill out of West Cross and turned right towards the farm. The caravan had also turned, and a glance showed Daniel that those behind had joined their mini convoy.

"What's with the caravans?" James was also peering backwards. "This road doesn't go to any campsites."

"God knows. Shall we park up in the same place as yesterday?"

"Might as well."

Half expecting the strange man to be in the road again, Daniel pulled on to the verge at the field entrance. Ahead of them the caravan had started indicating right.

"It's one of the travellers," James said as he got out. "That explains it."

They watched the other pair of caravans also indicate and turn into the traveller's encampment in the next field.

"Come on," James said, "Let's get this done." They started off across the field.

"Bloody hell!" The two of them crouched behind the hedge, staring in amazement. Yesterday's small ring of caravans had swelled to almost three times the size and more were arriving all the time.

"Where did they all come from?" James said.

"And why?" Daniel pointed along the hedge. "What are they doing?"

Along the hedge line adjacent to the road, travellers were wielding picks and spades.

"Digging," James said unnecessarily.

"You don't say."

While they watched, some of the diggers began uprooting the hedge to fill the ditch.

"Burying the hedge?" Daniel said as his subconscious worked through the ramifications. "What the hell would you do that for?"

Another man hurried over with a jerry can and doused the filled trench.

A sudden hollow rushing filled Daniel's ears and his stomach lurched as if he was falling. Flames flared across his vision, roaring greedily along the length of the ditch. Screams rose to join the cacophony, agony and loathing in equal measure; words just beyond the edge of understanding.

"Dan! Dan!" James was shaking his arm, yelling almost into his face. "Dan, what is it?"

"It's not good, it's ... I'm sorry, Jay, I really don't think we want to be here."

"Too bloody right," James agreed with fervent speed. "Sod the bike. I think we ought to tell the inspector what they're doing."

"I don't think that's a good idea," said a voice behind them. "I think you better come with me."

*

Zoe stepped out showing more confidence than she felt. She didn't want to go back so near home; so close to her mother's grasp and the searching police. Gwion had been persuasive though and his assurance that the travellers were moving on had swayed her. If they agreed to hide her for a little while – and Gwion seemed to think they would – then she could leave Fenwick and all its memories behind her.

The walk through the deserted town in the frosty half-light of early morning had been pleasant and Zoe hoped the travellers could supply a good breakfast. The toast David had provided was a distant memory.

She felt a twinge of regret about David – he'd been so kind to her yesterday, the only person in a long while who'd made any attempt to understand her. She hoped he wasn't going to get in to too much trouble from the policeman. Gwion said a constable had been watching the Foundation but he'd been 'encouraged to sleep'. Zoe hadn't dared ask what the old man had meant.

The three of them began the long climb from West Cross, uphill towards her parents' farm. Zoe peered ahead.

"There's more travellers," she said, surprised. "Do they ... well, sort of gather when they're moving on?"

"No," Gwion said grimly, "but the more the merrier."

Lacewing stopped. "We should split."

"I'll need your voice, later," Gwion said.

The girl raised an eyebrow and then grinned, a feral light to the emerald eyes. "Old magic," she said softly, "it's been a while."

"Magic?" Zoe demanded. "What magic?"

"Music," Gwion said, "not magic, just a song." It sounded like a warning.

"Of course," Lacewing agreed quickly and set off again. "Moving on music. Sometimes people stop listening."

"I don't understand." Zoe hurried to keep up, the uncertainty she'd been attempting to bury all morning growing within her.

"It's nothing," Lacewing said cheerfully. "Come on." She led the way into the camp.

Some sort of commotion was happening.

Many people were digging ditches around the perimeter and

building barricades but almost as many again had formed a crowd around a small group to the right of the entrance.

Two men faced each other across five yards of open space and between them…

"That's James and Daniel," Zoe said, her heart leaping for no unexplainable reason. "What are they doing here?"

"Fools!" Gwion frowned. "Why do the young never listen?" He began to push his way through the gathered travellers, Zoe and Lacewing at his shoulder.

Once they were close enough to hear, it became apparent that the two lads were in trouble.

"They were threatening to go to the police," one of the men was saying. He was tall, slim and dark and Zoe felt a shiver of something between fear and pleasure slide down her spine as he looked round and his gaze swept over her.

"So?" The other man was as tall but broader built, his brown hair pulled back in a ponytail. He looked the more annoyed of the two. "I doubt they can make the police think any worse of us. They know the sort of things travellers do when facing eviction." He sounded very bitter.

"Luke, they are–"

"We do not kidnap people. Do you understand that?" Each word bitten off.

Zoe shrank back slightly. She recognised a man at the end of his tether. Shortly this 'Luke' was going to start hitting people.

"I think," Gwion stepped forwards from the crowd, "that these are friends of Zoe's here."

Zoe suddenly found herself the focus of attention. She heard several people recognise her as 'the missing girl' and could feel colour slowly flooding her face.

"Zoe?" Daniel looked round. "What are you doing here?"

"Zoe needs your help," Gwion continued, blithely ignoring the stir he was creating. "She has to hide from her father's killer. She wishes to come with you."

In the uproar this announcement created, Luke said, "But we're not going anywhere, old man." He turned to Zoe. "Try police protection. It's not our job."

"She's family," Gwion said sharply.

"So newly arrived, you dare to claim–"

"I can." The dark-haired man took Zoe's wrist, sending a jolt through her. "I claim her as family."

Luke gaped at the two of them. "What?"

"At least let her step out of sight while we agree," Gwion said.

Luke glared from Gwion and back to Zoe and then threw up his hands. "Connor, put her in my caravan. While you're at it, stick them," he indicated James and Daniel with a jerk of his thumb, "in there too. I can't discuss this now. We need to be ready for the police." He turned on Gwion. "If you're here as 'family'," the word dipped in acid, "then make yourself useful."

As Zoe followed the man instructed to lead them away, she caught Luke's glance at the man who had spoken up for her. The hate in the look almost took her breath away.

*

Connor slammed the caravan door, locked it and – with a building sense of unease – went in search of Luke.

The travellers' leader was standing part way up the hill overlooking the activity surrounding the expanded encampment.

He looked solitary and unwelcoming and Connor hesitated before approaching. Then, straightening his shoulders, he climbed the slope.

"We can't keep them," he said when he was close enough for

Luke to hear. When the other man didn't answer, Connor added, "I won't be part of a kidnap."

"Who is he?" Luke said, as if Connor hadn't spoken.

"Who?"

"Raven."

"I ..."

"He's after my role. You know it was him called the family in; told them we were digging in."

"Really?" Connor turned to follow Luke's gaze. Raven was talking to Niall and Terry, directing operations by the main entrance. Connor looked round but there was no sign of the white-haired old man who'd delivered Zoe or his flame-haired companion. "I don't know who he is or what he wants but I really don't think hiding someone the police are looking for is a good idea." He made some effort to get the conversation back on track.

"You think I do? Or this?" Luke waved his arm in a wide circle. "This is madness. I want a home not a fucking battle ground. Do you know what's going to happen here?"

"You're resisting being evicted," Connor said slowly.

"And do you think that ever bloody works?"

Connor opened his mouth and then shut it again. He'd seen it on the television, back in the days when the closest he'd got to travelling was watching documentaries by Ray Mears. "No," he said after a moment, "probably not in the long run."

"No!" Luke agreed, snapping the word out.

"So tell them to go. It's your camp."

"The police are telling us to go. I lost my chance to make that decision last night." Connor nodded, hearing Luke's defiance in the firelight again.

"He pushed you into it." Luke's stand against Raven's insistence that they were going to be evicted.

"Oh yes, he played me." Luke's voice was bitter. "Once I'd said we were staying ... he probably had Niall ready and waiting."

"But why?"

"Because some bastards thrive on this sort of thing. There's rotten apples in any basket, Con. If I'd recognised him as one, then he'd never have got in."

The two of them stood in silence on the hill.

"You could leave," Connor said eventually. "We could. Take those who want to go."

"No-one will go now."

"But–"

"Family, Con. A year and you still haven't clocked it."

"But they're YOUR family. If you say–"

"But I said we're staying."

"And you can't change your mind?"

Luke let out a snort of laughter totally devoid of humour. "Change my mind? It's obvious I haven't, I've called the bloody troops in."

"But you didn't."

"Who believes that?"

"I do." Connor could feel his own anger rising.

Luke turned to face him and gave a sudden swift smile, brief and unexpected.

"But you're different. I don't think you're really one of us." Luke reached out and gripped his shoulder. "You go, Con. No blame for wanting to."

Connor had a sudden flash – this man grasping his shoulders in just such a way to pull him free of a falling caravan roof totally heedless of the danger to himself.

"I'll stay," he said. "I owe you."

Luke held his eye for a moment longer and then sighed. "See, you do understand."

"No," Connor lied, "but you saved my life."

"It's what we do for each other. Living and dying." Luke set off down the hill. "But it's mine to say so and that bastard's going to learn it or go."

Connor watched him leave, his unease sharper than ever. He'd totally failed to resolve the issue of the three people he'd shut in a caravan and he'd just agreed to stay for a battle he didn't want.

With his heart sinking in his chest he watched a police car pull up at the main entrance.

"Now it begins." He hadn't noticed the old man arrive beside him.

"What does?" Though Connor thought he could hazard a good guess.

"A day to remember, boy, and a journey for life."

*

They returned to the station via Museum Street. The massive gothic structure of the Smith Foundation Library dominated the town centre street. Its huge wooden doors stood invitingly open at the top of a flight of stone steps. A hunched figure lay crumpled in the doorway.

Marshall leapt up the steps and crouched beside the figure of a young police constable.

"Is he all right?" Mark joined him. "What happened?"

Marshall felt the man's wrist and, on finding a strong pulse, prodded the constable gently. The man stirred and opened his eyes. He stared in bleary bewilderment at Marshall before recognition flooded his face with colour.

"Sir, I'm sorry, Sir. I don't know what came over me, sir."

Marshall assumed the poor man had already spent a couple of sleepless nights around Hill Farm. "You went to sleep. Don't worry, it happens to the best of us on boring night duties." Marshall helped the young man up. "I don't suppose there was any sight of Zoe Faulkner?"

"No, sir, I'm afraid not. The last thing I remember was an old man with a flute who came out of the library, sir. He offered to play me a tune and then I think I must have dozed off."

"Old man? Flute? That sounds like one of the pair Daniel Calver said was with Zoe," Mark said.

"Some welsh name," Marshall agreed, "Gwion wasn't it?"

"Daniel said the bloke affected his sleep or his dreams ..." Mark caught Marshall's stare and tailed off. "Just a thought. Perhaps he has some sort of hypnotism thing with his flute, puts people to sleep."

"I've never done it before, sir," the constable said.

"Well, write it up, including the man and the flute." Marshall dismissed him. "I assume Zoe is long gone by now but let's go and see if David the librarian is in."

A man of about fifty was sitting behind the computer desk in the entrance to the library. His dark hair was streaked with silver, his blue eyes surrounded by laughter lines.

"Inspector," he came around the desk, his hand outstretched. "How lovely to see you. Do come back to the office." It was as if he greeted a long-lost friend and Marshall felt strangely cheered. He paused, caught in the act of removing his warrant card from his pocket.

"You know who I am?" It should have been worrying but it felt gratifying.

"But of course, Inspector John Marshall and Sergeant Mark

Sherbourne. You're on the trail of Zoe Faulkner. I'll make you some coffee, you look like you've been up a while, and we can chat." He led them between towering oak shelving, past hidden corners occupied by opulent armchairs and through to the office at the back of the library.

"Seems nice," Mark muttered.

Marshall just nodded. He hoped he was fairly good at spotting innocent from guilty, but he didn't usually feel quite this happy about any potential witness or suspect on a first meeting.

The office was a large L-shaped room with the right-hand side as they entered disappearing back further than the left. A roaring fire in a stone fireplace filled the nearer part of the right-hand wall and was surrounded by comfortable armchairs. There was a living area beyond with fridge and cooker and a bed in the alcove at the back of the room. To the left of the entrance stood a large leather-topped desk surrounded by bookshelves and display cabinets full of a wide array of interesting relics. Behind the desk, on the wall facing the door, hung a full-length mirror. It looked to Marshall more of a stately home drawing room than an office and the electrical appliances looked distinctly out of place amongst the cabinets full of ancient artefacts and weaponry.

"You live here?" Marshall was surprised.

"Part of the job, Inspector." He bustled around making coffee. "One of the conditions of service, so to speak."

"I never realised the library was so big," Mark said, relaxing into a chair by the fire. "It must go back quite a way."

"An amazing old building," David said, handing out mugs. "Quite a few secrets in this place, I imagine. White, one sugar, isn't it?"

"How did you–"

"Lucky guess," David said.

They sat in silence with their drinks while Marshall considered how to start. David wasn't at all what he expected, except he couldn't have said what he had expected from DI Cole's files. He was also slightly discomfited by David's anticipation of them and their needs and the feeling of being at home. For all the oddness of the office, he felt perfectly at ease.

"Did you have questions, Inspector?"

Marshall gave himself a mental shake. "Zoe Faulkner came here last night?"

"Quite a crowd of people came here last night, Inspector, but Zoe Faulkner was one of them."

"I'd quite like to talk to her. I don't suppose she is still here."

"No, she left earlier."

"Alone?" Mark said.

"With friends."

"Yours or hers?" Marshall said.

David considered the question with a wry smile. "I'm sorry, I should rephrase that. She left with people who mean her well. She is not at risk."

"So you say."

"So I believe, Inspector, or I would not have let her go. She is a very unhappy young woman and has suffered. I would not inflict more on her."

"Did she leave willingly? We have had a suggestion that force was being used."

"She understood the need," David said.

"What's that supposed to mean?" Mark leant forward.

"She wants to get away from home so was doubtful about returning so close but Gwion assured her the travellers would take her with them when they go today so—"

"Go!" Mark choked on the word. "The travellers aren't going."

"Gwion was quite–"

"What would he know; you've said he was here. No offence," Mark said, "but last we heard the travellers were digging in. She's gone back to the middle of a riot."

David shrugged; it was an eloquent raising of the shoulders which dismissed Mark's words and expressed a belief that whatever Gwion said must be so.

"You're saying," Marshall wanted to clarify events, "that Zoe has gone back to the travellers at the farm along with these other itinerants?" Back to people who were top of his list of possible suspects. "I'm really not sure she's safe doing that."

"I am, Inspector. Gwion will take care of her."

"I'm afraid I don't share your faith in Gwion," Marshall said, though he could see that David's belief was genuine. "These people may have had something to do with the murder of Zoe's father."

David leant forward, frowning, and paused before saying; "I doubt it. My feeling would be that Zoe probably killed her father."

"I beg your pardon? Did Zoe tell you–"

"No, no, Inspector, she didn't mention him, but she is full of pain and unresolved conflict. I would say she was capable of it."

"And thinking that, you just let her wander off? You didn't think to phone the police?" Even as he said it, Marshall knew the answer; they would have paid no attention to what they would have thought was a crank caller and his feelings.

David obviously followed the train of thought. "I'm sure you get enough 'help', Inspector, without me phoning you to tell you my opinion of Zoe." He smiled at Marshall who found himself smiling back. For all the oddities of this meeting, there was something reassuringly open and honest about David.

"So you know nothing that can help me about the murder of Thomas Faulkner more than an instinct?"

"No, I'm afraid not."

"How about Philip Knight? Laid himself out in a ditch and died on Wednesday night."

"Claims to have seen a woman dancing out there," Mark added.

"Ah yes, that happens on occasions, I believe," David said. "A local phenomenon I suppose you'd call it."

"I'd call it an unexplained death and I have a file of my predecessor's which suggests you might know something about it. Did you know Detective Inspector Cole?"

"Yes, Inspector, he used to come to dinner occasionally."

Marshall glanced sharply at Mark; that didn't fit with their suspicions at all, though Marshall was honest enough to admit that he gave no credence to the criminal mastermind theory now he'd met David.

"So DI Cole was a friend?"

"An acquaintance. I'm not sure we ever became friends. He didn't really believe, you see. You are a different type of man altogether. I think we might be friends."

"So why would he think you knew about these deaths?"

"I have no idea, Inspector." Marshall was fairly sure it was the first lie the librarian had told; his eyes dropping to study the cup he still held.

"And Philip Knight?"

"Sounds like he fell afoul of a local legend. I wish I could help, Inspector, but I think I would need to be more certain of our friendship before I converse on impossibilities."

While Marshall was trying to work out what that meant, David stood up and collected the coffee cups. "I'm sure you're a busy man,

Inspector, but do call again."

"I will." And he meant to. Marshall was intrigued; he also thought David knew more than he was letting on. And then there was the possibility of friendship.

He'd definitely be back.

Craig Hickson and Liza Trent were waiting for Marshall when they got back to the station. The doctor was chatting to Helen Lovell while Hickson had found the stack of unsolved case files on Marshall's desk and was reading through them.

"Don't you just love unusual phenomena," he said by way of greeting.

"Not if it involves people dying," Marshall said. "You?"

"Love a challenge." Hickson grinned and Marshall decided he probably meant it. His limited experience of Fenwick's forensic expert had shown him a man who got progressively more cheerful the more complex a case became.

"Seeing as we're all here, and I'm hoping you've got news, let's have a team meeting." Marshall dragged a couple of extra chairs into his office so filling it beyond its natural capacity and opened his notes on his desk.

"Right, let's look at what we've got so far and see if we can get further because at present I feel we're floundering a bit. Victim one is Philip Knight."

"Corpse," Dr Trent said, "but not sure we can call him a victim."

"Go on."

"I've looked at everything, John, and as far as I can tell his heart just stopped."

"Before or after he laid himself out in that ditch?"

"Oh, I'm not saying that everything's above board, just that I'm not sure we're talking murder. At least, I can't prove it at present."

Marshall nodded. "Point taken. So, body number one is Philip Knight who miraculously managed to die while lying in state in a ditch. He seems to be an aggressive animal rights protestor who got up people's noses. Last seen by Curtis Yates at eleven twenty or thereabouts when he left The Highwayman to go in search of a naked dancing woman whose existence is only suggested by the presence of long white hairs on the body. Did you get anything from those, Craig?"

"Nothing you want to know," Hickson said slowly.

"Don't tell me, it was a Dalmatian or sheep or something."

"Oh no, largely human." Hickson was obviously enjoying himself.

"Largely?"

"Tested each hair because I didn't believe the results the first time. DNA had a number of strands in common with human DNA and a slightly smaller number were animal."

"Animal? What do you mean animal?"

"Hare, I think, well, I'm fairly sure."

"So," Marshall said, "some of the white hairs belong to a human – woman? – and some to a hare. That makes sense because Curtis told us that Philip saved a hare from the hunt so–"

"No, John, hate to ruin the lovely picture you're building up," Hickson leant forward. "In layman's terms, each hair I tested belonged to some creature that is part human, part hare."

"That's not possible," Mark said.

"No," Hickson agreed. "Fascinating, isn't it? And, if you're interested, the red hairs we found in the shelter along with Zoe's are also registering as part human and part animal though the animal in question this time is a fox."

As far as Marshall could tell, though Hickson was finding the news highly entertaining, he wasn't in any sense joking.

"How is that possible?" Marshall said eventually.

"It isn't."

"So?"

"So I've checked all the machines, I've done a couple of base assessments to make sure. All the equipment is working fine. Really, John, I have absolutely no idea how it's been done. All I can do is give you the results and tell you I'm working on it."

Marshall hesitated and then made a note of the results though it seemed fairly pointless. His notes on this case were turning into gibberish what with Curtis Yates and his banshee and two-hundred-year-old unsolved cases with the same MO. "Right, er, where was I?" He was totally thrown off track.

"Philip Knight," Helen prompted.

"Yes, so, apart from a woman or possibly a hare, maybe even Jessica Rabbit, have we any suspects?" he caught the doctor's sceptical glance. "Always bearing in mind, of course, that we have no cause of death but someone must know and have laid him out like that."

"Curtis Yates was the last person to see him," Mark counted off, "but has no motive that we know of. Members of the hunt might have had motive, but we have no reports that any of them were there. Daniel Calver, the cousin, seems the most likely if we believe him to have wanted the shop but he claims he doesn't. He was out at the farm but not until the next day – though obviously that doesn't mean he didn't go out there before. He does have a reason in the shape of his friend's stolen bike."

"Well that about sums it up," Marshall agreed. "So, not necessarily a murder and no evidence of anyone murdering him just a dead body that could in no way have been lying like it was without there being some foul play. So, moving on, let's consider body two – Thomas Faulkner."

"Victim, this time," Dr Trent said. "Definitely a murder. Hit over the head with a blunt instrument."

"Spade," Hickson said. "His own spade, to be precise."

"General feeling – his wife aside – is that it couldn't have happened to a better person." Marshall checked through his notebook. "Last seen before he went out to dig up some ancient gypsy box from the tree roots according to his wife who is not the world's most reliable witness. Timing is non-existent and our main witness or possibly suspect is on the run and managing to avoid us quite comprehensively. Suspects for this one are literally queuing up. Mark?"

"Well, Luke, the travellers' leader, was up there at some point that evening though he claims he didn't do it. There was possibly another traveller who convinced the wife not to phone the police or at least, that's her story. I think the wife herself is doubtful and most people we interviewed obviously felt she would have been right to take up that spade herself. The daughter ran away with suspicious speed and, despite all our efforts, is avoiding us. Then there are these mysterious other gypsies, Gwion and this red-haired girl, who have taken up with Zoe or possibly taken her as hostage of some sort though she seems to be with them willingly from eye-witness accounts. Anyone else?"

"I did add Miss Shaw to the list as she wants the eviction though I don't seriously think she went around killing people to get it," Marshall said.

"Technically then, for the sake of completeness, I suppose we ought to add Philip Knight to the suspects and whoever killed him as they were wandering round the hill that night too," Mark said. "There may be a connection."

"If we're being complete," Helen said, "I went through the travellers names and put them into the computer to see if any of them had form. There was one called Connor—"

"Bloke who gave up everything to go travelling when his wife died," Mark said.

"That's him," Helen agreed, "gave up everything to go travelling when his wife was murdered."

"Not by him, surely?" Mark said.

"Unsolved case."

"Another one?" Marshall said. "I am sick of these things cropping up. Any evidence to suggest it was Connor?"

"A little, not much and the police couldn't shake his alibi. It's still an open investigation but they seem to have written Connor off as a suspect. I just thought it was interesting that he'd left everything and vanished really."

"Well we'll add him to the list, but I seem to think he was being crushed by a caravan at some point." Marshall ran his hands through his hair. "I'm not sure we're getting anywhere. I want to talk to Zoe and I'd quite like to drag some travellers down to interview rooms, take them out of their comfort zone."

"I'd like to have another go at the wife," Mark said. "Her stories don't make sense."

"All right, Helen, I want you to get hold of the notes on this Connor in case there are similarities. Hickson, try and solve the problem of the hair and Liza I want anything you can give me that proves there is some foul play related to Philip Knight. I'm going–"

DCI Edwards stuck his head round Marshall's office door interrupting his flow. "They've gone to serve the eviction notice. Twenty-four hours to leave."

"Won't happen," Marshall said. "They've been arriving all night."

"It doesn't have to mean–"

"Oh come on, you know what it means."

"You've dealt with these before."

Marshall glared at his superior. "No way, I've got a murder investigation here."

"I need someone on the ground, John. Someone with experience. Mark can handle the murder and you—"

"I don't—"

"It's not open to negotiation, John. I need an inspector in charge on site and you've done this before."

"And have no desire to do it again."

"I know. I need your common sense and judgement, John."

"My judgement," Marshall snapped, "was to tell that bloody woman to take a hike. I knew—"

"Enough, Inspector. Get out there and keep the situation contained."

"Yes, sir." Marshall resisted the urge to throw something until his superior had left the office.

Mark caught the stapler as it flew over his head towards the door.

"I'm not sure that will help."

"No. Just thought I'd get my shot in first. I imagine I'm about to become target practice for a field full of Irish yobs."

"They seemed nicer somehow, yesterday," Mark said. "I didn't expect—"

"Yesterday we weren't trying to deprive them of a place to stay. Yesterday some brainless moron from the council hadn't decided to plunge West Cross into anarchy. Yesterday—"

"We get the point, John."

"You also get the job of tracking down a murderer. As of five minutes ago, I'm in charge of traveller eviction."

"Well, according to David, our chief suspect and/or witness headed that way so you may get to speak to her if we go out there. I shall come too and speak to her mother."

Marshall gave his sergeant a grateful smile. "I'd appreciate the support. Let's go survey the extent of the problem." He picked up the file of notes. "I'll take this. We might get time to read them in between ducking. I do hope Miss Shaw realises what she's let herself in for."

"Let us in for," Mark corrected sourly. "God, what a way to start the New Year."

*

Daniel slumped on to the double bed at one end of the caravan beside James. "We should have brought our homework with us."

"They can't keep us here," Zoe stood in the middle of the cramped space, her hands on her hips.

"Reality check," James said. "Look around. They have done it. And I thought it was what you wanted."

"Not this, no. We have to get out."

"You don't say."

"We could break a window."

"Did you see how many people are out there?" James demanded. "How far do you think we'd get?"

"They can't–"

"They can! They have! They did! For fuck sake, woman, wake up."

Zoe took a step closer.

"Shut up, James, before she hits you again," Daniel said. He meant it lightly – a joke to defuse the tension – but Zoe paled and her head snapped back as if it was she who'd been hit.

"Oh nice one, Dan," James said.

"Sorry, poor taste." Daniel patted the bed. "Come and sit, Zoe. I don't think we're going anywhere and we might as well relax. I wasn't trying to offend you."

Slowly she came and sat alongside him. "I'm sorry I hit you,

James," she said, not looking at them.

"No problem," James grinned. "Dan often tells me that I ought to learn when to shut up."

"Sometimes two or three times an hour," Daniel agreed which won him a swift glance and a half smile. "In fact, I should have told him to shut up when he suggested coming out here again."

"But then I'd be all alone," Zoe said, staring at her feet again, "and, well ..." She paused, took a deep breath and then looked properly at Daniel. "Well, then I'd have no-one to hit."

They all laughed. Zoe took the rucksack from her back and pulled herself further on to the bed. "So how could we get out?" she said to James.

James reached in his pocket and pulled out his mobile phone. "We phone someone who'll come and get us."

"Who?" Daniel peered out of the window. "Who'd come through that lot?"

"That Inspector."

"Oh great, he'll be pleased when he told us to stay away."

"Any better ideas?"

Daniel shook his head. "Fire ahead. We're in enough trouble as it is."

"Inspector?" Zoe looked worried. "You mean police?"

"Yes. We saw him last night and he told us not to come here but of course James knew better and had to get his bike back."

"I don't really want the police," Zoe said. "If there's another way. I don't want to have to go home."

"You don't have to. You're old enough to–" Daniel began but James had already put his phone away.

"Get real, Dan. The poor mother reunited with missing daughter. No way they'll ignore that."

"So?" Daniel said. "Is that as important as—"

James shrugged. "We can do it later if we can't come up with something else."

"You're serious?"

"How would you feel if I said to stuff your feelings and go and work in the shop because that would make other people happy and their lives easier? Sod your dreams, do what your parents want?"

"Point taken." Daniel sighed.

"She probably wants to get away from home more than you do."

"I said, point taken."

James grinned. "I know. I just thought I'd prove my inability to shut up."

"You're running away too?" Zoe looked at Daniel with interest.

"No, I'm going to university."

"His parents don't want him to," James added.

"But you're going anyway." Zoe smiled. "Thanks. I'm sure we'll think of a way out."

Daniel wished he could be so sure.

"I'm starving," James said, "let's see what we can find. That'll take our minds off things."

"This is someone else's caravan, James, we can't just—"

"Why the hell not? They shut us in it."

James proceeded to start opening cupboards and drawers, getting out crockery and food as he found it. After a moment's hesitation, Zoe joined him.

"Oh, wow, look at this," James said as he opened the latest drawer. "Nice piece of work." He held an ornately carved box, the picture on the front showed a man dancing through woodland followed by a file of animals. Zoe let out a gasp and grabbed it off him.

"Oh my god," she said. "It's like mine."

"You've got one? Where did you get it? It's beautiful."

"It's ancient," Zoe said, "been in the family for years. Look." She grovelled in her rucksack and produced an identical box. "It's my flute," she said, showing them.

"So this guy plays too?" James opened the second box but there was no instrument.

Inside lay a lock of white hair and a magnificently crafted crystal hare.

CHAPTER 8

"Where did they all come from?" Marshall gazed out of the farmhouse window. The travellers' camp now sprawled across half the hillside. In the crisp January light, he could see groups of people busying themselves around the perimeter of the caravans.

"They have a 'family' network." Miss Shaw had opened the door to them which hadn't improved Marshall's mood. The fact that her visit had stoked Eileen Faulkner's fanatical desire to be rid of the travellers merely annoyed him further. The poor woman had had to be sedated again.

"A network? I'm sure they do. Did you have any further reason to be here?"

"I thought I might be of service. As Traveller Liaison Officer–"

"You've done quite enough already, thank you. I'll call if I need any advice on travellers that I think you can give me."

She ignored the implied offence. "I really think we need to work together on this to–"

"You served the notice; they've got twenty-four hours, now we wait. You might as well go and get some work done while you wait. I'm investigating a murder while I still have suspects."

"But we need to plan ahead because–"

Marshall opened the back door in a pointed manner. "I am so far unimpressed with your ability to predict the future, Miss Shaw. I'll be in touch." Behind the woman he could see Mark trying not to laugh.

Marshall shut the door firmly but gently behind her. She didn't merit the satisfaction of a slammed door.

"We probably should plan ahead," Mark said.

"Oh, I know, and I will but first I'm going to attempt a little tact. Luke seemed a reasonable man so let's try being reasonable."

"You think you'll talk him into going quietly?" Mark sounded disbelieving.

"Going or staying, I'm hoping he'll do either quietly."

"You can see what they're doing down there. Not much hope of it, I'd say."

"We'll try anyway."

Doctor Gillespie appeared in the doorway to the hall. "Inspector," he looked worried, "all this upset has been too much for my patient. She has become obsessed with the idea that the gypsies have killed her husband and taken her daughter and I'm not sure it's healthy to have a constant reminder of their presence."

"These things take time, Doctor. We're–"

"No, no, forgive me, that came out wrong. I was suggesting attempting to move Mrs Faulkner elsewhere until the situation is resolved."

"Yes, please do, if you can." Marshall was sympathetic to the woman's plight, but Eileen Faulkner's near-constant state of hysteria was wearing on all his officers.

"Any news on her daughter?" Doctor Gillespie asked.

"We believe she's alive." Marshall wished he had something more comforting to say.

"Another thing to talk to the travellers about," Mark said.

Upon Marshall's request, Luke came to meet him at the field gate – Marshall hadn't been at all sure he would bother.

The tall leader looked as if he'd had a sleepless night; dark shadows rimmed tired eyes.

"I had a couple of further questions," Marshall said without preamble. "Do you have a couple of minutes?"

"About the dead man?"

"About his daughter."

Luke frowned and Marshall waited patiently while the request was considered.

"Go on," Luke said at last.

"Have you seen her since we last spoke? She was reported to be heading this way."

Luke was silent a long moment and then he said, "Yes." One word snapped out and then his whole face closed down.

"Can you tell me where she is now?"

"No." Just as abrupt.

Marshall hesitated; this wasn't the same man they'd spoken to yesterday.

"Is she alive?"

Sudden startlement thawed Luke's frozen stance. "Of course, what do you take me for?"

"But you won't tell me where?" Marshall let his eyes sweep across the encircling caravans, taking in the increase in vehicles and people.

"Her choice," Luke said. "And she's been named as family."

"I could search."

"You'll not get in." The welcome of the day before had vanished.

"It doesn't have to be like this." Marshall cringed inwardly, listening to himself. He sounded like some policing manual. Next he'd be telling everyone to 'step away before someone got hurt'.

"It does, Inspector."

"You're a sensible man."

"I'm a traveller."

"The two can–"

"And my family have come to ..." Luke paused and then looked Marshall straight in the eye. "To make sure I behave like one."

Marshall blinked in surprise. "I understand, I think. Are there no other ways to behave appropriately?"

"Too late, Inspector." Luke turned his back and walked away. After three steps he halted, hesitated and then returned to lean in close to Marshall. "I'm sorry, I chose wrong, I should have gone but I wanted this to be home, so I'll fight for it." He strode away without another backwards glance.

Marshall watched him go. "She's here and, I expect, safe."

"But we can't get to her?" Mark said.

Marshall looked round. The gate was shut and several men watched the two of them intently from beyond it. No-one made any threatening moves, but the promise of violence hovered just below the surface in hard eyes and curled fists.

"No," Marshall said, "not at present."

"So what now?"

"We wait."

*

Maggie Arkwright stared at her blank screen and changed her mind, for the twentieth time, about tomorrow's headline.

She ought to be celebrating; for the fourth day in a row she was to get the front page. Fenwick was suddenly full of crime stories; dead bodies and missing persons proliferating at an alarming rate.

That was the problem.

Try as she might, Maggie couldn't find a way to satisfactorily link all the stories together into one coherent whole so she was stuck with deciding what would make the biggest impact as a lead.

Should she go with the total lack of real news on the missing girls or the thousands of possible sightings all over Fenwick? Then there was the dearth of evidence about Mr Knight, but she could possibly make something about his visions of naked women she'd picked up in The Highwayman. Alternatively, she could run with a 'Bully Gets Comeuppance' slant on Thomas Faulkner. At a real push there was this 'beast' angle she'd heard rumours of.

What she really fancied was 'Who Stole my Car' but she doubted the editor would find that amusing. Amongst murders and possible abductions, the theft of a fifteen-year-old mini was irrelevant to all but her. It was just making her travelling life a real pain at a time when she'd been gifted a wealth of stories to investigate.

Her mobile rang, a welcoming distraction from the empty screen. It was Kate, a school friend who now worked as a secretary for Fenwick Council and occasionally passed information her way.

"Just been asked to minute a meeting here," Katie informed her in barely a whisper, "they'll be here in a mo so I better be quick."

"What sort of meeting?"

"On a traveller eviction, out by West Cross."

"And?"

"I heard it might be turning into a battle. Police involved in force. That sort of thing."

"Anything happened yet?" Maggie made some notes in her jotter.

"Notice served, I believe. One of the clerks comes in that way, says there's caravans arriving, camp getting bigger." Before Maggie could formulate any more questions, Kate continued, "Shit, here they come. Let you know any more if I can." The phone went dead.

Maggie frowned, not really a lot to go on. She should head out there, take a look and see if she could make it a story. She was standing before she remembered and let out a small scream of frustration. No car, no taking a quick jaunt out to West Cross.

"Maggie, everything okay?" Jess from the front desk had appeared in the doorway.

"Car," Maggie said by way of explanation, "keep forgetting it's gone."

"I know, pain isn't it?" Jess sympathised. "If it helps, you can borrow mine."

"Might do, cheers, if I can decide which story to actually run with."

"Got a lady at the desk asking to see you, says she can help you with that."

"Someone else thinks they've seen the missing girl?"

"No, she said she had a front page for you."

"That's not the problem," Maggie sighed, "I've got half a dozen of those already. I can do without another."

Jess shrugged, "She said to tell you this was the link you've been looking for, if that means anything."

"Who is she?" Maggie frowned, trying to remember if she'd mentioned trying to link the stories to anyone outside the office. She couldn't remember doing so.

"No idea. Never seen her before. Isn't one of the usual suspects." There was a range of local busybodies who had a slant on any story and thought they could write better than Maggie or, at least, spot a story faster than she could.

"Five minutes, that's all, then I've got to make a decision."

The girl at the desk was of indeterminate age, her auburn hair falling in ringlets to her waist. Her green eyes had a trick of focusing just beyond Maggie as if she was looking through her. The clothes were a mismatch of purples and greens which she managed to inhabit with effortless grace.

"That's her," Jess said unnecessarily.

"Can I help you?" Maggie leant on the counter.

"Maggie?" The girl's voice was low.

"Yes," Maggie resisted the urge to correct her. She disliked total strangers adopting first name terms but rather a lot of her readers assumed they knew her because she 'spoke' to them every day.

"I know who stole your car."

"I beg your pardon?" Maggie gaped at the girl, "I ...I thought you had news."

"Isn't that news?"

"Well, yes, but not the sort I can put on the front page."

"Not if they're also responsible for thefts across Fenwick and the fight which is about to happen because of the eviction. Maybe even the murders."

"Travellers? You're saying it was them?"

"Of course."

"Have you proof?"

The girl smiled, showing too many teeth. Maggie took an involuntary step back.

"Not enough for the police, but enough to convince."

Maggie hesitated, "I don't want to get the paper in trouble. There is such a thing as libel."

"I'm offering you the most 'influential' piece you've ever written," the girl said earnestly, "for your second edition."

"We don't normally–"

"Today, you should make an exception," the girl flipped the

counter up so she could join Maggie on the other side of it. "I'll help."

"But–"

"I promise you; your words will never again have such force."

Maggie found herself almost towed back towards her desk. "If you don't like it, you don't have to use it. But I think you'll be persuaded."

The strange girl pushed Maggie into her chair and pulled one up alongside. "Let me show you what I mean."

Maggie nodded helplessly as the girl started typing.

*

An uneasy quiet had settled across the hillside. Connor watched from a vantage point halfway to the farm and worried. He'd made a pact with himself. Come nightfall he would free the three young people from the caravan. He would stay himself to see the fight out – he owed Luke that much – but he wouldn't be party to kidnap. As soon as the early January dark descended, he would creep in.

He had a feeling that Luke knew precisely what he had in mind – the man wasn't stupid – but Connor thought he might be allowed to get away with it. Luke was doing a good job of avoiding the subject altogether. His only reference to it had been to assign the late afternoon watch on the caravan to Connor. Connor had decided to take this as a hopeful sign.

While he waited, he contented himself with watching the activity below. It brought to mind siege preparations and futile ones at that.

"How did I get here?" he said to the hillside at large.

"The roads we walk are not always straight."

Connor whirled round to confront the old man who'd arrived earlier.

"Will you stop creeping up on people like that; it's bloody scary."

The man smiled, "My apologies. I am Gwion."

"Connor."

"You think it's time to move on?"

"I suppose. I quite enjoy the travelling. New places, new sights. Cindy was always more one for standing still."

"Your wife?"

"Yes."

"She's with you." It wasn't a question.

"No." Connor turned away, feeling the old griefs rise. "She's dead."

"You carry her with you," Gwion said.

"Memories obviously, she—"

"Chains. Like Zoe. Chains that bind. To travel freely all chains must be broken otherwise you merely run blindly in circles."

"I gave up everything to travel," Connor argued, "I could hardly be more free."

"Grief, anger, hate? Did you give those up?"

"I ... but ..." Connor stopped. "What the hell is it to you?"

"Travellers should travel. They need someone to find the road for them. I think if you were whole, you could do so."

"Find the road? For who? What, you mean lead? Luke leads."

Gwion moved away from him to look down the hill. "Does he?"

"What's that supposed to mean?" Connor failed to inject the right amount of outrage. Luke was losing his edge here, Raven pushing for control, recent events made that clear. But if Luke lost it, it wouldn't be Connor stepping into the breach, not with Raven hovering.

"Luke is leader," Connor said more firmly, ignoring the flash of desire that suggested it would be good to set out taking the caravans with him. They would have to go where he wanted and there were still so many places he wished to see. Places he'd been going to show Cindy except that 'the future' had become thirty-six hours and a criminal merry-go-round. Places he'd wanted to go before some maniac had slit her throat, soaking his future as well as their bedroom in scarlet.

How was he supposed to leave the anger and grief behind? He'd walked away from a house he could no longer live in and communities he couldn't visit without the sharp stab of memory, but the loss was a constant hole in his heart.

"Luke has lost his desire to travel," Gwion said, "this mess is of his making. You should have gone before Christmas."

Connor knew it was true as Gwion spoke. Ill winds blew and nothing would be the same. He shuddered, a chill of premonition catching him unawares. "I don't want to fight."

"Or steal."

"I haven't ... well ..."

He eyed the old man warily – did he know about the caravan?

"The road and what we meet along it will provide," Gwion said.

"If you say so." Up until now he'd provided for himself; one of the benefits of having sold everything. A tinge of guilt drew his eye to where his stolen home was parked. He could have paid for it several times over. The pride in their efficient theft now seemed ugly and wrong.

"I should give them some money," he said, ignoring his audience.

"Probably." Gwion didn't ask what he meant; the all-knowing eyes watching him closely.

"For the van."

"A purpose in life is good."

"You're odd," Connor said, without malice. "If you don't mind, I've got things to do."

"Wise things?"

Connor laughed. "No, probably not. Honest things. Honourable things." He set off. "Well, I think so."

"I think so too, Connor Myers," Gwion said behind him.

Connor paused mid-step at his full name being spoken aloud but then forced himself to continue. An irrational itch told him the man would no longer be there if he looked back.

*

"Pretty," James said, turning the crystal figure to catch the light, "Why do you suppose he kept it hidden in a box?"

Daniel was looking at the two cases lying side by side on the bed. "Why's he got a case like Zoe's?" He rubbed at his forehead, "I've seen it before as well, something like it, recently."

"In your dreams?" James suggested. "Did you predict this?"

"No, I've seen it, I'm sure," but he wasn't, not now James had suggested dreaming it; perhaps that was all it had been.

"The story is that a gypsy gave the flute to my family a couple of hundred years ago along with a magic box as some sort of thank you though no-one has ever said what they did," Zoe said.

"So did the man who owns this," Daniel waved his hand round to encompass the small caravan, "do something too? Is there a connection or something so he came here?"

"I never heard of anything." Zoe opened her box and ran a finger along the flute inside, "This gives me the creeps."

"Got it," Dan said, the sight of the flute bringing the memory back, "Gwion has one."

"What?" James and Zoe gaped at him in astonishment.

"When I first saw him the other morning, I stopped and put money in it for his playing."

"Are you sure it was the same?" James sounded unconvinced.

"Yes, when I left you and went back past, he'd stopped, and the box was shut. I didn't really notice except vaguely to think it was nice and seeing Zoe's brought it back. I'm sure they are the same."

"That is creepy," James said, "First Gwion, then Zoe, now this traveller guy. Bit too much of a coincidence."

"But mine used to be grandad's and his grandad before him," Zoe said, "it can't be related to what's happening now."

"Hang on, you said something about a magic box, what was that?"

"Just part of the story. I never saw it. Dad kept it hidden."

James slapped his forehead dramatically, "Stupid," he announced, "come on, what do travellers do best?"

"Travel?" Daniel suggested.

James thumped his arm lightly, "No, steal, obviously."

"So you say. So what?"

"Two identical boxes, one in the caravan of a thief. It's not creepy or anything, they just stole the other one off Zoe's dad."

"It's a possibility," Dan admitted though Zoe was shaking her head.

"I'm a genius," James said grinning, "problem solved."

"Luke wasn't like that," Zoe argued but Daniel touched her arm lightly.

"Gwion's box?" he said and James deflated.

"Well, not quite so weird," he suggested, "either way I think this is stolen property, so we'll take it back." He placed the crystal back in the box and put the two boxes into Zoe's rucksack.

"We don't know that–" Daniel began but Zoe stopped him.

"It feels right," she said, "they were meant to be together.

*

Marshall had covered the dining table in files and paperwork so that he and Mark could trawl through it. They'd found nothing so far which threw any light on the current cases though they were gaining an insight into his predecessor's obsession.

Marshall's phone rang; it was the station.

"Helen?"

"No, sir, PC Martin."

"PC Martin," he repeated for Mark's benefit.

Mark stuck his thumbs up, "Used to be Helen's partner," he mouthed, "good cop. Widower."

"What can I do for you?"

"Just had a woman in here with a strange tale. Wouldn't normally bother CID with it, sir, but the interview records show that you had her son in last night and it was him she was worried about, so I thought I'd let you know."

"I interviewed–" It took Marshall only a second, "You've had Mrs Calver in?"

"No, sir, Mrs Scafell."

"James' mum?"

"That's right, sir."

"What did she want? Has he done something stupid?"

"She doesn't know. She's worried he has but she thinks he's missing."

"Missing? He was fine when he left us."

"Yes, sir, and he went home and then went out again this morning."

"Where?" Marshall had a sinking feeling he knew the answer to that one.

"Well, that's the point, she doesn't know, only suspects. She thinks it was something to do with the bike he had stolen. He took a tool kit with him."

"I told them," Marshall slapped his hand down on the table, disturbing several piles of paper, "don't people listen to the police anymore?" He took a deep breath, "What's worried her, constable?"

"She says she phoned him to find out if he'd be home for lunch and he said, to whoever he was with, 'it's my mum, I could tell her' and a female voice said 'no, she'll tell the police'. Then he covered the mouth piece she thinks because she couldn't hear what he replied but when he spoke to her again the female voice had 'won' – as Mrs Scafell put it – because James just said he was out with Dan and wouldn't be back for lunch."

"And she's worried he's done something wrong so has told the police anyway," Marshall gave silent thanks for sensible parents.

"Possibly, sir. Just thought it might be relevant to the interview."

Marshall glanced out of the large bay window across the garden and away down the fields, "I think, unfortunately, that it is amazingly relevant to this mess. Thanks for the call and do let me know anything else that bothers you."

"They're down there," Mark made it more a statement than a question as Marshall put his phone away.

"I have a dreadful feeling," Marshall filled his sergeant in on the details.

"And the girl he was talking to? Zoe do you suppose?"

"Good guess I'd say. I think there was more to this meeting they had last night than they let on."

"So what can't he tell his mum because she'll tell us?" Mark went to stare out of the window. "Is it just that they went there when we specifically told them not to?"

"You met him, Mark, if James Scafell went to get his bike back and couldn't get it, what would he have done?"

"Marched in here, complaining loudly," Mark said without hesitation.

"Which he hasn't."

"Meaning?"

"I'd say he got in but if he got out without the bike he'd be here, and if he got the bike he'd have gone home. So–"

"So, he didn't get out again," Mark finished for him. "Bugger!"

"Fits the facts," Marshall thought for a moment, joining his sergeant to watch the activity in the fields below. "Yesterday, he said Dan drove them. Find out what car he's got and see if it's around here somewhere."

"And if it is?"

"Fuck knows, Mark. We're never going to get in there without precipitating a full-scale revolt." He sighed, "Go and talk to his mum and suggest – if you can do it without worrying her too much – that she phones him and gets him to talk to you. If necessary, get her to suggest to him we think we know where he is and we're just wanting to know that he's all right. Whatever you think best, just get to talk to him. Don't tell him off. Try not to alarm them but they need to keep in touch to let us know they're okay. If you can get him to admit that Zoe is there, so much the better, but don't alienate him."

"And Daniel?"

"And, I suppose, any female albinos if they're being spirited away down there."

"What'll you do?"

"Go and meet dear Miss Shaw and refrain from strangling her."

"Good luck with that," Mark grinned, "I'm not taking bets."

*

James snapped his phone shut, "I don't think she believed me."

"To be honest," Daniel said, "you weren't amazingly convincing."

"Well, I'm sorry, just couldn't think of anything to make up off the top of my head and she'll ring again if I don't turn up for tea. Surprised your mum hasn't phoned too."

"She thinks I'm avoiding dad."

Zoe sighed, "It's all my fault. I should just have let you tell them where you are."

"Your mum'll be worried about you too," Daniel offered warily.

"I hit her, you know," Zoe said, focusing hard on the caravan floor, "the night I left. Just like dad used to."

"How many times?" James asked after a slightly awkward pause.

"Once!" Zoe blazed to her feet, glaring at James.

"There, see, not 'just like dad' at all," James pointed out. "You stopped, you left."

Zoe sat down again though she kept staring at James, "But I can't go back in case I do it again. You do see that, don't you?"

"We don't want to force you to do something you don't want to," Daniel said, though he was beginning to feel less sure about it, "But actually James probably doesn't because he's never run away from anything in his life."

"Hence being stuck in a caravan," James said cheerfully, "which I think we ought to try and escape."

"We've been through this," Daniel sighed.

"I know, but I had an idea. How about we make a lot of noise, screaming and so on, and then we barge out when they come to see what the matter it."

"You watch too many movies."

"Won't know if it works unless we try," James pointed out reasonably.

*

The meeting with the council had been a waste of time as Marshall had suspected it would be. Frightened by the chaos they'd pulled down on their heads, the Traveller Liaison Team had done their utmost to off-load any responsibility onto the police.

Marshall sat and fumed in his car behind the block of plush new offices taxpayer's money had provided for the council and wondered what he should do for the rest of the day whilst he waited for the travellers to fail to leave.

He was getting nowhere with the murder investigations; or nowhere which made any sense.

He picked up the slim file of cuttings from the passenger seat. They still told him nothing except that Fenwick had a range of unsolved cases – just like any town. Normally they were petty thefts and car crime rather than ancient serial killers. At best it suggested some sort of copycat killing but it seemed like an awful lot of trouble to go to for Philip Knight and it didn't explain Thomas Faulkner's death at all.

He threw the file down again; it didn't help his mood sitting staring at the results of his predecessors' obsessions.

On impulse he left the car where it was and walked the few hundred yards through town to the Smith Foundation Library.

David was behind the desk with a teenage girl. She was demonstrating something on the computer though Marshall would have said David was paying very little attention and was only too happy to leave her to it and join Marshall in his office.

"What do you know about Thomas Faulkner's death?" Marshall said without preamble, trying to ignore the feelings of cosy familiarity the library brought on.

"Which one?" David said after the briefest of pauses.

"Which–" Marshall stopped and did a quick re-assessment. "The one two hundred years ago," he said, acting purely on instinct.

"I think there may be a piece about it in 'Fenwick – a History'," David said, "I'll see if we've got one on the shelf."

He disappeared and returned almost immediately with a book that was distinctly larger than the pamphlet Marshall had expected.

"There's a paragraph on page one hundred and twenty under

unsolved mysteries."

"Is it worth reading?"

"You tell me, Inspector."

'One of the unsolved mysteries of Fenwick involves the death of Thomas Faulkner, a sheep farmer from West Cross, and the disappearance of his twin daughters. The presence of a gypsy band on the farm was blamed at the time though nothing was ever proved. Anne Faulkner, the farmer's wife, claimed she had been given gifts in recompense for the loss of her husband but would never admit precisely what these were or who had given her them except to say it was 'the gypsy'. It is noticeable that the Faulkners and their farm have avoided much of the ill fortune which has plagued local farmers in recent years. The only bad luck seems to have been a string of similar unsolved deaths on the farm following that of Thomas Faulkner. All the victims claim to have seen a white-haired woman dancing on the hillside in the days before their death. It is not recorded whether Thomas Faulkner witnessed the same phenomenon.'

"Sounds like history repeating itself," Marshall said sourly.

"Do you believe in coincidence, Inspector?"

"No, there is usually a perfectly logical explanation which fits the facts."

"And the logical explanation here?"

"Which fits the facts?"

"But, of course, Inspector."

Marshall shrugged; he had no idea what game David was playing but he knew the answer that was expected. "Two-hundred-year-old gypsy serial killer," he said with a smile.

David also smiled slightly, "Don't dismiss it out of hand, Inspector. I hope you have a more open mind than your predecessor."

Marshall stared the librarian in the eye, but he didn't blink; definitely didn't look like he was joking.

"What do you know?"

"Nothing. I've made assumptions but you wouldn't believe them."

"Try me."

"Not today, Inspector, not till we know one another a little better." David stood and held out his hand, "Do call again."

Marshall took his time getting up. "May I borrow the book?"

"We're a library. That is the general idea."

Marshall sighed when it became obvious he was going to get nothing more. "Back to the siege, I suppose. If I survive it, I'll be back with more questions."

*

The bottom field looked more like a caravan park than any sort of animal home. Ditches had been dug along the hedge line and there looked to be people among the treetops – a hive of industry which all paused to watch as Mark drove slowly past.

Beyond the rows of vans in varying stages of repair, a movement caught his eye and he jammed on the brakes. Standing just inside the tree line was a tall, slim figure with long white hair almost to her waist. Her pale hair and skin stood out in stark contrast to the gloom under the trees.

Before Mark could open the car door, she had turned towards where he sat as if – even at such a distance – she could feel his eyes upon her. Then she slipped between the trunks away from the camp.

Mark released his grip on the door handle without opening it. There was no point trying to get into the travellers' camp to go chasing her when she had probably vanished comprehensively amongst the trees.

Realising, belatedly, what sort of obstacle he was making in the road, he set off again though he was concentrating more on the albino's appearance than the road and narrowly missed a fallen branch before he got his mind back on his driving.

Melanie Scafell was everything Mark expected having met her son; tall, blonde and beautiful with the same infectious smile. She viewed her son's scrape with tolerant good humour.

"I expect he went to chase down his bike. He got it at Christmas and was very upset about it."

"We did tell him we'd sort things out," Mark said, following her into a cluttered lounge.

"Oh, I'm sure you did," she smiled and moved a pile of ironed clothes so he could sit down, "but he does like to do things for himself."

"I don't wish to worry you," Mark said gently, "but there is some upheaval today at the travellers' camp. I don't suppose you could try ringing again so I can check he's not caught up in any bother."

"Sure, not a problem." She went in search of her mobile phone and Mark relaxed. The armchair was comfortable and he could feel his eyes dragging closed after his recent lack of sleep. He pushed himself upright and nosed around the room a little in a bid to stay awake. His wife would call it 'organised chaos'; there were piles of paperwork on the mahogany dresser and mantelpiece and a stack of new DVDs beside the television cabinet but all, he was sure, awaiting storage or some further process in order to be dealt with.

"Here we go," Melanie Scafell waved her phone at him, "shall I call or will you?"

"No, fire ahead, give him a number he'll recognise. Tell him he's not in trouble, I'd just like a word."

She rang and almost immediately began speaking, "Hi, Jay, it's mum." There was a pause, "I know, I'm not badgering, it's just I've got a policeman here says he needs a word about your bike. Can you talk to him?"

She nodded – pointlessly – at the phone and then handed it to Mark, "Best way with James," she mouthed, "spring it on him, you'll get the truth if he's no time to think."

"Hello James, Sergeant Sherbourne here, we spoke last night."

"Yes, hi," Mark could almost imagine the young lad rolling his eyes at Daniel – always assuming they were right and the two of them were together.

"It's about your bike."

"Have you got it?" Slight belligerence to the tone.

"I'm afraid not. I was ringing to tell you we've a bit of a problem with the travellers this morning so it might take us a while to deal with your bike issue."

"Okay." The voice sounded more relaxed and Mark guessed James was trying to decide whether he should attempt being annoyed about the lack of progress when really he was relieved he wasn't getting a telling off for going after the bike himself.

"In fact," Mark said cheerfully, "we think your bike may be part of the problem," he paused and then said bluntly, "or you are."

"Er ... well ..."

"You see, we're fairly sure you went to get it back and are now in the middle of a travellers' camp getting ready to fight an eviction," Mark kept his voice deliberately light. "Would we be accurate in such a guess, James? A simple 'yes' or 'no' will suffice if you're unable to talk."

"Yes," James said swiftly and definitely.

"Can you get away?"

"No," said just as firmly.

"You and Daniel?"

"'Fraid so," a slightly rueful tone to the voice, "his mum'll be worried sick."

Mark looked at James' mum who currently seemed more resigned than worried, "Yours too," he suggested.

"Yeah, sure, tell her I'm sorry but I'm okay."

"Will do, how about Zoe?" Mark slipped it in and let out a thankful sigh as James answered.

"She's fine. She's with... that was a mean trick."

"Sorry," Mark smiled and, remembering his journey down, added, "any sign of this missing albino girl?"

"None, no, it's just the three of us."

"Well, sit tight, don't do anything stupid and I'll send you a text now I've got your number so you can get hold of me if you need to. We'll get you out as soon as we can. Keep in touch." Mark cut the call before James could ask him to give any details on a rescue that he wasn't in any position to make and noted down the number to store in his own phone.

"Are they ok?" Melanie asked, presenting him with a coffee. "How worried should I be?"

"They seem fine and fairly cheerful and he was quite open and does have his phone so he may not be in too much trouble. We'll keep in touch with you and him and hope to have him away from there soon."

Mark hoped he wasn't being too positive. Nothing about this case was straightforward and it looked like he could tell Marshall to add some form of abduction to the list of crimes alongside unsolved murders, missing girls, stolen bikes and a traveller eviction.

He'd had easier starts to the New Year.

*

Marshall pulled into the row of parking spaces outside the offices of the Fenwick Advertiser. Taking the history of Fenwick book in, he greeted the girl at the front desk warmly. He had made a passing acquaintance with her and Maggie Arkwright, the crime reporter, over the last six months and was pleased to find that the paper managed to avoid some of the worst excesses or, alternatively, boredom ratings he had seen in some local offerings.

"Can I help?" Jessica Smith smiled at him, "You're keeping Maggie really busy, you know."

"Don't I know it," Marshall agreed.

"Brought the London crime wave with you?"

"I hope not." Marshall put the book down on the counter. "I've been given this as a potential lead. I don't suppose you have news articles from a couple of hundred years ago do you? I'm looking for reports of a disappearance at West Cross."

"We've been putting stuff on the computer," Jessica smiled helpfully, "I can have a look for you. Do you have a name?"

"Yes, but it's going to give you all the recent stuff. Try Thomas Faulkner, or his wife who was called Annie. He disappeared along with his daughters."

Jessica busied herself with the computer on her desk behind the counter then waved him through, "Come this side, I think this is what you want. There isn't a lot and it's only been scanned in, so the quality is a bit rubbish."

The article explained that Thomas Faulkner and his twin daughters had gone missing. The farmer had been found dead, seemingly having been beaten up, the girls had never been found. There was a black and white picture of the twins – a pair of pretty girls in their late teens or early twenties. One had dark hair, the other was white, both falling in long waves to almost their waists.

"Would she be blonde?" Marshall asked, pointing at the photo, "it's difficult to tell in black and white but it looks very white."

"No, that's odd, looks almost as if she did have white hair."

"Albino," Marshall said with a certain sense of inevitability.

"Where did you get that?" a voice demanded behind them. Marshall whirled to confront Maggie Arkwright who looked as if she'd seen a ghost.

"This? Just checking up on an old story about West Cross and a disappearance there. These are the girls who vanished, a pair of twins. Jess kindly found it for me in the archives."

"Disappeared? When?"

"A couple of hundred years ago."

"Bollocks," Maggie said, regaining the fire Marshall recognised though she was still white as a sheet, "that girl," she pointed at the darker of the two, "was in here this morning."

CHAPTER 9

"That was the police," Zoe accused as James snapped the phone shut.

"Yeah, I know."

"And you told them—"

"Hold your horses," James held his hand up, "they told me. They seemed to know all about it. Don't know how but they'd worked it all out."

"Probably me," Daniel said sourly, "everyone seems to know what I'm doing before I've even done it these days."

"You think Gwion told them?" Zoe asked.

"Wouldn't put it past him."

"But he brought me here," she argued.

"And why did he do that?" Daniel shook his head. "Absolutely positive, wasn't he, that you'd be off with the travellers. That's what you said. But, as far as I can see, no-one's going anywhere."

"Fighting an eviction, that copper said," James added.

"There you go. I think Gwion's several sandwiches short of a picnic."

"Got his own agenda, my dad would say," James said.

"Agenda? I think he's writing his own bloody script and expecting us all to act to it."

"So?" Zoe's shoulders slumped, "What can we do about it?"

"Well," James said, "he's got us shut in a caravan on the wrong side of the gypsies–"

"And the police," Daniel put in.

"Quite, and the police. And there's a fight about to start."

"So?" Zoe said again.

"I suggest we get out of here."

"James, we've talked about this and–"

"No, seriously, it works in all the movies. We scream a lot and when someone comes, we overpower them and run off."

"I'm not really the 'screaming' type," Zoe said dryly, "I found it easier not to."

There was a slight pause and then James grinned, "Leave that to me."

Before Daniel could point out that it might be an idea to add more details to the plan than they were currently working with, James let out a blood-curdling scream.

He then threw himself against the door of the caravan and let out another high-pitched squeal.

Daniel couldn't tell what effect the noise was having on those outside but, after a moment's horror-struck silence, Zoe had collapsed into fits of hysterical laughter.

James looked slightly hurt as he re-doubled his efforts at throwing himself round the caravan yelling at the top of his lungs.

Abruptly the caravan door was thrown open and Raven filled the doorway.

Daniel hesitated. Zoe wasn't fit to run anywhere, and James had swallowed his last scream and stared at the tall gypsy in silence.

The forgotten feeling of terror from the dream swooped on Daniel and he took a step back though Raven, in fact, looked highly amused.

"You are here," he said, "for your own safety while those outside fight a battle which isn't yours. Do be a good boy and keep the noise down." He left, leaving the three occupants of the caravan staring at the closed door.

"Arrogant prat," James said, with feeling.

"Patronising," Zoe agreed though she sounded like she was trying not to laugh again.

"Oh well," James gave a rueful grin, "worth a try."

"You think?" Daniel shook his head, "That was trying, was it?"

"I did my part. Never heard a scream like that before, have you?"

"No," Daniel agreed before joining Zoe in her renewed fit of giggles, "I wouldn't go into acting if I were you."

James joined in the laughter, "We'll try again when it gets dark," he said cheerfully.

"Only as long as you promise not to scream again," Daniel assured him.

"So what do we do while we wait?" Zoe asked.

"Play us a tune on your flute," James suggested.

"Well—"

"Don't you play it?"

"Well, yes."

"I bet you're good. Pretend we're not here," James pulled open her bag and took the two wooden boxes out. "We'd love to hear you. Wouldn't we, Dan?"

Daniel had opened the second of the boxes and removed the crystal, turning it so it caught the light. "Yes, of course," he said absently, "Why is it stuck in a box? This should be on show."

"Mum said the flute and its box was hundreds of years old so perhaps that is too."

"All the more reason why it should be on show."

"I agree," Zoe took it from him, "Mum would have had it in the glass cabinet if it was ours."

They watched the play of light in the crystal as she turned it over and over.

"Perhaps she didn't know about it," Daniel said eventually, "and what's the hair for?"

"Perhaps it's hare hair – get it, hare—"

"Don't be daft, Jay," Daniel stretched the lock across his fingers, "what size of animal would have hair this long?"

"King Kong?"

"A giant rabbit?" Daniel rolled his eyes.

"Hare," James corrected.

"Whatever. This is human hair."

"How about," James said slowly, "your mum didn't know about it because it belonged to your dad and this is hair from a lost love of his which he keeps hidden to remind him. That would be romantic."

"My dad wasn't romantic, he was a thug," Zoe said.

"Perhaps a lost love did that to him," James said.

"And the box? The fact that Gwion has one?"

"Perhaps," Daniel said before an argument developed, "we'd better put it away as it isn't ours and we don't really know who does own it."

"Spoilsport," James said, "I quite liked the idea of a lost love of your dads—"

"He probably hit her too," Zoe said sourly, killing the conversation.

"Put it away," Daniel said, "Come on, play us a tune, it might make you feel better."

She offered him a tremulous smile, "Okay, do you play?"

"No, but James sings almost as well as he screams," Daniel said which earned him a proper smile.

"Then perhaps I better drown him out," she said and picked up the flute.

*

"I saw the albino, John," Mark greeted him as the Inspector arrived back at the farmhouse.

"No, you didn't."

"I did, large as life, down by the trees."

"She vanished two hundred years ago," Marshall sank into a chair beside the Aga and put his head in his hands.

"A different person wouldn't you say?"

"I don't know any more, Mark. An albino and her twin vanished from this farmhouse two hundred years ago when their father died in suspicious circumstances."

"And I saw an albino down by the trees earlier today, it was no ghost, John."

"Oh, I know, and her twin was in the Advertiser's offices earlier. Gave Maggie Arkwright quite a turn."

"So what does it mean?"

"It means," Marshall said with a sigh, "that someone knows their history and is going to a hell of a lot of trouble to recreate things even before we knew what we were dealing with."

"Some sort of revenge?"

"Well, you could look at it like that as they've killed Thomas Faulkner, sent his wife off her rocker, kidnapped the daughter – quite comprehensive revenge, wouldn't you say, if that is the case? No idea how Philip Knight fits into it all, though."

"Zoe's in the camp with James and Daniel, I've just found that out."

"Then it looks rather like whoever is behind all this is in that camp and now has Zoe Faulkner and Daniel Calver, close kin to two dead men."

"So, what do we do?"

"Unfortunately, until they've had their twenty-four hours, I'm not sure there is much we can do. Getting a warrant to go in there is only going to turn the whole bloody mess into a riot that much sooner. We'll have more help come the morning when we start trying to turf them out, so I vote we set up a perimeter in case anyone tries to escape and sit tight. Meanwhile, seeing as we're here, let's see if there are any details in the farmhouse about why someone is raking up a two-hundred-year-old story and what they are trying to achieve."

The scrap book was buried at the back of a shelf of photograph albums. It held an almost identical set of articles to the file Mark had found amongst the unsolved cases at the station – back copies of the Advertiser and other newspapers detailing disappearances at the farm over the last two hundred years. The earliest was a twin to the piece Marshall had seen on Jessica's computer earlier.

"Yes," Mark said, "I see what you mean. It was at a distance, but this could be the albino I saw this morning." He read the article in more detail, "And it says her sister was a red head. Is this the girl who has been following Zoe round, or possibly leading her round?"

"Told Maggie how to write a front page this morning as far as descriptions go."

"But none of this tells us why," Mark said in exasperation. "If we assume that someone is dressing up as this pair of girls who disappeared, then why? What's it got to do with the current family? I don't get it."

"Me neither," Marshall agreed. "Anything at all about Thomas Faulkner's cause of death? The first one, I mean."

"Nope, don't think they had forensics back then. All this says is that he looked like he'd been in a fight, but the locals reported that he'd been fighting the gypsies on his land. Some suggestion that he'd done it for money."

"Another Faulkner who was useful with his fists, then."

"Looks like it. Yes, here, 'the victim, who had been reprimanded for being drunk and violent outside the Highwayman on more than one occasion'."

"I don't suppose there is anything about Philip Knight in all that?"

Mark spread the contents of the scrapbook over the dining table but there was no reference to the Knights or the Calvers, just articles about the deaths on the farm alongside those on the sale of part of the land for an Estate at West Cross and a couple about Fenwick missing out on foot and mouth disease. "No help," Mark said, "except to tell us what we already knew." He paused, "We could try asking Eileen Faulkner, see if it jogs her memory any now we've got some more facts."

"More facts?" Marshall sighed and cleared all the bits of paper back into the scrapbook, "Conjecture, rumour and wild assumptions based on a picture from two hundred years ago and some spurious identifications by people who didn't even realise they were seeing impersonators. Not sure it's a lot of use, Mark."

"So?"

"So we plan an eviction very carefully because there are, as far as we know, a whole set of people now in that camp we don't want to go anywhere. I want to speak to Daniel Calver and Zoe Faulkner, not to mention an aged flautist who put one of my officers to sleep this morning so the girl could escape and this errant redhead who has been leading us on a wild goose chase. And there seems to be a real albino girl who is the only person we have concrete evidence – from the victim himself – was on that hillside when Philip Knight died so I don't want her slipping through the net either."

"I take it the two investigations are now one with the Traveller eviction so the DCI can't complain if we work together."

"I'd like to see him try," Marshall said grimly, "because I have really had enough now."

*

Helen arrived mid-afternoon clutching a copy of The Advertiser.

Marshall and his sergeant had spent a frustrating couple of hours discussing the welfare of the travellers and looking through the council assessment – a fairly pointless exercise as over half the group had arrived since Miss Shaw had carried this out.

Her report, summarised, amounted to 'no pregnancies, no very young, no very old, no infirm' and, therefore, no reason why removal should not be quick and efficient. The ditches filled now with lit branches and the rapidly constructed tree houses, tunnels and watch posts suggested Miss Shaw's report wasn't worth the paper it was written on.

By the time Helen arrived, Marshall was ready to strangle someone. The only good news, as far as he was concerned, was that a highly sedated Mrs Faulkner had been collected by taxi just after lunch.

"I could give you another target," Helen said, throwing the newspaper on to the kitchen table. "The Advertiser's outdone itself."

"Rid Fenwick of Murdering Scum!" blazed the headline. The article quoted Mrs Faulkner's ravings at length and blamed the travellers of every wrong in the town for the past few months. It then accused them of kidnapping Zoe Faulkner and half a dozen other 'possible missing people' and blamed 'ineffectual policing' for failing to remove the 'blot on West Cross' landscape'. The article finished by calling for people to 'act now'.

"Oh my God, is this crap having any effect?"

"Haven't seen any problems yet but that's second issue which is unusual and it's only just out. I brought it up as soon as I saw."

"Maggie's usually more rational than that." Marshall would have said the crime reporter, for all her shock earlier, had her head screwed on right.

"According to the grapevine, her car was stolen," Helen said.

"Yeah, she mentioned it," Marshall hadn't realised it was such a big deal. "I'll arrange a better presence up here in case it encourages any drunken hotheads later to head this way."

"On a more positive note," Helen said, "I have got a fairly comprehensive timeline of Zoe's movements two days ago. She was definitely running from something."

"And now she's hiding," Mark said, filling Helen in on recent developments.

"That is one young lady I would love to talk to," Marshall said, "but I can't risk starting the riot I can feel brewing by marching in there just yet."

"We're going to have to start evicting them tomorrow," Mark said. He didn't bother to add 'if they don't go'. No-one watching the camp – not even Miss Shaw – could mistake the actions there for preparations to leave.

*

Roger Scafell picked up the paper from the mat, "That's odd, we've had an Advertiser today, haven't we?"

Melanie nodded, "Came this morning as usual. I'll recycle it." She took it and then stopped in the kitchen doorway. "It didn't look like this though."

She opened it up and the two of them stared in amazement and growing anger at the front page.

"So James was right about his bike," Roger said, feeling slightly guilty about his own dismissal of his son's claims.

"Yes," Melanie said distantly.

"Where is he, he ought to see this."

"He went out with Daniel. Sorry, Roger he went to try and get it back – the bike. I think he may have got a bit messed up in this." She tapped the picture which showed a man called Charlie Monaghan being arrested for GBH. "The policeman said he seemed okay, but I think I ought to contact them again."

"Police?" Roger scowled, "Leave it to me, Mel, I'll go and get him."

"I'm not sure–"

"We'll not have murdering scum like that in Fenwick. Like the paper says, it's time to do something about it."

"What can we do?"

"Go and get my son back for starters. Don't worry, I'll be careful."

Leaving Melanie frowning at the back door, Roger left. He was gratified to see that several of the neighbours were also standing at garden gates holding copies of the Advertiser. "I'm going to go and get James," Roger told the world at large, "Melanie says the gypsies have him. And they stole his bike. We can't just sit here and let them do this."

"Have you seen this?" Tom asked at number Twenty-Seven, "This man was arrested in the pub, I was there, knifed a bloke for spilling his pint. If we don't do something, we'll all be dead."

"So what do we do?" another asked, the paper clutched so tight in his hand it was beginning to tear.

"Come with me, get James, tell them it's time they moved on."

"I'm with you," said Tom and several others nodded agreement. By the time Roger set off again they were a group of eight. He didn't stop to think about taking the car, that would be daft with so many and a rational part of Roger's mind had worked out that parking would be difficult in the lanes around West Cross. The irrational part told him that walking wasn't too difficult, and it might enable them to gather a few more bodies.

By the time the group reached the edge of town and set off up the lanes for the traveller's encampment it had built to several hundred people, many waving copies of the Advertiser, most complaining about thefts. The fact that some of these went back to long before the travellers had arrived had not occurred to most of them. Spurred on by the fire in the writing and the many perceived injustices, the townsfolk followed Roger out of town.

*

A large bonfire had been lit in the centre of the camp and Raven was putting rosin on his bow as Connor passed on his way to his stint on watch.

Connor paused to listen as Raven stroked the first notes from his fiddle. A yearning tune seeped out, barely heard above the flames greedy cackle but it made the hairs rise on the back of his neck.

Raven caught his eye. "Calling on music," he said.

"What?"

"Calling on." The man grinned, his eyebrows raised sardonically. "Come along, come, my boys." He began to hum in time to his lazy bow across the strings.

Connor paused a moment and then hurried on, feeling uncomfortable. The music was insidious, following him, getting under his skin. Like an itch he couldn't scratch and impossible to blot out. "It didn't sound so loud," he said to the surrounding dark and moved faster from the fire.

The tune followed him, drifting amongst the caravans as far as Luke's.

Terry was on duty.

"About time," he said tossing over the keys. "What's the noise?"

"Raven's playing his fiddle again."

"Played better last night. I'll get him to do something livelier." The older man stomped off in the direction of the fire but, though Connor listened, no change came.

He waited a while to be sure Terry wasn't coming back and then took a deep breath and let himself in.

Even inside the caravan he could feel the music, just on the edge of hearing. He rubbed absently at his ear while studying the three young people sitting on the bed. They watched him warily and with a certain amount of calculation.

If he didn't speak, he'd lay money on the blonde lad stating the obvious fact that he was alone. Connor briefly considered letting them go without saying a word – allowing himself to be overcome – but he'd made a decision and that should be manifest. It would be cowardly not to stand by his choice, even if only he knew it.

"You can go," he said.

"What?" Shock registered on all three faces.

"Just like that?" Zoe said. "What's the catch?"

"On my part, no catch."

"But–"

"I," he stressed the word, "am letting you go."

"I see," the dark-haired lad stood up. "We better get out then." He pulled Zoe to her feet, grabbed the rucksack and headed for the door.

"Why?" Zoe resisted slightly as they came alongside where Connor had stepped back to let them pass.

"I'm no kidnapper," Connor said. "Now go."

The three of them went, leaving him standing alone in the darkened caravan listening to the unsettling fiddle music.

*

"That was nice," Daniel said as they ducked behind the caravan in the dark and paused to get their bearings.

"Even nicer if he'd done it bloody hours ago." Even with the games they'd found in a cupboard it had been a long and boring day and James' temper was distinctly frayed. "My parents are going to be worried sick."

Daniel's buoyancy dropped. "My mum already thinks I'm not talking to dad."

"Chin up, mate, let's get home."

"What about me?" Zoe looked small and frightened.

"You can come with me," James said. "I'll look after you." The two exchanged a glance which excluded Daniel so completely he might not have been there.

"Let's go then," he said brightly, tapping James' arm. "Any idea which way?"

Objects loomed in the dark and flickering flames could be seen from several directions.

"This way," James said confidently and headed off between two caravans. Zoe and Daniel crept along behind. The orange light flared brighter as they went. James stopped and peered round the end of the caravan; the other two crowding behind.

"Oh fuck," James said, "they've lit them."

The firewood filled ditches they'd seen being built earlier in the day were now merrily ablaze. Dark figures were silhouetted against the light all along the perimeter of the camp.

Daniel staggered; a roaring filled his head. The flames leapt higher and higher, people screaming and yelling, chaos.

"Dan! Dan!" James hissed in his ear, his hands holding Daniel firmly upright. "You went again."

"Got to get out."

"I know that, you idiot, I just don't know how."

Daniel rubbed hard at his eyes, trying to banish the screaming visions. "Up hill? Towards the farm?"

"No, the stream," Zoe said, pointing away from the road. "Mill Brook runs down that way in the trees. They can't have set fire there."

She seemed to be right; the ditches ran as far as the tree line but not along it.

"What's past the brook?"

"More of our fields. But we can head down the stream to West Cross and come out by The Mill."

The Mill was a posh pub-restaurant on the outskirts of the village. Daniel had been to a wedding reception there when he was younger and seriously annoyed his father by paddling in the stream in his best suit.

"OK, we'll try it." He stepped forwards and hesitated as the fires swam in his vision. "Jay, will you lead? I can't stop what I'm seeing." Nor control the quaver to his words.

James gripped his wrist tightly. "I've got you, Dan. And when we get out of here we're going straight to that policeman. I'm going to get fucking everybody banged up."

Dan did his best to smile but his heart felt in his boots. Non-existent people still shouted and screamed in his ear and he had to resist the urge to duck as missiles only he could see hurtled out of the air above. A sudden lurid vision of James flashed across his sight —

James grinning manically while his head hung at an impossible angle on its broken neck.

"We ..." Daniel began and then stopped. What did it mean? He had only seen things that had happened before. Was this the future he was seeing now? If so, what would happen to James? Perhaps they should stop, or he should warn him or ... "I ... Jay, help me, I don't know what to do."

"We're getting out of here."

"But, I saw ... I saw ...I ..." He couldn't say it.

James hit the side of the caravan he was standing beside with a deafening thud. "I'm going to kill that old man! Fuck knows what he did to you but–"

The caravan door flung open and an old woman glared at them, her eyes glowing red with reflected firelight.

"Oh shit!" James grabbed Dan's arm again. "Come on, run!"

He dragged Daniel along, Zoe pointing the way beside them.

Behind, the woman raised her voice in protest.

*

The uniformed back up made it to West Cross before the mob from town but only just.

Marshall barely had time to organise a cordon of officers with riot shields before he saw the light of torches heading up the lane from West Cross.

"Did everybody round here get a dose of insanity for Christmas? What the hell do they think they're doing?"

Mark watched the advancing crowd with him from their vantage point outside the camp entrance. "I wish I knew, John."

"Is this an excuse to wade in and start locking travellers up before the twenty-four hours are up?" Helen suggested.

"If they get involved," Marshall said.

A glass bottle flew over their heads from behind and smashed in the road in front of the advancing town folk.

"Well, that answers that one," Mark said, ducking as a brick flew back in the opposite direction.

"Keep the idiots out of the camp. Push out." Marshall ordered.

The night became a whirling chaos of hurtling glass and rock. Fire rained down. Branches and stones smashed into shields. Men screamed and yelled. Hate and insults flew.

Under it all, a constant thread, Marshall was sure he could hear a fiddle, though that was plainly impossible.

CHAPTER 10

"This is madness." Marshall shoved with his shield, whipping his baton across an unprotected leg as another youth charged the line. A sympathetic ache began in his left arm where it had been crushed by a collapsing tunnel last time. He shook his head, trying to clear the memories. Dark and firelight and people become animals – Marshall had hated every last minute of it. How ordinary humans could behave so out of character was beyond him, and then there was the citizens of Fenwick who, he would have said, were the cream of respectability and normality yet here they were standing in a fire-lit lane in the middle of a January evening hurling anything they could pick up.

"Get back. These people have a right to leave peacefully." He might as well have whistled down the wind. "Get back! Such idiocy!"

"I can stop this 'idiocy'." An old man stood, suddenly, in his way. "Shall I stop it for you?"

Marshall gaped at him in total amazement, aware that around him the turmoil had swept away. "Stop? Be my guest. That's a trick I'd like to see." His breath came in gasps already. "The world's gone mad."

"There is a price."

"What?" Marshall ducked as another branch whirled towards his head and was gone.

"There is a price."

Marshall looked properly at the man and the shouting and screaming milieu of humanity which had ebbed away from them.

"What price?" He was wary now; something was wrong and suddenly the fiddle was louder, disturbingly so. The white-haired man didn't look so old at a closer glance. His eyes stared hard into Marshall's, laughter lines at the corners but no laughter at all in the face now.

"All travellers will be gone within twenty-four hours and you will not see them again."

"That's what—"

"Even if that includes your murderer."

"My ...Who the hell are you?"

"Someone who can help. Do you wish me to?" Bright blue eyes held Marshall.

He watched the lethal projectiles as if from a distance, his memory supplying pain and screaming enough. "You manage to stop this and get rid of these travellers without further riot or harm and I'll accept your price." He might have to start again to find the murderer, always assuming he could ever make sense of who had killed Thomas Faulkner, but he would be spared nights in freezing tunnels dragging screaming maniacs out against their will.

The world and its noise rushed back and a branch crashed against the shield, almost toppling him.

"Trust me," the old man said and vanished into the crowd.

Marshall shook his head, forgot the strange man and his impossible promise, and pushed on.

*

Luke stood behind the double barrier of police cordon and a flame-filled ditch and watched the night splinter into chaos. Any fool's hope that he could stop events or build a home smashed into pieces alongside the first thrown bottle. The travellers leapt to the defence of their camp as word spread of the advancing town folk but each missile they hurled hammered another nail into the coffin, entombing any hope they might have had of staying. The police would come in with force now. A shame, Luke thought, because the police inspector had been human and reasonable.

"People are going to get hurt," Connor said, appearing at his elbow.

"Probably."

"And once the police have got rid of them out there they'll be in here to get rid of us."

"I know."

"So?"

"So? What can I do, Con? We should have gone last night, okay? That make it better? I didn't want to be thought a murderer and I didn't want that man telling me what to do so my pride kept us here. I was wrong. I expect I'll pay for it. I've lost my group, possibly my freedom for this ..." Luke took a shuddering breath. "I should probably invite the bloody cops in because I sure as hell can't stop them now and the longer these idiots fight, the worse it'll be."

"I can stop them." Gwion stood in the entrance to the camp. "I can keep anyone from entering this camp."

His voice carried and several travellers nearby stopped to look at the old man with his shock of white hair glowing orange in the firelight.

"Pull the other one," Luke said bitterly.

"I guarantee. No-one will enter." He said it with such certainty that Luke could feel himself wanting to believe.

Luke laughed. "Fine, you go ahead. We'll do things our way."

"There is a price."

Luke gaped at him in amazement and then laughed again, feeling the hysteria tingeing the sound. "Old man, if you stop everyone from getting in here it'll be worth the price."

"It—"

"Still talking about it?" Luke turned away and picked up a branch. "I guess I'll have to trust more solid measures then. Let me know if whatever you're doing works."

For answer Gwion took a flute from the inside pocket of his coat. "You'll know," he said. "Join me, fiddler. We have a tune to play." As he began, Raven appeared from between the caravans carrying his now silent fiddle. Gwion nodded briefly to the younger man who raised his instrument and began playing, accompanying the beautiful melody pouring from the flute. Side by side the two men – old and young – playing without pause, set off walking anti-clockwise along the border of the camp.

"Do you suppose…" Connor began.

"No," Luke said firmly. "I don't." Wielding his branch, he headed for the back of the police line.

*

Daniel stumbled over something else lying on the ground. The whole camp was littered with items designed to impede their flight. His shin was scraped raw from a deck chair he'd fallen over and he'd jarred his ankle catching himself when a tumble of bikes appeared in their path.

James had fallen headlong over the bikes and now hobbled along, slowing progress considerably.

Not that they were going anywhere fast.

What really held them back was the music; a yearning fiddle tune that got inside their heads and called them back.

Zoe now had to be dragged along to keep her moving at all and Daniel could feel his own movements slowing, fighting against moving on. This was despite the fear of what was behind them. The screaming in his head was now happening for real and a battle seemed to be happening across the further side of the camp.

"The camp isn't this big," he said.

"I know," James looked wild-eyed in the flashes of firelight. "I can't find–" he waved his hand vaguely towards the trees.

"But it's there." Daniel pointed to the tree line visible over the roofs of the caravans; a darker shadow against the night.

"I bloody know."

They ground to a halt; their feet unable to go any further.

"That tune," Zoe gasped as if they'd run miles whereas Daniel had a dreadful feeling they'd simply been charging in ever-decreasing circles.

"I wish it'd stop," James said. "I can't think straight."

As if his words were all that was needed, the fiddle tune paused. Before they could move, a second, livelier and somehow harder tune began.

It was as if a cloud had been lifted. Daniel could see where they needed to go. "Come on, this way." He led them out into the open and managed three paces across the space towards the trees before walking into a figure who materialised from between the trunks.

"We need you," Lacewing said, looking beyond him to Zoe.

The auburn-haired girl looked wild and fey in the firelight and Daniel had a sudden insight; this woman standing in front of a thousand fires down a thousand years.

"Haven't you done enough already?" James demanded. "We

wouldn't be in this fucking mess if you–"

He might as well have saved his breath.

"We need you," she stepped towards Zoe. "Play me a tune."

"Are you totally fucking insane? Now is hardly the time for–"

She glanced, eyes hard, at James. "You were told to stay away."

"What?" His mouth dropped. "Well, cheers, thanks, don't mind me. Now, fuck off, you crazy woman. We're going home."

She shrugged. "Go then. Zoe, we need you to play the tune."

"She's coming–"

"Play!" The force in Lacewing's voice silenced James.

Zoe held the other woman's eye a moment longer and then she knelt and removed the two boxes from her rucksack. She handed the second to Daniel with a small smile and then turned her attention to the flute box. She paused in the act of opening it to let her trembling fingers slide in a caress across the wood. Then, moving faster, she pushed the flute together and re-stowed the box.

Daniel reached down to help her to her feet and then shouldered the pack. "I'll take this too while you play."

She gave a small smile and looked at Lacewing.

"Play what you hear."

Around them the fiddle swelled, accompanied now by a breathier sound – a flute, soaring in harmony.

Zoe listened, her eyes unfocused for a moment, and then she raised her instrument to her lips. The tune leapt from her fingers almost as if the flute played itself, notes tumbling out in a wash of sound.

"Bloody hell, she's good," James whispered.

"Of course." Lacewing turned away from them. "Walk with me, Zoe."

She set off around the border of the camp and as she went, she sang. There were no words that Daniel could understand, the language was something he'd never heard, but Lacewing's voice was as clear as crystal, rising into the night. The words wrapped themselves around the flute music, filling the dark around them as they walked.

Feeling foolish and unnecessary, Daniel followed in Zoe's wake as if she was some modern pied piper.

"Is that foreign?" James sounded awed. "It's beautiful."

"It's ancient," Daniel said, knowing the words true as he spoke. Like his glimpse earlier, he was sure Lacewing had sung these words and walked this circle many times before. For they did walk a circle; striding anticlockwise around the perimeter of the camp, just inside the fires.

No-one hindered their progress. People stopped and stared, open-mouthed at the sight – or possibly the sound – of them. All other noise had been sucked from the night. There was only the tune – voice and flute and fiddle, endlessly repeating.

It became the world – firelight and music – and Daniel walked on, James beside him, treading the circular path blindly.

*

The tune built through her, flowing out of the pipe, becoming almost solid in the air. Zoe played; her eyes fixed on the singing girl ahead of her. The music carried her, so she stepped without faltering across the uneven surface, round and round.

Ahead of her, half a circle distance, the other pipe echoed hers. Or perhaps she echoed it, the notes repeating back and forth across the camp as they travelled. Around the twinned notes, the fiddle wove an intricate countermelody, filling the gaps.

Above all, Lacewing's voice soared, a song in a language unknown.

Zoe gave herself to the music. The wooden flute she treasured had been made for moments such as this.

She was vaguely aware of people watching as they passed, faces turned to listen, and of Daniel and James pacing behind but they didn't matter. Once she thought she saw a white-haired girl standing amongst the trees at the edge of the caravans, but she couldn't stop to see.

The huge hound, Merlin, appeared beside her on their third circuit, slipping silently from the trees as they passed. It paced beside Lacewing, uttering an occasional eerie howl that somehow complemented the words she sang.

It was only as Lacewing's voice died away and the leaping notes grew to a crescendo and faded that Zoe realised how tired she was. After the emotional exhaustion of the past week and a day spent with little food, the playing had taken everything from her.

She swayed where she stood and James leapt forward, his arms round her keeping her upright.

"What did we do?" She knew it had been something beyond the music. There had been power in the night as they walked.

"Ancient words," Lacewing said, sounding hoarse and drained. "Ancient powers."

"Doing what?" James demanded.

"The tune from my dream, the 'moving on music'," Daniel said. "It sounded like that a bit except there more to it. It was different somehow."

"Very good," Lacewing said, her green eyes bright in the firelight. "More indeed. A tune to keep people out."

"But," Daniel frowned, "I'm sure it was that fiddle music calling people here, we couldn't move away because–"

"Too sharp," the dark-haired man – Raven – had joined them, clutching his fiddle. "We could hardly stop something that wasn't happening now, could we?"

"I don't understand," Daniel said. The tune was still echoing in his head which wasn't aiding his thinking though it had pushed the disturbing visions away. In fact, he didn't understand this strange fiddler at all. First he'd dragged them in to the camp and insisted they were trouble, then he'd stood up for Zoe and demanded the travellers look after her and told them he was keeping them out of trouble, now he seemed to be admitting to playing both the tune which had caused the riot and the one which – supposedly – was going to stop it. "I don't understand at all," he repeated.

"Not yours to understand." Raven nodded to where Gwion stood with Luke. "Gwion calls the tune."

Daniel wasn't sure that reminding Gwion of their presence would be sensible. The old man had been quite clear in his order to stay away.

Beyond the gate, Daniel could see Inspector Marshall as well; someone else who wouldn't be happy with the pair of them.

"We probably ought to be going now," he said to James, "before all those idiots out there start throwing things again."

Caught by the music, all activity within and without the camp had stopped. All eyes were fixed on Gwion where he now stood in the camp entrance, halfway between travellers and police.

"They can throw all they like, nothing will pass," Raven said.

"Seriously?" James diverted his attention from Zoe.

"Seriously."

"Wow, some tune."

"It will cost," Lacewing said. "Ancient magic comes at a price."

"I don't think the travellers have a lot of money," James said. "I suppose they could give you a car or something."

"Not gold," Raven said. "The price for such a tune is paid in blood. Old ways need red power."

*

The tune pulled at Marshall. There was no way two flutes and a fiddle should have been so audible over the chaos, but the music drowned every other sound almost as if it was playing inside his head. It spoke of roads to travel but not for him; the gates were closed. He could sense the path weaving into a distance he couldn't see.

Marshall became aware that the crowd of youths before him had stopped throwing things and now stood in wide-eyed wonder, listening to the music.

The police were also distracted, glancing behind them more often than ahead.

Abruptly the music died and silence fell into the night.

"Wow," Mark breathed, "that was ... awesome."

Marshall nodded; it had been powerful music; he wasn't sure what it meant.

He watched one of the lads from the town – a face he recognised from an occasional drunken night in the cells – shake himself as if rising from deep waters. The youth reached down, picked up a stone from the side of the road and threw it.

Hundreds of pairs of eyes watched it go, looping high over the heads of the police. Somewhere above and just behind Marshall the stone hit solid air, lost all momentum and slid gracefully down a non-existent wall to the ground.

There was a collective gasp. Several more projectiles followed in a half-hearted attempt to break through. None did, all falling softly to earth just behind the police line.

"That better be a two-way barrier," Mark muttered as one of the travellers swung back his arm to launch a bottle.

It was. The glass shattered harmlessly on the ground beside the other objects.

Marshall stopped watching. He had no idea what was stopping the items, but it obviously worked. Now he needed to deal with the crowd from town while they were still dumbfounded.

Grabbing a loud hailer from the ground by the gate, he leapt atop a tree stump and raised the hailer to his lips.

"Ladies and gentlemen, there is nothing to see, it is time to go home. Please disperse in an orderly manner. The removal of travellers is a police matter. Please leave now to avoid further trouble and arrests."

He signalled along the line of officers and they began moving forward, repeating his words and pushing people back.

From his vantage point Marshall watched confusion spread across the faces of the crowd. He might almost have believed that most of them suddenly had no idea what they were doing in a lane outside West Cross.

Groups began to turn and wander off towards town. In a fairly short space of time the lane in front of him emptied. Barely a dozen remained, and these seemed more interested in the properties of the invisible shield than in causing trouble.

"Does it stop people?" one lad asked as Marshall stepped down from his tree stump.

Marshall glanced at Mark and gave a brief nod.

"Why don't you try?" Mark offered, inviting the lad through the cordon.

"Really?" The young man headed for the camp at a run and, just past Marshall, ran solidly into nothing and stopped abruptly. Even half expecting it, Marshall blinked in surprise.

"Are you hurt?" Mark went to the lad.

"No," he sounded puzzled. "It's like running into ... er ... like a pillow or something. It's soft like but totally not letting you through."

Marshall helped steer the lad gently back through his police line. "Go on, I think it's time you all went home." After some hesitation and muttering the youths began heading down the lane.

"They'll go 'round the side for another go," Mark said, "bet you."

His words were born out by several of the lads turning left into the next field entrance.

"Let them. I don't think there's much harm in that. I don't know how it's possible, but they obviously can't get in." Marshall turned to stare into the camp where the travellers were all gathering to stare back at him. "The question is; can they get out?" The strange man had promised all travellers would be gone within twenty-four hours but Marshall didn't see how that would be possible if the police couldn't get in to move them and the travellers couldn't get out.

"I think that might be occurring to them too," Mark said.

"Possibly." Marshall thought that rather a lot of the travellers were also wearing the dazed 'what am I doing here' expression that he'd seen on the faces of those in the lane.

*

Connor could still feel the music, running through his blood. It spoke of roads to travel and places to see. He could almost smell the newly washed aroma of grass after rain, rich loam under the trees, cow parsley on the summer wind. Sometimes the tune spoke of streams rattling over stones, leaves rustling in the autumn winds, waves crashing on a lonely shore. He couldn't spend his life in this field, he had to be going.

"What have you done, old man?" Luke demanded, breaking into Connor's reverie. "Are we trapped in here?"

"You may leave," Gwion said.

"Right," Luke said, striding towards the barrier, "let's see, shall we?"

"No, Luke don't." The warning was out of Connor's mouth almost before he'd thought of saying it. That word – leave – bothered him, the slight stress he thought he'd heard.

"What is it, Con? You think he's lying?"

"No," Connor said slowly, trying to put his finger on what worried him. "I'm just thinking that people out there can't get in so what happens to you if you go out there?"

Beyond the shield Connor could see the police inspector also giving the question careful consideration.

The travellers were mostly silent, and Connor wondered how many others were fighting the desire to just leap in their 'vans and go. The road was calling. Just beyond conscious hearing the music still played. What did it matter if they couldn't return to the camp?

"If I go out," Luke said slowly, "you're saying I can't get back. Is that so, old man?" The travellers' leader stepped menacingly closer to Gwion, towering over the older man.

Gwion was unperturbed. "You may leave," he repeated.

"You double-crossing bastard. What have you done? We'll starve here if we–"

"You can leave," Gwion said, enunciating each word slowly and clearly.

"The whole bloody point of this," Luke waved his hand at the still blazing fires, "was that we didn't want to fucking leave. They," he stabbed his hand towards the waiting police, "they want us to leave and you were supposed to be stopping them."

"I offered to keep them out, to stop the violence. We are not fighters."

"'We?' What right have you got to say 'we'? You're not one of us. If we want to fight for our home then–"

"Travellers have no home, they travel."

Connor remembered the old man saying the same thing earlier. Again, he caught a snatch of tune, a breath of wind in the barley, moonlight on the high moor.

Luke clapped his hands to his ears as if he too had heard and didn't wish to listen. "I want a home," he said. "This was to be my home. How dare you take that from me?" He raised his fists, the veins standing out on the side of his neck. "How dare you." He stepped closer still to Gwion.

"Mine," Raven said, pulling Gwion out of the way as he moved forwards. "My fight. My blood if need be."

"No." The shout came from the inspector, helpless beyond the boundary. "You cannot."

"You have no say," Raven said bluntly.

Luke's fist smashed into the side of the fiddler's head as he turned to speak to the inspector.

"I knew," Luke snarled, "I knew this was what you wanted. This group is mine, you bastard, this land ... you won't have it. I might have known you were in it with him." He lashed his foot out towards Gwion.

Connor stifled his own shout. This pair had been heading for a fight all day, there was nothing he could do except get himself hurt trying to stop it. What's more, he understood – this was the way the travellers settled disputes. Luke had to prove himself.

Terry showed less understanding, or perhaps just a greater pull had hold of him from the music which still echoed. "Luke, he's right. It's time we moved on."

"What?"

Several heads nodded around the camp. Even Niall who had been so quick to arrive for a fight was nodding agreement. Voices reiterated Terry's words.

"There'll be snow on the hilltops," Terry said, warming to his theme, "and I know a good pub on the–"

"Then fuck off. Go on, go. I won't be magicked into leaving." Luke swung another punch at Raven who saw this one coming. He raised his arm, deflected the blow and retaliated. His own fist slammed into Luke's chin, cracking his head back.

Luke leapt forward and the two men became one swirling mass of snarling rage.

Connor couldn't tell who was winning. First one was on top, then the other. Fists flew, knees and feet hammered home.

Despite the intensity of the battle, he could feel his attention wavering. The starlight would be crisper away from the orange streetlight glare of town. If he set off now, he could make it out into open moorland before daybreak.

Out of the corner of his eye he saw that several people had already left the crowd round the fight and were packing items into caravans.

A cry of exertion drew his attention back to the fight. Luke had picked Raven up and thrown him violently away from him. The fiddler fell and lay still momentarily before groggily beginning to rise to hands and knees.

Luke leapt forward, sweeping a broken branch up as he did so. He swung it high over his head.

"No!" Connor's voice joined several others. He thought the policeman's was one but loudest and highest was Zoe.

She rushed forwards to stand over the fallen man, her face drained of all colour. "No, please no, you can't."

Luke paused, his breath coming in gasps as he lowered the branch slightly. "Move, you stupid bitch, move!"

Zoe shook her head. "No, I'll not see ... not again." Her voice shook but she resolutely stood her ground.

"Bloody fool," Luke said. He pushed her violently backwards so that she sprawled across Raven's kneeling form. Luke raised the stick again.

As Zoe attempted to regain her balance, a body hurtled in, yelling, "Leave her alone!"

With a sickening thud, the branch connected.

*

Daniel wasn't sure what they were still doing there, particularly not with the music calling him to go.

He could see the road from his dream rising to meet him and ached to put his feet to the path.

James and Zoe hesitated though, caught by the drama playing out in front of them.

Daniel had to admit there was a certain dreadful grief to Luke's desperate anger. He fought knowing that he'd lost all that really mattered. Daniel thought what Gwion had done to the traveller was unforgiveable. The old man had deprived Luke of his dreams as surely as he'd handed Daniel his. It was unfairly cruel, and Daniel could understand why Luke had to hit out.

Beside him, Zoe was getting paler and paler. Several times she put her hand to her mouth as if to catch the words which tumbled out. "Please stop, oh, please, no."

Belatedly, Daniel remembered what he'd heard about her father and his violence. He could see the same compassion in James' face as he held the trembling girl.

As Raven was thrown to the ground in front of them, Zoe pulled away from James. He tried to hold her back, but she was determined to stop the fight.

As Luke raised the wood a second time, Daniel felt the world slip sideways. He was almost fast enough to prevent what happened, but realisation came a fraction too late.

He reached wildly for James but it wasn't enough.

The snap as his friend's neck broke was louder than any sound he had ever heard.

CHAPTER 11

Roger found himself humming as he strolled back down the lane towards the estate. He thought it was probably the tune he'd just heard played though he struggled to hold it properly and it was beginning to lose its coherence the further he got from West Cross. Around him his neighbours were questioning just why they'd thought it so vital to rush out there to get rid of the gypsies. Roger couldn't remember being that fired up about anything for years now and was on the point of agreeing with Tom that they'd all rushed off for no reason when a thought struck him.

"James, I was going because of James."

"What, his bike? The police will sort it, that's what that Inspector said."

"No," Roger stopped in the middle of the road in amazement that he could have forgotten so fast, "James is out there, that's what Melanie said."

"Well, the police will get him too, won't they?"

"I suppose, but I didn't even ask." Why hadn't he? All excited about the gypsies going and he hadn't given James a thought. He'd rushed off telling Melanie he was going to get James back and then he hadn't even asked, just got caught up in throwing things. And when the policeman had said it was time to go home, he'd just turned around and headed off like an obedient schoolboy.

Roger hesitated, unsure what to do. None of what he'd done this evening now seemed to make much sense. If the police had said they would find James, why had he suddenly thought it was a good idea to go racing up there throwing stones? That wasn't him. But as he'd gone, Melanie would be furious that he hadn't enquired.

Roger sighed, "I'm going back."

"Don't be daft," Tom took his arm, "they told us to go home."

"But my son might be there and I didn't find out. Melanie will go ape."

"Do you want me to come too?" Tom gave his shoulder an understanding pat. Roger knew he had the reputation as the loud one but when it came to it, Melanie was in charge and everyone knew it.

"No, go on, go home. I won't be long, just so I can say to Mel that I made an effort. I'm sure the police know what they're doing." Which, in itself, was strange because earlier he'd been convinced the police were a total bunch of idiots who couldn't do anything without a mob of local hooligans telling them what to do. Roger shook the feelings away and told himself to stop trying to work out why on earth he'd thought any of his actions this evening were a good idea. He'd concentrate on James and then go home.

Sighing again, he turned around and began trudging back up the hill which seemed a good deal longer than it had done the first time he'd charged up it.

*

Luke dropped the branch and fled, running off between the caravans.

Marshall reacted as fast as he could, dashing forwards only to find himself bouncing violently backwards. He swore loudly, "Round the perimeter, move. You need to take him if he comes out, if he leaves this ... this thing."

Police officers scattered left and right following the perimeter of the camp.

"John, some of the caravans are starting up," Helen yelled as she set off.

"Shit," Marshall grabbed half a dozen officers, "Here, stay here and search every vehicle that leaves."

"You think he'll go," Mark said, "he's safe in there because we can't get to him."

"He just killed someone, he's hardly rational."

"We don't know–"

"That was his neck, Mark, I know." And he'd told the lad to stay away from here.

"So you think he'll hide in a caravan?"

"I would," Marshall said shortly. "So we take every single one apart until we've got him." He couldn't believe he'd just had to stand by and witness a fight to the death and be unable to do a thing about it. It was insulting.

Helen re-appeared. "Cordon established. Officer every five metres as close to the... whatever it is as we can get. It runs all the way round and into the trees as far as The Mill Stream. We need to move lights under the branches as it's a bit dark to see much. Shall I get an ambulance too?"

"For all the use they'll be until we work out some way to get in."

"They could bring him out," Mark pointed out as Helen started phoning.

"Neck injury," Marshall said perversely, ignoring his earlier argument that the lad was dead, "On the off chance it wasn't fatal they shouldn't try and move him."

"Probably too late for that," Helen said, pointing to where Zoe clung to the still form, wildly sobbing. Daniel crouched beside her.

"Do you suppose he killed her father too? Is that what she meant?" Mark asked.

"Very possible," Marshall rubbed his eyes, "not really a conversation I want to have with a distraught victim across this much open space."

Mark slammed his fist against the still resistant air, "We need to get in, this is ridiculous."

"I know," Marshall felt like hitting someone himself. Miss Shaw was top of his list of preferences though the old man ran her a close second; he could think of various orifices he could ram a flute into.

He could see the flautist just beyond his reach, talking to the singer. He guessed this was the girl he'd been hearing reports of with her long auburn hair and the large dog sitting beside her. After some moments of whispered conversation, she said something to the animal and it set off, following the route Luke had taken.

"Sent the dog after him," Mark said.

"But I don't know whose bloody side they're on, Mark. He may have gone to attack him or we may end up fighting some half-wolf when we get in there. God, what a mess!"

"Steady, John. You've got all the angles covered as best we can when dealing with the impossible. No-one gets out of there without going through us."

"I know, it's just ... I actually told that man he could do this. What was I thinking?"

"That he was nuts. Whoever heard of magic, invisible barriers?"

Marshall sighed, "Well, yes, there is that."

"None of this is your fault, John."

"I don't know, if we'd gone into the library last night like you said–"

"Against people with that sort of power? I'm rather glad, having seen what they can do, that we didn't."

Marshall gave up. His sergeant was always much too reasonable when he was trying to beat himself up about cases. It was part of the reason why Mark was so good with victims.

"Sir," Helen said, "could be more trouble."

Beyond the barrier, those travellers not already packing were gathering round where James lay.

*

Daniel wiped his face and climbed to his feet. He could no longer stare at the reality of James' bulging eyes.

He looked round. Gwion stood with Lacewing, Raven sat – holding his head – on an upturned crate.

"Blood price?" Daniel said going to stand in front of the fiddler, "How could you?" He knew the man hadn't swung the branch but, as far as he was concerned, this was his fault. His and Gwion's.

Raven raised his head, his face serious. "Not his, Luke's. It wasn't meant to be like this. If he hadn't–"

"Oh, so now it's James' fault he'd dead? How–"

"You were told to stay away," Gwion said, which acted like a red rag to a bull on Daniel's temper.

"He got us shut in a fucking caravan when we tried to go away!"

Raven laughed mirthlessly, "I told you you'd be safer shut up rather than wandering around."

"So now it's my fault, is it," Connor said softly, moving forwards, "for letting them out?"

"No," Daniel said, "of course not."

"No," Connor came to stand in front of Daniel, between him and Raven. "I'm sorry for your loss but truly, and it saddens me to say it because I like the man, James' blood is on Luke's hand alone. He wielded the branch. He chose to fight." He held Daniel's gaze until Daniel nodded heavily and looked away. Connor turned on the seated man, "I do, though, hold you responsible for what happened to Luke. You came with the whole purpose of pushing him to this."

"It was necessary," Gwion said, "he had lost his way."

"No," Connor said again, "he had lost your way but that doesn't make him wrong."

"He was a traveller," Gwion said, implacable, "not a thief or a vandal, someone to be feared. To travel is to be one with the land, a welcome return with the turning of the year, giving and receiving along the journey. That is how it always has been. That is how it will be. You feel it, he no longer did."

"What right have you—"

"Every right," Lacewing said, and Daniel glimpsed again the weight of years.

"The moon has grown old since first I walked this land," Gwion said, "there is power in the journey; ancient ways that need our steps to feed the land, to keep the music alive. The travellers feed the lore of the isle, the magic at its core."

His words woke the music again in Daniel's head, tinged now with grief. He saw the same recognition in Connor's face, but the older man shook his head slightly.

"I know the tune," he said softly, "and I will follow but there are issues of leadership to be dealt with first."

"Leadership?" Gwion smiled. "A man follows his own path."

"These people chose to follow Luke."

"Then let them choose another," Raven said.

"You intend that to be you, I suppose," Connor said.

"No, the four ... five of us travel alone."

"Five?" Connor asked.

Daniel also looked round at the three of them – Gwion, Lacewing and Raven. "There's the dog, I suppose but," he paused, suddenly remembering his circling in the dark, "you mean Zoe?"

"Of course," Lacewing said as if this was obvious.

"Doesn't she get a say?" Daniel couldn't believe they were still acting in such a high-handed manner. James' death had taught them nothing though, if Gwion was right, perhaps they were all too old to care anymore.

"Zoe needs to leave; she can't stay here."

"I think that's her decision. Zoe?" Daniel wondered whether the sobbing girl was even paying them any attention where she was slumped over James.

"I need to think," she muttered, pushing herself to her feet. She stumbled away from them towards the trees.

They watched her go and then Connor turned on Raven, "You're not going to fight me to lead? You were fighting Luke."

"Fight, why should we? If they choose to follow you then lead well." Raven finally got to his feet to stand by Gwion and Lacewing. "My fight was merely part of the price, the risk I bear."

Connor looked round the diminishing crowd of travellers.

"Go on," Terry said.

"North," Connor said after a moment, "Anyone who's with me. We go North. I'll join you shortly," He looked at Raven, "Where did he go?"

It was Lacewing who answered, "That way, to his home, I think."

Connor set off at a run, Daniel close behind.

*

The first of the caravans arrived in the entrance blocking Marshall's view. Behind it several others queued.

"Are we searching, John?" Mark asked, waving the driver to a halt.

"Yes, we don't believe her word," Marshall said, "take your time. As soon as they're past the barrier stop them and make it thorough. Those behind can wait, however much they now want to leave."

"Just searching for Luke?"

"That gives us a reason but you see anything suspicious, Mark, anything at all and you deal with it." He'd had enough of the whole affair and the soft approach really hadn't worked all that well so far with the travellers.

Mark waved several uniformed officers forward, "Take it apart," he ordered.

As Marshall went to help, a taxi screeched to a halt in the road outside and a woman leapt from the back of the car and ran towards them, leaving the car door wide open. The driver followed her out, "Oy, love, are you going to pay?"

"What's going on?" Mark caught the woman as she hurtled past him; it was Eileen Faulkner.

"I saw her, I saw her, she was here, I saw her."

"Saw who?" Marshall joined them, his heart sinking. He thought the woman was safely away and he could have sworn she hadn't been here so far this evening.

"Zoe, I saw her."

"Well, yes," he could hardly deny it. The girl had been sitting sobbing on the floor just yards away not two minutes earlier. "Unfortunately, we can't get to her at present."

"Liar," she fought Mark's restraining hands until he sighed and let her go. She charged straight at the camp and flew backwards violently as she ran into the obstacle her daughter had helped to create. "What have you done?" She whirled on Marshall.

"I did nothing."

"But she was in there, I saw her."

"Madam, I–"

"Saw her? How?" Helen said crisply, cutting to the heart of Marshall's own concerns. "How did you see her?"

"Here," Eileen held out her phone which quite clearly showed a picture of Zoe walking along playing her flute, "I was sent this. They said they were going to put it on Youtube."

"Youtube?" Marshall looked round. "Mark?"

"Shit, John, I'm sorry. I was only looking for cameras. I never gave phones a thought in that mayhem."

"Most people left," Helen said, "but some did head off across the fields, they could have taken anything."

"They could still be there," Marshall said, "waiting for more and people can upload to the internet straight from phones these days I believe so don't need to go home to do it."

"I suppose," Helen agreed.

"So we could have Mr and Mrs Scafell here any minute having seen a video of him dying? Tonight just gets better and better."

"What now?"

"You keep searching those leaving. Helen, go 'round the outside, take officers out of the cordon and get them sweeping outwards. Clear all fucking media and anyone who even looks like they might own a bloody phone well out of the way of this blasted magic wall." He took a deep breath, "I'll deal with Mrs Faulkner," not a prospect he embraced with any great fervour. "Actually, Helen, phone the station too. If we've got anybody left in town, get them to the Scafell's and the Calver's. Let's get to their parents before anyone else starts sending photos out."

"Okay."

"Sir," a young policeman waved to him, "have you a moment?"

"No," Marshall muttered under his breath, "what now?"

He strode across the road, "What is it?"

"This gentleman just arrived back," the PC indicated a man in his late forties, stockily built, with greying, receding hair, "he was here earlier but says he has calmed down now and remembered why he came up in the first place so he'd just have a word."

"And you are?"

"Roger Scafell," the man said, completing Marshall's nightmare of an evening, "I told Mel I'd see what had happened to James."

Marshall resisted the urge to swear and took the man gently by the arm, "I think you'd better come with me," he said.

*

Luke was taking his caravan apart, frantically searching it, when Connor and Daniel arrived in the doorway.

"What are you doing?" Connor stopped in amazement, but Daniel pushed past him, a sudden certainty hitting him. He dropped Zoe's rucksack off his back and plunged his hand into it. He pulled out the carved box with its crystal and hair contents.

"Looking for this?"

Luke gaped at him, "How ... of course, you were in here, you took it."

"So did you," Daniel said, certain of it though he hadn't been earlier, "It's not yours."

"Maybe not."

"Why?" Connor took the box from Daniel and opened it. "What is it?"

"I've no fucking idea," Luke snapped.

"What?" Daniel snatched it back and stared at the contents as if the answer might be staring back at him. "We thought it was important?"

"So did I."

"So did you? You mean you don't know?" He felt like the ground had suddenly disappeared from under him.

"The bastard was digging it up in the middle of a hurricane. I figured it meant something."

"So you took it?"

"Yes, and it turned out to be rubbish, except that it must be important in some way."

"I don't–" Daniel began but Connor interrupted him.

"Luke, the police are after you, you just killed that lad, why the hell are you looking for an unimportant box? You're as mad as he was if he was digging it up in a hurricane. You need to get out of here."

"Do you think I can escape?" Luke asked softly.

"No!" Daniel spat out. "I'll make sure of it." Only the conviction that he would probably come off worse in a fight with the tall man was stopping Daniel launching himself at Luke.

"I think the Inspector will make sure of it," Luke said.

"So why the box?" Connor pressed, "I don't understand."

"If I'm found with it, they'll think I killed Thomas Faulkner too," Luke said after a pause.

"You want to get rid of it," Daniel put the box behind his back.

"No," Connor said slowly, "he came back to get it when he could have left it here and ran. He could have claimed one of you three planted it here during the day."

"What, but we–"

"Think what he said," Connor took the ornate container from Daniel's unresisting fingers. "Tell me why, Luke."

Luke hesitated and then shrugged, "They've seen me kill once, they'll believe twice."

Connor held the box out to him, "Why, though?"

Luke looked at him, briefly at Daniel, then grabbed the box and pushed past Connor out of the caravan. "Payment," he yelled over his shoulder as he set off for the trees.

After a moment Daniel said, "He wants people to think he killed Zoe's dad when he didn't?"

"Wants? No, I just don't think he cares and it makes sense to take the blame. The police want a killer and they know he is one."

"Why would he do that?"

"Oh, come on, Daniel, work it out. Payment!"

Daniel held his eye for a long moment and then sighed, "He knows who really did it."

"I think we can be even more definite than that," Connor said, "you saw her reaction just now and she also headed that way. Come on."

He set off after Luke. Daniel resisted the urge to tell Connor that Zoe wasn't like that because his heart was telling him the traveller was right. He could see again the tarot card from the library except that this time Zoe quite clearly held the spade.

"Oh shit," he said to the empty caravan and leapt down the steps after Connor.

CHAPTER 12

Zoe stumbled into the trees desperate to get away from the death she'd witnessed and the accusation in the music. She could still hear it, flute music playing in her head. It was deep inside her, linked by blood to her and the land; she understood that now. The tune she'd weaved pulsed in the ground beneath her feet and drummed in her veins.

Blood magic, the fiddler had said.

Ancient power and the price paid for it.

Zoe wept as she ran; for James but also for herself and her mother and the life and love she'd never felt she had.

Gwion and Lacewing seemed to think she was going to head off into the wild with them, but she didn't know if she could do that: she wasn't sure she was going to get a choice.

Running blindly in the dark under the trees she almost ran into Luke. The travellers' leader was standing on the bank of the Mill Brook, looking back towards the camp. He caught Zoe and kept her from falling into the water.

"This magic of yours stops here," he said harshly, "across the brook the police can get to you."

Zoe stopped, "The police? I ..." She didn't know what to say or what she wanted. She'd spent all day convincing James not to let the police know where she was and now he was dead. Perhaps she should just stop running.

Luke let her go and calmly crossed the stream. He then sat down with his back to a tree and gave her a small shrug she barely saw in the gloom. "I'm not going any farther to meet them. They can come to me."

"You're going to give yourself up?"

"I don't kill people usually," Luke said dryly, "but I do take the knocks for what I do wrong. I'm sorry about James, I wasn't aiming at him ... or you."

"I know," Zoe whispered, "but you could go and escape."

"That policeman is a good bloke, he won't let me go." Luke leant forward to stare harder at her, "And he's got two dead bodies to charge me with."

"But you–" Zoe stopped and then she crossed the stream slowly and crouched down beside him so she could see his face clearly. "You didn't kill my dad."

"How would you know?" He smiled and then leant back against the tree trunk. "Don't worry, you don't have to answer that. I came up to give him the rent. I saw."

"And didn't tell anyone?"

"Deserved every blow," Luke said, reaching out to wipe the tears from her cheek, "and if your mum hadn't got in the way, I'd have done it for you when we first arrived. No-one hits a woman like that around me." He picked something up from the ground beside him and held it out to her, "I think this might be yours. Your dad was digging it up. I was going to give it to the police as evidence of the truth of my claim, but you can have it if you like. If you need it."

"I don't know what it is," Zoe said, "well, I do because we looked at it earlier in your caravan but I've no idea what it means. You can keep it."

"No," said Gwion, "I can't let him do that."

"What the hell business is it of yours?" Daniel had also appeared at the other side of the stream from a slightly different direction, Connor silently watchful beside him.

"Because it isn't hers," said a new voice, soft in the gathering dark, "and it isn't her father's." A tall, slim girl with white hair falling in curls to her waist stepped from between the trees and walked in the silence she had created to stand beside Luke. "It's mine."

*

"Sir! John!" Helen waved her radio frantically at him from beside the hedge. "They think he's in the trees by the stream. It's a bit dark but they swear it's him." There was agitated buzzing coming from the flailing radio.

Marshall paused, torn between wanting to make the arrest and having to deal with two distraught parents, stuck outside the invisible shield.

"Go on, John," Mark said, "it's your case."

"Technically, Mark, I've no idea about that. My job is to get rid of travellers; you're supposed to be running the murder case."

"Sir," an older police constable, about mid forties, stepped forwards from beside the gate, "Ben Martin, we spoke earlier. Can I be of any assistance?"

"Well–"

"Come on," Mark grabbed Marshall's arm and pulled him in the direction of the path towards the woods, "Ben'll be fine." He turned and yelled instructions at the other man, "As soon as you can get an ambulance in there, you get Mr Scafell to his son. Get the doctor to

Mrs Faulkner."

The two of them broke into a run, Marshall cursing the mud which hadn't got any easier in the last few days after all the rain.

In a very short time, they found a young police constable gesticulating with a torch in the dark beside the copse. "Over here, sir. I think he's in there and he's stopped. There's more than just one of them so I didn't think I ought to go in alone."

Marshall nodded, "We'll borrow your torch, if we may. Stay there, direct people this way if Helen manages to round up anyone else." He wasn't sure how likely that was; they were spread very thin tonight.

"Quietly," he cautioned Mark unnecessarily and led the way into the dark under the trees.

They didn't have far to go before they came across the Mill Stream and heard voices ahead. Marshall cautioned Mark to slow down and crept ahead to where he could see. The trees thinned by the water, allowing moonlight in from above and Marshall could just make out the people gathering in the clearing.

Luke sat with his back to a tree on Marshall's side of the stream, Zoe crouched beside him. Across the water, as he watched, Lacewing and Gwion arrived, Raven a little way behind and, off to their right, Daniel and Connor burst through the tree-line.

Marshall glanced at Mark and saw his own thoughts reflected in his sergeant's face – they had no idea how many of these people were friends, how many enemies.

Luke and Raven had just been engaged in a fatal fight. Were they about to continue and, if so, would the others there stop him interfering?

He sidled slightly closer, trying to see if the giant dog was also about.

"No," Gwion said loudly, bringing Marshall to a halt, "I can't let him do that."

"Do what?" Mark hissed in Marshall's ear as Daniel said, louder than Gwion, "What the hell business is it of yours?"

"Good question," Marshall said softly, "though I get the impression that old man makes everything his business."

Mark suddenly grabbed his arm, directing him to a movement in the trees behind Luke. As they watched, a tall, slim girl stepped forwards to stand beside Luke. She bent down to take something from him. Marshall couldn't see properly in the moonlight what it was but the girl was perfectly clear in her claim; "It's mine."

"Our albino," Mark said, forgetting to keep his voice down.

Fortunately, Daniel was louder, "Yours? Who the hell are you?"

"You!" Luke said and then let out a laugh which silenced the rest of the group in the clearing, "So the madman in the pub was right. Were you dancing naked out here for him?"

"Madman?" Daniel said, sounding stunned, "Phil? You killed Phil."

Marshall thought that was a bit of a leap but one he wasn't prepared to argue about after what he'd seen so far today.

"I–" the woman began.

"Quiet, girl," Gwion ordered, "it's not their tale to know."

"He was my bloody cousin," Dan said, "and you've been telling me none of this is my business but I'm still here and still seeing things. I saw what he," he jerked his finger in Luke's direction where the traveller sat quietly chuckling against his tree, "did to James ages before he did it and then you killed my best friend and my cousin's dead and Connor says–"

"He deserves the tale, tell him."

Marshall blinked; the order came from Raven. It also seemed to surprise Gwion who turned to glare at the tall fiddler behind him in the dark.

"I think you've forgotten the risks involved, piper," Raven said, stepping forward into the moonlight, "something I never do."

"You chose your way."

"Indeed, as a balance to yours. And a large part of this tale was begun by me, I could be said to stand blame for it. So, I say it needs telling to these people most affected."

"And if they tell the police?" Gwion demanded.

"It comes with risk, like all I do. I am prepared to accept the consequences; you know that," Raven looked up and straight at Marshall where he stood hidden, "I am not sure our tale fits any policeman's view of the world." Marshall wondered how much the man could see in the dark or whether he was just firing words blindly into the night.

"Tell it then and be quick, we need to travel on."

Raven paused now he had Gwion's agreement until all eyes were on him and then he nodded to the white-haired girl, "Answer his question. Tell him who you are."

"She's my sister," Lacewing interrupted, confirming Marshall's suspicion from earlier, "we're twins."

"Hardly identical," Mark said, pointlessly, under his breath. Marshall put his finger to his lips; he didn't want to miss a word of this.

"So?" Daniel shrugged. "What's that got to do with anything?"

"Two hundred years ago, I killed their father," Raven said bluntly.

"Two-? Oh do me a favour, you–"

"You asked for this tale," Raven said sharply, "you will listen to it without interruption."

"But–"

"Daniel, hush," Connor laid a hand on the young man's arm.

Marshall echoed the sentiment; he was intrigued to hear how this story went. He remembered the picture in the paper and Maggie's disbelief from earlier. So far, Raven wasn't saying anything he hadn't already contemplated – however much he hadn't believed it.

"Two hundred years ago, I killed their father," Raven repeated. "He was violent and drunk but I did so deliberately in order to use his years."

"What?" Luke leant forward, "Explain that."

"I have an extended life, a gift of the piper's magic or his music, one or the other, perhaps both. To maintain it, I use the music to 'borrow' years from those who do not need them. Those who are using their years badly, I remove, and take the remaining years as my own." Raven shrugged, "I don't expect you to believe, I only know what is so. I made a pact with myself when I first joined the piper, that I would not take life without risk. I offer all my ... donors the chance to fight. If I lose, I die – my risk. If I win, I take their years. In the case of Thomas Faulkner, I fought a drunk and so I won unfairly and I widowed his wife and left two young girls without a father."

"It was badly done," Gwion said, "and not according to your own rules."

"I accept that," Raven shrugged again, "as I have said before. The piper said we owed a debt, so we gave the same gift of extended life to his daughters. The box contains her totems. I don't fully understand and have never asked, but some part of us is no longer human and, in some way, we have the durability of the crystal." He turned to Daniel fully, "Lacewing chose to travel with us. Her sister did not."

"This was my home," the albino said, "I wished to stay here and keep an eye on my mother and my family down the years."

"And you killed Phil," Daniel said, though he sounded less belligerent.

"I made a different vow," she said after a slight pause, "I can become the hare of my totem, so when I need more time, I look for someone with the heart to rescue a hare. If they would risk their life to save mine, then I assume they would be happy to give their years to me. The dancing," she smiled at Luke, "is a dream I give them as a gift to lift their last days."

Marshall remembered Daniel talking of the old man being in his dreams and shuddered slightly at the thought of the power gathered in the glade in front of him. He would have liked to maintain his scepticism, to brush it all aside as nonsense, except his shoulder still smarted from where he had run into apparently solid air earlier and the picture from the paper was still in his pocket.

"And Phil saved the hare," Daniel said shaking his head, "him and his bloody animal rights. Mum always said it would get him killed but I don't think that was quite what she meant."

"So," Connor said, "did you kill the farmer too?"

Raven turned towards him and Marshall leant forwards; this was what he needed to know. Doctor Trent couldn't even prove Philip Knight had been murdered so he could forget the strange girl's even stranger claims, but Thomas Faulkner was a murder victim and he needed a killer.

"No, I was going to offer to fight him. I went up there the night of the storm. The reports were of a nasty, violent thug who didn't deserve to live, so I thought he was perfect for my style of justice. Unfortunately, someone got to him first." The fiddler turned towards where Luke and Zoe huddled by the tree.

"That was me," Luke said, loudly, "precisely because he was a nasty, violent thug. Particularly because he was a nasty, violent thug who got his kicks thumping women. Found him digging up your lady friend's box and hit him on the head with the shovel."

"I bet Zoe saw," Mark whispered, "that's what she meant earlier by 'not again' and why she ran away."

"Perhaps," Marshall wasn't sure, mainly because both Connor and Daniel had given a slight start at Luke's voice and he would have bet money that Raven was talking to Zoe, not Luke. In his mind he could hear David telling him that he thought Zoe had probably killed her father.

"But—" Daniel began.

"Of course," Raven nodded, and Marshall thought he heard respect in the man's voice for someone he had been trying to kill barely an hour earlier, "the prices we pay for our acts. I applaud it; the man deserved to die though I would have made better use of his time."

Marshall had a dreadful feeling that Raven, with his strangely formal acceptance, was instructing his friends in what they should do. He took a deep breath and stepped into the glade. This had gone on quite long enough, and this was something he recognised as being within his remit. "Luke," he paused momentarily thrown; he didn't even know the man's surname. "Sir, I am arresting you for the killing of James Scafell," he thought a good defence would probably get away with calling it manslaughter.

"And Thomas Faulkner, yes, I know," Luke said for him before he could decide whether he was going to add that one to the tally.

Marshall hesitated and then turned to the young girl squatting beside Luke, "Zoe Faulkner, I've been looking for you, I have some questions you need to answer about the night your father was killed."

"She saw me hit him and ran away, Inspector, I'd have thought that was obvious." Luke spoke before Zoe even had a chance to open her mouth.

"And then she came back here?" Marshall wasn't going to tamely accept the story they were feeding him without some investigation.

"I persuaded her that Luke had done her a favour," Gwion said, stepping across the stream to join them. "That he was no threat to her."

"Why not encourage her to come to me?" Marshall demanded, annoyed with the way they seemed to be closing ranks against him. It looked like the old man had taken Raven's cue.

"Did you just hear Raven's story, Inspector? What policeman was going to accept that?"

Marshall gritted his teeth, "Zoe could have come to me and told me she saw Luke killing her father without having to reveal any of your nonsense, Sir!" He stepped closer to the old man, using his height to intimidate, "Her actions in the last few days have suggested to me that she was running away from me."

"Running away from me," Luke said, "I just said that."

"Running away from home," Zoe said quietly, "from dad. I couldn't stand it anymore, so I was going." She looked Luke in the eye then gave a slightly lopsided smile, "I saw Luke and thought I was free and actually went home and told mum it would be okay, that dad was gone."

"And?" Marshall prompted when she stopped.

"And she cried," Zoe said, her voice suddenly harsh, "she asked me what she was going to do without him, how we were going to cope. She clung to me. So, I hit her and that's just what dad used to do. So I decided I had to run away anyway."

Marshall felt most of it had the ring of truth but he asked again, "You saw Luke kill your father?"

She barely hesitated, the briefest of glances at the travellers' leader, "Yes, like he said."

Marshall gave up, "Then, Luke, I am also arresting you for the murder of Thomas Faulkner." He ignored what sounded like a collective sigh of relief from others around the clearing. "But," he turned on Gwion, "I think, as you all seemed to know about this, I ought to throw some charges of conspiracy to pervert the course of justice at the rest of you."

There was absolute silence and then Gwion grinned, "I rather like you, Inspector, and I think you'll work well with David to maintain the law in Fenwick, but you have to accept the things you simply cannot do."

Marshall hadn't expected the compliment but wasn't totally surprised by Gwion's words, "Cannot?"

Gwion whistled softly and the giant dog stepped from beneath the trees behind Luke, "We will be leaving, Lacewing, Raven and I," he glanced at Daniel thoughtfully and then added, "and Zoe too if she'll have us. I think Blanche may also be persuaded to come now."

"Blanche?" But even before he'd finished saying it Marshall realised that Gwion was talking of the albino girl.

"Luke, you may do with as you will, but we are subject to different rules."

Marshall matched him, eye to eye, for several long moments whilst he considered the sense of calling the man's bluff. No-one else moved, even Mark waited silently for his decision. In his head Marshall thought he heard the music again from earlier though he was never sure afterwards whether it had been his own memory or a reminder from the strange gypsy before him.

Just briefly, Marshall wrestled with the idea and then accepted everything he'd heard. He broke eye contact and looked up at the fiddler who also met his eye. "There is a price," Marshall said, taking his cue from the tales he'd heard and the old man's bargain earlier.

"Of course," Raven said with the same respect that Marshall had heard offered to Luke, "that is always so."

"You need to remove the barrier so I can get to James' body."

"And," Connor suddenly stepped forwards, his voice urgent, "you need to stop Luke hearing this music of yours. I can go, but if he's going to be locked up, it would send him mad. You've done enough to him, now leave him alone."

"You can still hear the music?" Marshall had thought his mind was playing tricks.

"If we were inside the ring, yes, I think it's a spur to encourage us to move on," Connor said, continuing to stare at Gwion and Raven, "but you can't do that to Luke if he's," he seemed to catch what he'd been about to say and then began again using Marshall's own words. "Consider it the price you pay for gaining Zoe."

Raven laughed but he was already removing his fiddle from its case, "I think, Piper, that we have taught the people here more than you intended of the old ways," he said. "Walk with me. A final tune and we will be gone, Inspector, though time may return us with the seasons as it ever has." He pulled his bow across the strings and set off through the trees. After a moment Gwion lifted his flute and followed, Lacewing a step behind, the dog pacing beside her.

The white-haired girl, Blanche, bent and offered a hand to Zoe, "Coming?"

Zoe stood slowly and then crouched again to give Luke a brief, hard hug. She turned to look at Daniel who gave her a small smile, "Your decision," he said, "not theirs."

She nodded and then raised her own flute to her lips. Following Blanche, she set off after the fiddler.

Marshall could never afterwards remember the second tune, though the first sometimes came to him in dreams. The fiddle scattered across the night, disjointed and yet strangely haunting, the flutes adding a soft undercurrent of breathy harmony. It gradually faded and Marshall was sure the strange assortment of gypsies had gone with it.

"Thanks, Con," Luke said, disturbing Marshall's reverie.

"Least I could do," Connor said, offering the other man a hand to help stand. "I'll stay if you like, speak up for you."

"No, move on, forget me, forget your wife, learn to travel. I'll put my trust in the Inspector."

Connor also gave Luke a brief hug and then set off back towards the camp and the departing caravans. Marshall let him go.

"Cuff him, Mark," though it was a pointless gesture; as far as he could tell Luke had chosen to be here and wasn't going anywhere.

"And me?" Daniel sounded young and lost now everyone had gone. "James," he said suddenly and burst into tears before turning and running after Connor.

Marshall sighed, "God, what a mess."

"The travellers are going and you caught a murderer," Mark pointed out, "the chief is going to be delighted."

"Stop being so bloody reasonable," Marshall said, without heat, "you aren't the one who's got to write all that down in a report."

CHAPTER 13

Marshall pulled into Church Street carpark and paid and displayed. He'd done enough bending of the rules trying to clear up the mess left by the travellers and murders that he felt he ought to follow parking regulations even if what he was about to do probably meant throwing the rule book out of a very high window.

The Smith Foundation was open, its massive wooden doors standing invitingly wide. Marshall paused at the foot of the stairs leading up to them and then resolutely climbed up. Inside it smelt of old books and dusty age, belied by the fairly modern desk with its computer just within the doors.

David was standing behind the counter, his blonde assistant nowhere to be seen. "I was just about to close up, Inspector, do go through."

Smiling slightly to himself at the librarian's unflappable nature, Marshall meandered slowly through the library to the large office at the back. He hesitated in the doorway. A fire was roaring in the fireplace and two armchairs had been pulled up; one on either side, with a small table between them. Two steaming mugs of coffee, a bottle of single malt and two small tumblers were neatly arranged on the table.

Marshall shook his head, almost tempted to leave, slightly scared as to what he might be signing up to here with a man who seemed to know his every move.

On the other hand, Marion had joined the local church and WI, his girls were about to start the local school and he had a good team of officers. For all the strangeness of the past week, no-one had drawn a knife or gun on him, he hadn't had to chase anybody anywhere and no-one had accused him of being a 'racist pig' or any insult worse.

The pleasant dreams of strange music were a vast improvement on nightmares of dank basements full of chained Romanian slave girls and football riots full of rowdy drunks.

This seemed to be what Fenwick was; he could accept it or go back to ordinary crime on ordinary streets.

Taking a deep breath, he stepped into the room, helped himself to one of the coffees and sat down. Taking a long drink, he relaxed back into the chair and closed his eyes.

"Well done, Inspector," David said from the doorway, "I said I thought we could be friends. Help yourself to a drink, unless you're on duty."

"No, I thought I'd leave this until I wasn't officially being a policeman."

"So you wouldn't feel the urge to arrest me?" David said with a smile. He came to sit across from Marshall.

"Possibly, I'm assuming you knew what Gwion and his friends were up to."

David put his head on one side, regarding Marshall closely. "Is it time to discuss impossibilities, Inspector?"

"Impossibilities? That man created a barrier I couldn't get through by playing a flute and got rid of every traveller in Fenwick in under two hours. My forensic specialist claims he is getting DNA that can't possibly exist from a machine that works perfectly and several people I've met in the last week claim to be over two hundred years old. I've even got the pictures to prove it. So, yes, I think I'm ready to listen to 'impossibilities' because, actually, you're going to have to go some way to compare to what I've already swallowed."

David laughed, his eyes twinkling, "Can I ask, then, you say you've swallowed it. Have you really? Are these truths you can live with?"

"I'm a policeman," Marshall said, "I happen to think I'm a good one which means I work with evidence and I like to see things for myself. I've seen some crap in my life, things you wouldn't believe humans were capable of, but I've witnessed them and had the evidence, so I've had to believe. Why should I stop now? I ran into Gwion's barrier, I've seen the people face to face that I know were in a picture two hundred years ago. It would do me no more good to deny that than it would to tell you people don't traffic humans or kill other people over who has the tallest hedge."

"In which case, what can I do for you, Inspector?"

"John," Marshall said. "If we're going to be friends, it's John. Gwion said I'd be good for Fenwick if we worked together which I presume means you are, at least unofficially, a part of the law of this place. I'm assuming you have been here a while."

"I was here when Gwion first came and his fiddler friend killed the first Thomas Faulkner."

"So Gwion gave you—"

"No, I don't dance to his tune. My life belongs to the library. The Foundation is an unusual place. Mine is an unusual 'job' shall we say. Gwion is a friend who comes and goes with the seasons – he and the fiddler and the fox. I stay and do what I can for those who need something out of the ordinary."

"Daniel said something about a garden," Marshall said, "one that shouldn't be there."

"Indeed," David nodded towards the large mirror hung behind the desk opposite the door, "through there. I will show you one day but let's not stretch your mind to accept too much at once."

"That's where my car is parked," Marshall pointed out, leaning forwards to get a better look.

David raised his eyebrows, "Really?"

Marshall shook his head, "No, probably not, but you are going to have to show me at some point."

"Evidence of your own eyes," David said. He got up and went to the mirror. Marshall wasn't sure what he did, but it cleared turning into a doorway with a garden beyond it. "Happy? Would you like to enter?"

Marshall leant back and poured himself another whisky, "No, not today, one day." He smiled, "You're right, I think I've accepted quite enough already this week. So," he stretched his legs out, "tell me how I can write a police report that makes sense of the past week and my chief inspector will accept."

"Your chief inspector might surprise you."

"Or he might fire me for writing gibberish." Marshall said, though he stored that information away for further use. "Whatever, reports go on to the computer system and someone somewhere is going to start suggesting psychiatrists if I don't make up something a little more believable than what actually happened."

David leant forward, "Granted, let's see what we can do." He raised his glass to Marshall, "I think I shall enjoy working with you, John. Cheers."

*

Daniel stood beside the grave, his mind blank. Two funerals in as many days. He'd wept buckets for James but couldn't seem to find a single tear for Phil.

His mum put a gentle arm round his shoulders, "Come on, love, time to go home." His father, strangely subdued, stood on his other side.

Daniel rubbed hard at his eyes which stayed resolutely dry and then shrugged his mum's arm off. He turned to his father who refused to turn to face him.

"We need to talk."

"Dan, now isn't—"

"Of course it is, mum. Where else can we be straight?" He kept looking at his father, talking to him, not to her. "I've got to go, not because I don't love you, not to spite you, but because I want to see the world, travel, move on. Phil's dead and James," his voice hitched and he had to pause and regain control, "and that might mean to you that you need someone else for the shop, but to me it means that life's too short to do things you don't want to because you might die tomorrow. James would want me to follow my dreams so I'm leaving and I'm not going to argue about it again. I'm just going. I'd prefer to go with your blessing and know I can come home again but I'm going whatever."

After a two-minute silence while they stood and shivered slightly in the chill wind that blew through the churchyard, Joseph Calver finally turned away from the grave to look at Daniel.

"I'm sorry," he said, "sorry for the things I've said. I saw James' parents yesterday and it hit me then that I was being an idiot. You might be off but you'll be a phone call away and home for Christmas. If I don't let you go then I might lose you as thoroughly as they've lost James and I couldn't bear that, Dan." He paused and then swept

Daniel into a hard hug, "Go with every blessing, just make sure you come back."

*

Marshall knocked sharply on Chief Inspector Edward's door.

"Come!" Edwards waved him towards a seat. "Good result, John."

Marshall placed the folder he was carrying on the desk, "It's all there." It had taken many hours, several drafts, the entire bottle of whisky and a huge injection of realistic fiction to make it stand up, but he'd completed the case notes.

"Excellent," Edwards made no move to open it, as if he guessed there was more to Marshall's visit.

"Can I have a word?"

"By all means."

"Can we have a chat about the Smith Foundation?"

Edwards sat back; his face abruptly closed. "I'd prefer it if we didn't, John. I like you, I think you'll be good for Fenwick."

Gwion had said much the same in the moonlight by the stream, Marshall wondered if the two men meant the same thing. "So?" He asked.

"Shall we say that investigation into the Smith Foundation was what got your predecessor dismissed."

"Investigation or obsession?" Marshall frowned, wondering just how much Edwards knew. "Okay, just a question then."

Edwards didn't look happy but nodded.

"Do you know what such an investigation would find?"

"I have been given that information, yes."

Been given? No indication as to how much of it he was choosing to accept. "And do you believe it?" Marshall decided to push it.

Edwards sighed, "I have been convinced that that is a question that doesn't merit closer investigation."

Marshall nodded, "All right, well I'll tell you something. I want to stay in Fenwick, I like it here and Marion's delighted to be out of London, so I don't know whether it will make it more or less likely that you'll want me to stay, but I also know what I'd find if I investigated The Smith Foundation."

"And?"

"And after the week I've had, I'd believe every word."

"And you can work with that?"

Marshall smiled, "I think *you* probably wouldn't believe what I saw in London. I'd much prefer miracles and unexplained wonders than having to deal with the fact that every evil I encounter is the result of human perversion."

Edwards visibly relaxed, "Then I look forward to working with you in future."

"That," Marshall grinned, "is exactly what David said."

ABOUT THE AUTHOR

Emma Melville lives and works in Warwickshire. She is a school teacher of students with special needs who writes in her spare time, concentrating mainly on crime and fantasy short stories, often inspired by her involvement with folk dance and song. She has had several short stories published in anthologies and won several literary prizes. Many of her stories involve Inspector Marshall and fantastical crimes in Fenwick. This is her first novel involving him which was shortlisted by the Crime Writers Association for their Debut Dagger Award.